HORACE WINTER SAYS GOODBYE

Conor Bowman was born on a Thursday in 1965. He is left-handed and hates coriander. In 1986, he stood up Samuel Beckett and has always regretted it. Incredibly, he was once offered a place to study in Cambridge University and that year changed his life. His favourite writers are Graham Greene and A.M. Homes. Conor also writes songs. He has no mobile phone. He is not afraid of umbrellas and has an average sugar reading of 7.8. His hero is Elvis Presley. His favourite film is *The 39 Steps*. *Horace Winter Says Goodbye* was written in longhand over a period of eight years.

Conor works as a senior counsel and lives in Meath. He is married with four children.

Novels
Wasting By Degrees
The Last Estate
The Redemption of George Baxter Henry

Short Story Collections
Life and Death (and in between)
No Shortage of Long Grass

CONOR BOWMAN

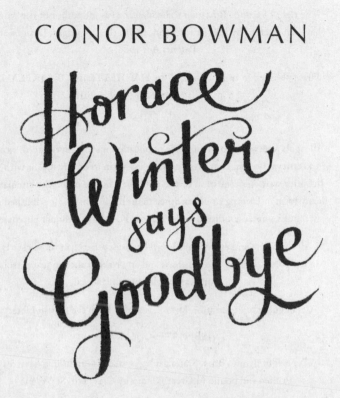

Horace Winter says Goodbye

HACHETTE
BOOKS
IRELAND

First published in Ireland in 2017 by HACHETTE BOOKS IRELAND
First published in paperback in 2018

2

Cataloguing in Publication Data is available from the British Library.

ISBN: 9781473641792

Typeset in Bembo Book Standard by Bookends Publishing Services
Printed and bound in Great Britain by Clays Ltd, St Ives plc

Hachette Books Ireland policy is to use papers that are natural, renewable
and recyclable products and made from wood grown in sustainable forests.
The logging and manufacturing processes are expected to conform to the
environmental regulations of the country of origin.

Hachette Books Ireland
8 Castlecourt Centre, Castleknock, Dublin 15, Ireland

A division of Hachette UK Ltd
Carmelite House, 50 Victoria Embankment, London, EC4Y 0DZ

www.hachettebooksireland.ie

For Zoe George Bowman
(who has difficulty seeing daffodils!)

It was a humanist service at Mount Jerome Crematorium in Dublin, in accordance with the wishes expressed in Horace Winter's last will and testament.

One afternoon, some weeks later, the executor of that will, his cousin Stephen McCullough, and Horace's solicitor, Emma Kelly, sat in her small but comfortable office in Smithfield Square.

'Does that name ring any bells?' she asked, pointing to the will.

Stephen squinted. 'No. But I barely knew Horace, really. I mean, we were pally as kids but not so much since. Apart from going to work, he kept to himself.'

'Well, I shall need to track her down. One possibility, of course, is that Horace was just confused about the address. I've checked the telephone directory but that's turned nothing up. I suppose most people use mobiles now and half of those aren't registered anywhere.'

Absent-mindedly, Stephen picked up a pencil from

the desk between them, then looked at the young solicitor. 'How *was* Horace in the last few months?'

Emma Kelly paused. 'I'm not sure I fully understand your question, Mr McCullough.'

'Well, I suppose … I mean, we hadn't spoken for years. We socialised a bit together when we both first started working. After that we kind of drifted. That's a long time ago now.'

A secretary came in with a tray of coffee and Rich Tea biscuits.

'My mum said that Horace's mother had always wanted a daughter …'

Emma Kelly poured the coffee. 'About the, em, the ashes, Mr McCullough. I think I'll just keep them here – in the office safe – until we can locate the beneficiary.'

'Fine.' Safe in the safe, Stephen thought. After all those years at the bank, Horace would have appreciated that.

CHAPTER ONE

Large Oakblue (*Arhopala amantes*)

'Don't replace the gutters unless it's absolutely essential', were the last words Horace Winter's mother had said to him. She'd died at home in the big bedroom at the front of the house, taken in the night without pain or warning. She had been ill on and off for the last twenty years of her life, but not with anything Horace thought would result in his losing her. They had drifted along for the greatest of time and then, one morning, he'd woken to find himself utterly alone in the world at the age of sixty-two. He'd delayed for hours before phoning for an ambulance. What was the point, he'd thought, of having a crew race out through the morning rush-hour traffic? There was nothing they could do, so why not wait until things were less hectic?

First, he'd telephoned the bank, one of the few occasions when he had ever lifted the receiver of the telephone on the hall table and dialled a number. It was caked with dust and cobwebs. He'd spoken to Sarah, his secretary, and told her he was taking one of his annual leave days, rather than burdening her with the reality. After that he'd made himself a pot of tea and some toast, and carried it into his mother's room. He'd sat in the armchair by the bed, surrounded by the television schedules she'd insisted on keeping, and had his breakfast.

In the hours that followed, he'd sat in silence, hearing nothing but the sound of his own breathing and the *snap*, at precisely 2.49 p.m., of a mousetrap in the airing cupboard. He had been too upset to cry. He knew that his mother had been a 'difficult' woman and, on occasion, she had even been a little unkind in what she had said to him. He remembered an incident when, a week after receiving his Leaving Certificate results, he'd spent an age trying to find the butterfly and moth collection he'd begun some years earlier. He'd turned his room upside-down and eventually had gone downstairs to ask his mother whether she'd seen it.

'I'm not having dead insects cluttering up the house, Horace. It's unhygienic. Death, death and more death. It's about time you grew up. Bedrooms are for sleeping in.'

All the same, a person had only one mother and, to Horace, grief seemed the appropriate response to her death. He knew, though, that he felt a different species of grief from that he'd experienced in the aftermath of his father's departure. His father had been taken from the world unexpectedly. He hadn't had any opportunity to say goodbye or – or anything.

Horace had had the house to himself for three years now. He turned the key in the front door and listened for the comforting rustle of post under the wood as it swept all before it in its journey across the red and white diamond tiles in the hall. Home was a Victorian redbrick terrace house. Fifty-seven Edenvale Road had been his mother's family home and she had bequeathed it to him, along with the contents of a post-office savings account and some Guinness shares.

He picked up the small heap of paper and recognised an electricity bill as the only item that wasn't junk. He discarded the pizza leaflets and other flyers in the bin under the kitchen sink. As the lid began to close, something caught his eye and he rescued a sheet of yellow paper. He smoothed it out on the kitchen surface before reading it aloud: '"Gutters replaced: free quotation."'

Horace stood at the window and looked out onto the street through a gap in the curtains. The sides of Edenvale Road were lined with parked cars, and the neighbourhood itself was as silent as a cloud or a library. He noticed something different about the house directly across the road. In the front garden, bathed in the backhanded illumination of a streetlamp, there was a large For Sale sign. Horace tried to recall who the owners of the house were or, if they'd already left, whether they had had children or a dog. He couldn't.

He knew very few people who lived on the street, apart from a couple of neighbours with whom he was on nodding terms. Somehow, when his mother had been alive, it had often seemed to him that no one else in the surrounding houses mattered. She had never encouraged him to mix with local children when he was growing up.

'They think they're better than us because we're not Catholic,' she had said frequently, in response to his requests to go out and play in the street. Horace often felt that perhaps his mother had meant the opposite of what she said.

Those other children had grown up and moved away. Many of the houses had been sold and turned into flats or bedsits inhabited by even more strangers, who stayed only for a year at a time. Suddenly, when he was about twenty-five, Horace had realised he knew no one else in the street to talk to. Even the few he did know to see began to dwindle in number. For that reason, the changing guard of inhabitants announced by For Sale or To Let signs were on the absolute periphery of his world.

He patted his clean cheeks with a dash of aftershave that had lasted years after he'd received it as a gift one Christmas from a pharmacy that banked at his branch. The scent was sweet and sour and reminded him of old but interesting books, the type you might find in an antiquarian bookshop where they knew the value of leather binding and gold-leaf inlay. In the en-suite bathroom, he brushed his teeth and then gargled some mouthwash before going downstairs to have his breakfast.

After the meal, he brushed his teeth again in the tiny downstairs bathroom, then straightened his tie in the hall mirror and left the house. He walked in the cold sunshine down Beechwood Avenue and into Ranelagh. Dublin, like Horace, was going to work on just another Friday morning. At the newsagent/deli's beside the bus stop, the clock on the wall said thirteen minutes past eight. The headline in *The Irish Times* concerned some new revelation about a politician's life, dredged up by one or other of the ongoing tribunals. A tiny photograph of a man in a pink shirt caught Horace's eye in the left-hand front-page miscellaneous column. It was of a cyclist in last year's Tour de France who had tested positive for some substance with three *p*s in its name. He thought of his aftershave. He picked up a copy and flicked through the pages. Inside, a lady was pictured with a monkey in a cage on the back of a huge tricycle, as a street festival raged in a country town.

'Hello, Horace,' said the shopkeeper. He intruded every single day with his voice, his smile and his bonhomie, and Horace didn't even know his name. He had been greeting Horace for years now, and his tone and demeanour had barely wavered. Horace had an idea that the proprietor was driven by the pursuit and accumulation of wealth: two assistants in green smocks manned the deli counter and busied themselves whenever their employer looked their way. The man reminded Horace of the caterpillar of the Large Oakblue butterfly, *attended invariably by green tree ants.*

His left hand shook slightly as he began to fold the newspaper. He lined up the pages exactly, then swooped it shut. Outside, a bus was stopping with a gush of air brakes.

Horace Winter joined the queue to get on, found his monthly ticket in his wallet and set out for the city centre, surrounded by dozens of strangers who were all travelling in the same direction as himself. From the top of the double-decker, he watched as Dubliners went about their everyday business. He felt in his suit pocket for a hanky in case a sneeze came, but it didn't. Along the Liffey boardwalk, couples strolled hand in hand and tourists studied maps they perhaps didn't understand. An adventurous lady with a double buggy containing sleeping twins crossed to the Italian Quarter when the pedestrian lights forbade it. The surprising November sun had drawn people out of doors, and they speckled in the light in wild yet gentle colours, flitting from door to kerb and on and on and on. Their individual patterns marked each out as different and vital. Horace looked down at his blue suit trousers. All butterflies and moths were different, he thought. Each had its own particular mix of colours, markings and habits that rendered it unique. Even within the same species, he doubted whether two specimens would be identical in every respect. Could you have twin butterflies?

Horace thought about the day trips he and his father had sometimes taken during the school holidays, out to Howth or down to Wicklow, in search of elusive species. Once they'd actually seen a Gatekeeper *and* a Silver-washed Fritillary on the same afternoon in a wooded clearing just south of Powerscourt waterfall. It had been a Saturday in August and Horace had been thirteen years old. They'd hidden themselves under a green rug and taken turns with his dad's old army binoculars. Horace recalled that, as they'd lain there in the shade, his father had talked about things he'd never mentioned before.

'The last time I did this it was under a camouflage net in a forest in Germany. A long time ago, Horace.'

'During the war, Dad?'

'Yes, Horace, during the bloody war. That forest was so dark in places that even in the daytime you sometimes couldn't see more than a few feet in front of you.'

'So why did you need to hide?'

A sad look had passed over his father's face. 'We were hiding from ourselves, I suppose, and from what was to come. War makes people different from how they would have been without it,' he said wistfully.

'Tell me more about the war, Dad,' Horace had said. 'Did you ever shoot anyone?'

'Ssh,' his father had cautioned. 'You'll scare away the Gatekeeper.'

CHAPTER TWO

Gum Snout Moth: (*Entometa apicalis*):
displays black patches when threatened; rests
by day on bark where camouflage is plentiful

Common Brownie(*Miletus chinensis learchus*)

It was Friday, 16 November. Horace Winter was retiring. He had worked at the bank for forty-eight years.

The solid partner's desk, with its brown leather cover and fantail gold edge design, was drawer-empty of contents. Only an emerald reading lamp bothered the vast expanse of its surface. He had sat at this desk for more than eighteen years. Three months and nine days more, to be accurate. He was certain that his calculations were precise. On the pale blue carpet, he could see the faint but definite path worn, from the coatstand to the window, by his routine each morning after he had closed the door on the world. He recalled the drip of raincoats and his attempts to save the carpet with the Health or Motoring or Property supplements from his daily paper. He went to the coatstand and turned right, skirting the bookcase filled with the black edges of ledgers and reports he would never read again. Seven steps carried him to the depression beneath the radiator adjacent to the window. The white-painted ropes slept in their pulleys and hung in two loops like wintering twine. He heard the scrape overhead of chairs in the boardroom being pulled out or pushed back into place. The view from his office was unchanging: a narrow glimpse of the universe between the corners of two very plain buildings. His office was across the corridor from that of the manager, which was entrusted with a view of the river. Long ago, Horace had expected to make the natural move to the other office but, after being passed over twice, he had eventually understood that he would never be promoted.

When he got to the boardroom, he took up a position by the window. It was a dull day. On the pavement outside the bank, a bevy of schoolchildren, on a tour of the capital, stood in a chitter of excitement as two teachers counted heads. A seagull squawked in the air over the river, then ambushed a discarded sandwich crust sitting in a tawdry tin-foil coat on the knobbled wall of Capel Street Bridge. A green-topped hotel, the Clarence, stood impassively in the lunchtime light and, like a colourful poster on a notice board, Sunlight Chambers guarded the right side of the horizon. Horace shaded his eyes and tried to look beyond the horror of the moment.

'Well done,' Sennan Callaghan said, as he offered his hand. Horace turned away from the window and deliberately misread the gesture.

'Thank you, Sennan,' he replied, as he lifted his untouched glass of champagne from the windowsill and handed it to the man who would replace him on Monday as assistant manager (branch). Callaghan was left with no choice but to take the glass, in much the same way as Horace had been left with no choice but to leave the bank. He had reached the magic age of uselessness: sixty-five.

This man is a moth rather than a butterfly, Horace

thought, as his replacement brought the glass to his lips and drank when he clearly didn't wish to.

'Butterflies at rest hold their wings together over their back,' Horace said accidentally, with little enough volume to carry past his immediate company.

'Oh, yes, I'd forgotten – you're a butterfly buff, aren't you? What is it again? It's not ornithology, that's—'

'Lepidopterology,' Horace said, with a smile. 'The study of butterflies and moths.'

'Well, you'll have plenty of time for that now,' Sennan said, between sips of the fizzy wine he was now apparently starting to enjoy.

Butterflies and Moths: A Beginner's Guide had been a gift from his father when Horace had had mumps at Christmas in his last year of primary school. Until then, he hadn't really been an expert on anything, but during those two weeks in bed with a swollen throat, he'd devoured the book from cover to cover dozens of times. He'd been fascinated by the vast number of different species that existed. Horace's father had been an expert on butterflies and moths for years. It was an interest he said he'd taken up 'during the war'.

Horace thought it unusual that anyone would

develop a hobby as gentle as the observation of butterflies during a war. He tried to imagine a Titania's Fritillary appearing on the Russian Front and capturing the attention of thousands of troops who were just about to attack each other. Perhaps it was precisely because of its incongruity that his father had developed his interest. Horace wished he'd asked.

Peter Lannigan, the branch manager, was deep in conversation at the other end of the room with the regional head of sales and marketing. Horace had mixed feelings about Peter Lannigan. He was a good deal younger than Horace and had started working in the bank many years after him, yet had been Horace's boss for almost a decade now. Lannigan was good at his job, though. Horace couldn't deny that.

Sarah, Horace's secretary, edged towards them through the sparse crowd, carrying a tray of canapés. Sennan Callaghan stepped out from in front of Horace and positioned himself where she would have to speak to both of them, if she dared to speak at all. Oh, yes, thought Horace Winter, definitely a moth. A Gum Snout, he reckoned. He could feel the energy draining from his soul as his rival finished the champagne, and the girl, who answered to the assistant manager (branch) in the Ormond Quay outlet of the Leinster Bank, leaned ever so slightly towards his rival. Horace wanted to cry out or to pull her his way but, of course, did neither. The smell of pâté on slightly stale salt biscuits invaded his nostrils, and he closed his eyes for an instant as though delaying the shutter speed to take a better photograph. He had spent long stretches of time in the company of Sarah Carolan. She was an excellent secretary, and knew his every habit and requirement. There had been times when he had wondered whether they could ever become something more than work colleagues. Of course, on grounds of impropriety and age, he'd pushed those thoughts away – but they had occurred to him. Even assistant bank managers were human. From today, however, he would no longer be her boss. Notwithstanding that, Horace doubted his feelings were reciprocated.

Horace Winter was five foot six in height and still had more hair than half the men he could think of who were years younger. 'It's not all about the hair, though, is it?' he imagined a sober voice saying.

'What will you do with yourself on Monday?' she asked, as she lowered the tray (to a point where Sennan Callaghan found it awkward to reach). It was clear from the combination of her actions that her question was directed at Horace, but before he could reply his successor interposed.

'I shall continue to wonder how I can ever fill the shoes of Horace Winter.' This was delivered with a supercilious smile flecked with biscuit crumbs. Horace was at once disheartened by the intervention and relieved at not having to answer the question.

'I was asking Mr Winter, actually,' Sarah rallied, in a minor display of mutiny. And Horace was reminded for some reason of the mating rituals of the Pale Clouded Yellow or *Colias hyale* ...

A cackle of laughter, from the back of the room, impeded his thinking. He'd always imagined that somehow he never *would* retire from the bank. It was that sort of life, wasn't it, one that went on and on, in and around the legs of other people's lives, without having to stop and examine itself? He'd been in the boardroom before: disciplinary hearings, warnings from the heart of Europe about interest rates, staff appraisals, occasional social events. This was the very room in which Anthony Avery had had his heart attack on the Saturday morning of a rugby international when the bank had entertained some wealthy account holders with drinks and smoked salmon. The death of the manager of another branch in *their* boardroom had shaken everyone.

Over the heads of two people talking, he saw the regional manager approach the lectern at the other end of the room and tap the microphone, which was obviously not turned on.

'Could I have everyone's attention, please?'

Horace Winter did not want to hear these words, not now and not ever. He'd hoped the people at Head Office would reconsider, ask him to stay on. Of course they hadn't.

★

Back in his office after the presentation, Horace clutched the wrapped gift with reluctance as he looked around for the very last time.

On the top shelf of the bookcase, between the ledgers, there was a space that had held the few personal belongings Horace had allowed to cross into his professional life: a framed photograph of a Red Admiral, a Bath White and a Monarch butterfly (simultaneously at rest on a whitethorn) and a model of HMS *King George V*. He'd carried the battleship carefully from home and into work on the bus one damp February morning some years earlier. If he were honest, this addition to the décor of his office had been an act of defiance. It was a statement of intent in the wake of his realisation that promotion was a mechanism he had exhausted. That small-scale reminder of battles fought at sea had been his way of telling himself and others that the fight was not over. But he had known in his heart that it *was* over, and that he had lost. One other personal effect had been ever-present in his office: the book about butterflies and moths he'd had since he was a child.

Adorning the wall opposite the bookcase, there was a large framed aerial photograph of the city of Dublin. In a way, it depicted an overview of Horace's life, showing, as it did, the parameters of his existence: from his house on Edenvale Road in Ranelagh to the bank, and beyond to the North Circular Road, the Phoenix Park and the zoo. With little variation, his world and his time were contained within the frame. Old buildings, old things and old people, he thought. What else is there?

He had been born in the Coombe Hospital and presumed he might die in another hospital in Dublin. He walked to the photograph and ran his finger in a direct line across the glass from his home to the river and the building in which he now stood. It struck him that, with all of the certainty he had enjoyed in this room, he had no idea where next to direct his finger or his feet. In that instant, he grasped that within a few minutes, when he left the bank for the last time, he had absolutely no idea where he would go or what he would do. Until that moment, he had not believed that he would ever have to retire.

'There could be twenty years or more ahead,' he muttered, and was filled with fear and isolation. What exactly were you expected to do when you stopped expecting to do what you'd always done? Horace felt the beginning of a headache and tried to think of cool water, a soothing stream, to carry off the pain. He didn't much like water, but he felt hot.

A hesitant knock on the door heralded the arrival of Sarah Carolan. Horace hadn't expected to see her again.

'I thought you'd gone, Mr Winter. This was the only place left to look,' she said, with a shy smile, as she entered the room.

'No, not gone yet, Sarah,' he said sadly. He pulled a handkerchief from his breast pocket and dabbed his forehead. He was mildly angry with her for having a life at the bank that would endure beyond his, but he was overwhelmed at that moment by a sense of loss.

'I knew you wouldn't leave without saying goodbye, Mr Winter.' She smiled again, uncertain now, as if she recalled the instant in the room above them when she'd leaned her body, and consequently her life, towards his successor as she'd carried the tray of nibbles. Of course she hadn't been disloyal. Horace looked beyond her at a space just behind her head, as if he were worried something or someone lurked there.

I've never been much good with the ladies, he thought. It was difficult to know what to say, and sometimes if you said nothing, it was as if you had said too much. He held out his right hand, the one he'd been taught to write with. His 'wrong' hand had been tied behind his back at school, attached to his belt, for five whole weeks until he'd 'come round'. His secretary, though only for a few more minutes, shook his hand firmly, then rooted in the pocket of her frock. A small package sat in her palm and she offered it to Horace, like a sugar lump to a horse.

'You can open it if you like,' she said.

He slid his little finger under the flap at one end and carefully unfolded the blue wrapping paper. He wondered if anyone actually reused wrapping paper or whether perhaps people only made an effort to unwrap carefully so that they would not appear greedy or rude. The paper was the colour of a pair of pyjamas he had at home. His secretary took the discarded paper and Horace Winter was left holding a small velvet jewellery box. He opened the lid and the hinge creaked quietly. Inside he found a gold tiepin in the shape of a butterfly. Horace's stomach lurched.

'I – I hope you like it?'

'Yes, Miss Carolan, I *do*.' Horace couldn't think of anything else to say but he knew more was expected. 'It's very … very shiny,' he said awkwardly.

'Yes, I suppose it is.'

Horace thought he saw a tear gathering in her eye and was suddenly seized with a wonderful feeling. He was sure that she was going to tell him that the powers at Head Office had changed their minds about his retirement; that they needed him to stay on.

'There's something you haven't told me, Miss Carolan, isn't there?' The Common Brownie, he mused: long antennae and a slender body; slightly drab in colour but found as far away as Java, Myanmar and Borneo. A beautiful butterfly.

'No, Mr Winter, there's nothing, I just … I'm sorry you're retiring and … I think it's absolutely unfair that you were never made branch manager just because you're unmarried.'

The pain in Horace's head increased tenfold and he gasped for air. Her words reverberated in his head, like liquid swilled in a glass. In his line of vision, he saw Miss Carolan turn away from him and grasp the door handle. As she touched it, the door opened. Sennan Callaghan stood there, rocking back and forward on his heels, grinning. Horace looked up into the bookcase and imagined HMS *King George V* in flames, torpedoed by a thousand tons of exploding golden butterflies.

CHAPTER THREE

Cranberry Blue (*Plebejus optilete*)

Spurge Hawk-moth (*Hyles euphorbiae*)

After he had got out of the taxi, Horace stood for a short time on the pavement outside his house. He had another headache. He'd had a series of terrible ones recently. He gazed into the pebbled patch that had once been a tiny lawn. Two huge terracotta pots housed the stalks of bushes he'd last seen growing in April. The enclave of clematis to the right of the front door resembled a pile of coats hung on a single hook. The pink and white blossoms teemed with bees and insects in the summer, always reminding him of the murmur of a motor. He looked to his right, to where his old green Morris Minor had been parked permanently since his mother's funeral. He hadn't made a conscious decision not to drive it any more, it just seemed that, well, there hadn't been anywhere to drive to. In his left hand, he carried a small carton of milk he'd bought in the village. The taximan hadn't minded stopping. His right hand fiddled in the pocket of his suit jacket and he felt a sharp point enter one of his fingers. It was the butterfly tiepin. It lay in his palm and the gold wings caught the tiniest glint of winter sunlight, then bounced it back into the sky.

On the other side of the road the driver's door of a parked car was still open. Horace's head began to spin slightly and he found himself swaying as he pushed open the gate into number fifty-seven. As it swung, so did Horace. He remembered that his keys were in his trouser pocket, then saw his green bin, on the short garden path, begin to move. His head hurt and his tummy swooped, as if it were trying to escape. He heard the noise of the two keys attacking each other on the keyring that carried the logo of the bank inside a small square of plastic. 'The bank with huge pre-tax profits but little heart', he heard a voice say in his head.

He fell forward but kept his balance by holding on to the railings that separated his garden from next door's.

'Help me!' he croaked, as he slumped to the ground about halfway along the path. He dropped the milk carton and heard the gate creak behind him.

'Gently does it now,' a soothing voice said. An arm was under his shoulder, helping him to his feet and allowing Horace to lean. He began to walk to the front door but it was not his hand that put the key into the lock and turned it. He stumbled but was steadied by the other person's body as he went into the hall. He needed a cup of tea.

Inside, with the front door closed, Horace looked at the floor and saw a worn pair of gardening shoes. He moved his eyes to the tiny strip of exposed ankle, then followed the dusty beige slacks up, until he found himself looking into the face of a lady he did not know. 'I'm – I'm terribly sorry,' he said. He was flustered beyond anything he'd experienced before. Collapsing in front of his own house and being rescued by a complete stranger. 'You see I've just been – I mean ...'

'It's perfectly all right,' the lady said. 'You've nothing to apologise for. You just had a little fall, that's all. Now, let's get you sitting down, shall we?

Perhaps you'd like some tea.' She took him once more by the arm. Horace was confused and upset, embarrassed and unsure all at the same time. This was *his* house, wasn't it? How could he be uncomfortable in his own home?

Just as he began to wish that the woman would leave him alone, she smiled, not just with her mouth but with her eyes. They were a shade of greeny-blue he had never seen before, like the swirl of colour inside old handmade marbles, and although he momentarily considered that she might be a Cranberry Blue, or even a Meleager's Blue, he knew she wasn't. Perhaps she was a species of butterfly he didn't know, a type that fell outside the remit of *Butterflies and Moths: A Beginner's Guide*. He would go to the library at the Royal Dublin Society, or perhaps to the catalogue room in the Natural History Museum. Surely he'd find her there.

He wished she would explain the world to him. He hoped there were some biscuits left in the tin in the cupboard.

The lady helped him to shuffle the last few steps along the hallway. 'You're lucky I spotted you before you fell,' she said, with a grin. 'I was doing some weeding across the road in my front garden.'

As they went towards the kitchen, Horace saw the

folded wheelchair compressed between the umbrella stand and the wall. The air in the house seemed thick, as though someone had refused to open a window after the rain had stopped. The lady had black sunglasses, which were pushed up on her hair. He heard the kettle sigh, then the chink of crockery.

'A nice cup of tea, that's what you need,' she said.

A few minutes later, it was steaming in front of him. 'I don't even know your name,' he said, as he helped himself to a spoonful of sugar.

'Amanda,' she said.

'I'm Horace Winter.'

'Will you be all right here on your own?' she asked.

Would he be all right here without her? That was what she was asking, wasn't it? He said he would.

'Okay, then.' She smiled and then gave Horace a wave, which reminded him of how small children waved: she opened and closed her hand rather than shaking it from side to side.

Then she went back to her gardening across the street.

On Saturday morning, Horace felt quite himself again and was embarrassed to remember the turn he'd taken on his doorstep in front of a stranger. But what didn't feel so fine was the question inside him: what would he do now, without the bank to take up all of his time?

Horace took the bus in to town. He needed to buy socks. Almost without his having noticed it, everywhere suddenly had Christmas displays of one sort or another. The lights on Grafton Street were fantastic and a busker outside Bewley's Oriental Café sang a song about a tavern.

His father had driven a 1933 Wolseley Nine saloon. Horace recalled the exultant hum of the engine as they had made the trip home from Rosslare together each summer, just the two of them. His mother had no interest in either 'chasing butterflies or catching up with relatives'. He and his father had been totally at ease in each other's company as they drove up through the countryside without a care in the world. Or perhaps they did have cares, but the cares were miles away. He remembered the softness of his dad's laugh and the warmth that had surrounded them on those trips. He couldn't bring to mind the details of their dialogue but he sensed that conversation had come easily between them. Horace wondered if people were only properly at ease talking to someone else when they were facing in the same direction; not face-to-face across a coffee table, but walking together side by side or sharing a trip in a Wolseley. He tried to revisit the journeys home, but could recall only ham-salad sandwiches on a newspaper atop the bonnet of the car. The paper had flapped and, in his mind's eye, Horace tried to read the print but saw only blurred ink, like a mortgage application smudged in a fax machine.

Above the clamour of the season, he heard another noise. Somehow it lifted him over the heads of the people around him so that he could narrow his hearing and follow the sound. It was a man's voice.

'I *said*, leave them there. We're in a fucking hurry. I've got to get Uncle Paul's present before the shops close.'

'Wait! Daddy, wait!' The young voice rose from between the feet of the last-minute shoppers. It was the voice of a boy trying not to cry, and Horace knew that he himself had used that very tone many years earlier, although he could not remember the words he'd spoken. He began to edge his way through the crowd now, following the voices.

'Get up for Christ's sake, Max! I've had enough of this nonsense about those bloody cards. Just leave them!'

'Please, Daddy! I want to pick them up – just wait for me.'

'No. Maybe it'd be better if I just left you on your own.'

Horace found his way to the far side of a wall of shoulders, coats and hats. For the first time, he could see the boy. He looked to be no more than eleven or twelve, and he was on his hands and knees trying to pick up dozens of coloured cards, which were strewn on the pavement. They seemed to feature sports people. One said: 'Defender: Arsenal'. Horace saw the back of the child's father, who was evidently determined not to help his son retrieve the scattered cards. In his right hand, the man had a carrier bag. Instinctively, Horace crouched on his hunkers and began to gather up the cards: West Ham, Bellamy, Rooney, Tottenham Hotspur, Gerrard, Sheffield Wednesday. The child glanced up from his task and smiled at Horace in gratitude. They were comrades in a crisis.

'*Come on*, for fuck's sake!' the man roared. There was a pause in the boy's collecting but then he resumed his task. Suddenly, a hand swooped down and grabbed him by the hair, wrenching him upright. The cards in the boy's grasp fell to the cobbled footpath as he was jerked around to walk down the slope of Grafton Street. The boy began to howl in protest but his father silenced him with a slap. Horace hadn't seen the man's face but he imagined that it must now be crossed with rage.

Horace gathered up as many of the cards as he could and began to follow the pair down the street, keeping his eyes fixed on the bright red bag the boy carried on his back. Once or twice, he lost sight of them in the droves of Christmas consumers, yet he managed to keep a general tracking direction and continued his pursuit past Brown Thomas's and around the corner into Wicklow Street. There could be no doubt about the identity of the man, he thought. He was a Spurge Hawk-moth: *A poisonous caterpillar. When fully grown, the moth seeks bright lights and conceals itself easily.*

As Horace watched, the man pulled his distraught son along roughly by his hand or arm, the boy struggling to keep up. They crossed Clarendon Street at the end of the pedestrian area just beyond Tower Records. As they did, a Greyhound refuse truck drove sharply around the corner, cutting them off from Horace's view. When the lorry had passed, he could no longer see them. He scanned the street. It was getting quite dark now, and, in the glare cast by the Christmas lights overhead, it was becoming increasingly difficult to separate individuals from the crowd. Horace looked forlornly at his two handfuls of football cards and crossed the street. At the next corner, where a café and a chocolate shop kept watch, he stopped for a moment to gather his thoughts. Then, he turned and retraced his steps, looking into each shop through its door or windows as he passed.

The weight of Christmas pressed in and down on Horace Winter, like a heap of visitors' coats on a bed at a party. He felt himself slowing in the treacle of passers-by but resolved not to abandon his search. He had no idea what he would do if he found them, but he knew he had to keep looking. He crossed now to the other side of Wicklow Street and began to work his way back towards George's Street, investigating shops in an effort to locate Max and the Moth. Just as he was about to admit defeat, he spotted the red bag through a gap between two other customers in a small boutique that sold leather goods. Horace went in.

The father was looking at a display of leather belts and riding crops. The boy stood in the middle of the shop, turning slowly on his heels. Horace proffered the two handfuls of football cards to him but the boy gave him barely a glance. His eyes were red from crying. Horace watched him unhitch the bag, and saw that it had been slung on his back upside-down. Wordlessly, the child accepted the cards and replaced them in his bag.

Horace glanced around him. The boy's father was now at the cash till, paying a pretty shop assistant. The man had put his carrier bag on the floor in order to transact his business. Although he had his back to Horace, Horace knew the colouring by heart: *forewings patterned in mid-brown and dark cream, hind wings dark brown, cream and pink.*

As he prepared to depart, he was suddenly seized with an inner rage. Without thinking through the rights and wrongs of his action, he used his elbow to nudge a wallet with a security tag off a display case. It fell soundlessly into the man's bag. Horace strolled out into the street and went on his way.

*

'Careful,' his father had said, as Horace held the jar while his dad spooned crystals of potassium cyanide into the large glass vessel. They'd both worn tea-towel masks over their faces and donned gardening gloves. Then they'd mixed plaster of Paris and poured on a layer, which covered the cyanide completely. On the following day, after the plaster had hardened, they had placed cotton wool over it and popped in the airtight stopper to complete the device.

Horace recalled the last specimen he'd captured – a White Ermine moth – about two days before his mother had thrown out his entire collection. He remembered the act of killing it: the fine pen dipped in oxalic acid pricking the under surface of the thorax. Death had been instantaneous and the moth remained in a perfectly relaxed condition for setting. He wondered whether his net was still in the house. As he searched for it now, he remembered his father's expression on an autumn day donkey's years ago. Horace had come home from school and was in his room writing an essay about Cromwell. He'd heard raised voices downstairs, then his dad had knocked on his door and come in brandishing the net, which he'd handed to his son. Then he'd picked up *A Beginner's Guide* from Horace's bedside table and flicked through it. Horace thought he saw tears in his father's eyes.

'You know what, Horace? Sometimes I think we'd all be better off being butterflies or moths. Life would be a lot shorter, and most of the time it would be sunny.'

It had frightened Horace to see his father sad.

Despite being retired and having plenty of time, he doubted he would have the courage or the interest to begin collecting again so, in a way, it didn't matter that he was unable to find the net. It had all started with the book his father had given him.

'There are more than twelve thousand types of butterfly and about eighty thousand different species of moth in the world, Horace. Of course, nobody could know them all, but this little book describes about three hundred and that's a fair chunk of information. If a person could just know the species in this book well enough to identify them on sight, he'd be an expert. And imagine if he went through his life and managed to see them all at some stage and tick them off as he observed them. *That* would be a life lived to the full.'

After he had recovered from mumps, Horace had set about trying to spot all of the different species contained in the slim volume he'd been given. The first few he'd ticked off had been easy enough to spot: Red Admirals, Clouded Yellows, White Ermine, the Cabbage White. Later, on holidays at his aunt's, he'd once seen a Holly Blue and a Bath White, but, as he had got older, the ticks had become fewer and further between. Horace had also realised, quite early in his adult life, that his job as a lowly bank clerk with a modest salary would never enable him to travel to far-flung places, to pursue rare species and note them in his log. Even later on, when he was assistant manager, he could never have found the time to devote to such a futile task. Some species in the book were now extinct and others so scarce that even experts could sometimes spend years trying to find their habitat. In any event, Horace had pretty much abandoned the hunt when he was in his late teens and had almost entirely forgotten the book until an incident had occurred in his branch on the Friday of the October bank holiday in 1973.

Horace had reserved a table in a fancy restaurant in Wicklow Street for six sharp. He was going to treat his mother to dinner out, then bring her to see a play at the Abbey. The date was ringed in red pen on the calendar on the fridge at home. But the date and day soon took on another, far greater, significance.

It was exactly three p.m. by the clock on the wall. The strict bank policy was that the main door was to be shut at exactly one minute to three and no further customers were allowed onto the premises. Anyone already in the bank could conclude their business, but they would be shown out carefully through the door, which would immediately be locked behind them.

As Horace let a customer leave, two student types – a youngish couple in their early twenties, with rucksacks on their backs – appealed to be allowed in.

'We're stony broke,' said the man. 'We really need some cash for the weekend. We've run all the way from Heuston station.'

'I'm sorry,' Horace said. 'The bank is shut. I'm afraid our policy is not to allow anyone else onto the premises once we close.'

'But that lady has only just come out,' protested the man.

'She was inside the bank before we shut the door,' Horace explained.

'*Please*,' the girl implored him. 'Our rent is due and we've no money for food or anything. We'll never last till Tuesday. It's not three o'clock yet. Look,' she said, twisting her wrist so that Horace could see her watch. He looked at his own, which tallied with the girl's.

Although he had an uneasy feeling about countermanding bank policy, his heart was strained by their dilemma. He was going out to dinner, but what would happen to the poor young couple? They might lose the roof over their heads. He had relented.

'All right,' he'd said. 'Come on in.' There was a large crowd of customers already on the premises and he supposed that no one would really mind an extra couple queuing to get funds for the weekend.

Indeed, no one had noticed – until the man pulled a pistol from the girl's knapsack and shouted, 'Everybody down on the floor *now*!'

The scene had disintegrated into chaos as people panicked and screamed. Some had started crying. *Bang!* A shot was fired and a fluorescent light-bulb showered down on customers and staff, like sharp flakes of snow. In a corner one man, filling in a lodgement slip at the high table, had remained with his back to the main floor of the bank, where a mass of terrified customers and staff were lying face down.

'Are you fucking deaf or what? I said, *down on the floor*!' the raider had screamed.

The female accomplice had started directing a frightened clerk behind the counter to fill both knapsacks with cash.

The man at the high table had turned slowly. Horace had glanced up from where he lay on the floor and saw that he, too, had a gun in his hand. Blast, Horace had thought. Two bank robbers in competition in the same branch. But he'd been mistaken.

'Special Branch. Drop your weapon.'

It's just like a television programme my mother might watch, Horace had thought.

The younger man hadn't hesitated. He'd aimed his gun at the plainclothes policeman's head and squeezed the trigger. There'd been a low *thok* as his gun had jammed. Then, there'd been an explosion. The detective had fired his own gun and the younger man's chest had seemed to fly apart. The female accomplice had started to scream and cry. The customers had all gone quiet.

Months later, they had still been coming across fragments of the dead man's flesh in the oddest of places at the Ormond Quay branch of the Leinster Bank.

An investigation had revealed that the clock on the wall of the bank was incorrect. No one had blamed Horace for letting the couple in. 'You couldn't have known,' people had said kindly.

But Horace had blamed himself. He felt he *should* have known somehow that those people were intent on wrongdoing. He remembered a conversation he'd had years earlier with a girl on a beach during a hot childhood summer. They had discussed the meaning of life and living, people, good and evil, and everything under the sun.

'I think people are a bit like butterflies,' he'd said. 'All kinds of different characteristics, colourings, interests and what-have-you, some good and some not so good.'

'You mean, some good and others pure evil?' she'd countered.

'Perhaps, yes, maybe. Although it's hard to think of butterflies as evil.'

'Oh, they're not the butterflies,' she said. 'They're the moths.'

In the aftermath of the shooting, and somewhat compulsively, Horace Winter had begun to evaluate people he observed or encountered as either butterflies or moths. To the other employees, his interest seemed a little eccentric. The *A Beginner's Guide* book had become a permanent fixture in his office (although it had accompanied him home each evening and returned to the bank each morning). He'd known that others thought his interest unusual, but he'd wondered how much stranger they'd think it if they'd known he saw *them* in that way, as a living, breathing conglomerate of human-sized, winged insects.

Horace knew that it was foolish to think of butterflies as 'good' and moths as 'bad', but this philosophy had never failed him. Everybody had an essence, and it was usually visible instantly to the discerning lepidopterist. In very rare cases, it was sometimes difficult to tell which category people fell into, and he was tempted to call them 'half and half', but that was always a mistake. People were either butterflies or moths, and, occasionally, all you needed to be sure of which they were was a little more time. The consequences of getting it wrong were potentially fatal so he supposed it was best to take all the time you needed. On the odd occasion when he required more time to observe someone before he decided, Horace would default to 'moth'. At least that way he couldn't be taken by surprise. From time to time, he encountered a new species, and when he did so, he made notes in the margins of the pages of the *Beginner's Guide* and ticked off another variety.

But what was the use of having a code to live by, he wondered, if your life could suddenly be snatched away from you? When monstrous corporations tossed their employees out into the maelstrom of retirement, how did they expect them to cope? Horace had no idea how to begin making a new life now that his old one had ended.

CHAPTER FOUR

Transparent Burnet (*Zygaena purpuralis*):
found in Ireland and W. Scotland; often hidden
among leaves; its wings are usually quite
easily seen through

The Monday after his retirement, Horace Winter rose as normal at seven o'clock and boiled a kettle for his shave. A little later, he watched the black specks swirl in the foam as he swished the water in the basin to hurry it to the plughole. He had woken during the night with a headache but had taken a tablet and just laid in bed, counting backwards from a thousand, until the pain receded and allowed him to fall asleep again.

In the bank, staff would be getting ready to open up. Piles of paper would diminish on desks only to be rebuilt later by commerce, ambition and, sometimes, error. He imagined the spill of coins into counting machines and the *frisssh* of notes in motion towards addition. Tiny pink and blue sponges offering moisture to thumbs.

On Grafton Street, he walked past four South American musicians in ponchos. They played melodies he felt he knew on instruments he'd never seen before, and they had CDs for sale on a blanket in front of them. Their sound trailed behind him as he passed the statue he hated – 'The Tart with the Cart', someone had christened it – a bronze sculpture of Molly Malone, the legendary Dublin fishmonger. She was depicted wheeling a cart that would never move.

On College Green, he turned left, away from Trinity and whatever knowledge it held. He felt a twinge of remorse as he recalled a question from a very long time ago: 'Discuss the role of mysticism and the occult in the poetry of W. B. Yeats'. Horace looked in through the window of a recruitment agency. He saw an advertisement for a receptionist and another for someone with fluent German. He thought about how many good German sailors had lost their lives on battleships when they could have worked instead at the Institute of Education for the 1940s, equivalent of twenty-three euro an hour. He lifted his newspaper like a baton and showed it to himself in the glass. It seemed to be someone else's, so he left it on top of the rattling box that signalled for pedestrians to cross at the next junction. It sat, balanced and alert, as Horace crossed the street.

The clock on the side of a silver column in the trophy-and-engraving shop display told him it was five past nine.

Horace reached the bank at exactly ten o'clock, just as the junior clerk opened the heavy bolts and folded back the solid door, granting access to a world of interest rates and overdrafts.

'Good morning, Jimmy,' said Horace.

'Good morning, Mr Winter,' the clerk replied.

Horace took a deep breath and climbed the single step into the premises. He glanced around with the practised eye of a gardener who knows exactly where every plant, flower and shrub should be, regardless of the season. All was well.

Business in the bank was always brisk on Mondays

before midday. Horace stood outside the main counter at the high table that held the plastic trays filled with lodgement slips, withdrawal dockets, and applications for bank drafts and express transfers.

'Good morning, Horace,' the branch manager, Peter Lannigan, said, surprise in his voice. He had emerged from the doors behind the 'Private, No Entry' sign and now stood beside his former assistant manager, dwarfing him. Lannigan was a broad-shouldered former county footballer who had a Minor All-Ireland medal and a string of connections. Horace's gaze was drawn to the solid gold band on the other man's left ring finger. The key to the kingdom, he thought.

'It's lovely to see you, Horace.' The tone of the manager's voice betrayed the untruth. 'Come to open an account, have you?' he asked, with forced jocularity. 'Or is there anything else we can do for you?

'No, not really,' Horace replied. 'I just thought I'd come in to see how things were.'

'Fine. Drop in anytime.' Lannigan looked at his watch and nodded inanely, as if to convey some impending task for which he had no stomach but no choice either. He patted Horace on the back, then made his escape across the main floor and disappeared into the warren of desks and low partitions known as 'Mortgages and Loans'. Horace stayed for another few minutes, then left the bank and wandered home.

He footled about the house for most of the week and tried to keep himself busy. He tidied the back garden a bit and even thought about a holiday. But where would he go? And with whom? He felt almost ashamed of his lack of hobbies, interests and friends. What had he done with his life, except work in the bank and be alone after the death of his mother? Horace resolved to read the newspaper from cover to cover at least twice each morning and to refrain from setting the alarm clock before going to bed. He was retired now and could do anything he wanted. But what *did* he want to do? He was adrift and unaccompanied.

On Wednesday, he took down the other two model battleships he owned from their perches on the bookcase in the front room. He dusted the shelves they'd occupied. He then used cotton buds and warm water to purge the ships of the dust and grime that had accumulated on them since the last time he'd cleaned them. *Warspite* and *Ramillies* had originally belonged to his father. He knew these ships had been involved in the war in which his father had fought, but that was all. His father had built the models from kits and Horace remembered the smell of Airfix glue. For years, the detailed models had simply sat on their shelves, in the background of the life that went on in the rest of the house.

Why had they been so important to his father that he had spent dozens of hours carefully constructing them from scratch? Horace remembered how on one occasion his mother had been dusting the shelves and had accidentally moved one so that it had fallen onto the settee. One of the gun turrets had come off and snapped in two. Horace's father had noticed the damage on the very next occasion on which he had entered the room. A few days later, a parcel arrived at the house by post. Horace's father had ordered a new model of the ship just so he could replace the broken gun-turret with one from the new kit. Afterwards, Robert Winter had thrown the remainder of the new kit into the bin. Horace often wondered why he hadn't kept the other pieces in case of further breakages. He now knew that it had been the very act of discarding it that had ensured it would never be needed. No one ever touched the models again. Perhaps his father had simply been returning a favour: protecting the ships now as they had once protected him. Horace carefully placed them back in the bookcase.

On Friday, Horace returned to the branch. Nobody seemed to mind his pottering around on the main floor and, anyway, things were slow so people quite frequently had time to chat to him for a moment or two. Shortly after noon, things picked up and he remained on the edge of the activity in the public part of the bank. An elderly lady recognised him from behind the safety of bottle-thick spectacles.

'Oh, Mr Winter, how *are* you? I thought they were getting rid of you.' The lady laughed and Horace shared her joke before handing her two lodgement slips on which he had already filled in her account numbers.

'Hard to keep an old dog down,' he said, grinning. She was a valued customer of the bank and had shared in a rollover jackpot two months after the National Lottery had begun. For years, he had kept her secret. Not even the manager at the time, Fottrell, had been taken into her confidence about the win. Horace felt warm inside.

A student, who owed more than he should have been allowed to borrow, waved at Horace as he left the bank just before lunchtime. Like clockwork, the young man would come in each week to pay off his debt with whatever he had earned as a DJ the previous weekend. Horace liked him and the knowledge that his faith in the youngster had been justified. That was the key to successful banking: the symbiosis between the institution and the individual. Every successful person started from zero and needed the support of an assistant bank manager to help them progress from the drip of the dream to the deluge of triumph. All around him, people came and went from the branch, braving showers of angry rain to go about their ordinary lives. Horace went home after he had been there for most of the day. He felt useful.

The following Monday, he returned to the Ormond Quay branch again. By two thirty, he had a migraine, but he remained at his post, fielding queries from customers about the arrangements for lodgements over the coming holiday period, and sharing kind exchanges with people he'd known for years. Sennan Callaghan, his successor, appeared once or twice to nod and smile thinly at Horace, without uttering a word, good, bad or indifferent.

Horace left the bank at five to four and had a late lunch in a small sandwich bar on Ormond Quay. He had dined there, on and off, since it had opened a couple of years earlier. It was an oasis of tasty soup and snacks in a district where solicitors' offices reigned supreme. He walked home to Ranelagh and found a letter from Head Office (Pensions Section), enclosing his lump sum gratuity: exactly one half-year's salary. The accompanying note, on heavily embossed paper, wished him well in his retirement.

Horace bought a new Hoover and vacuumed the house from top to bottom each day. He went for a walk to Herbert Park and fed the ducks. On Wednesday, he went to the bank in plenty of time to be there when the doors opened. He stayed until lunchtime. On Thursday, he attended at the bank again and this time remained on the floor until the close of public business. He began to notice a change in the demeanour of the staff. They seemed to take offence at his continued presence. On several occasions, he was fairly sure he heard his name muttered in muffled conversations between tellers.

'Miss Reynolds?' he said sharply. The younger of the two employees looked up in shock.

'Yes, Mr Winter?' Horace knew there was no need for him to admonish her: she would learn from her mistakes without further fuss.

'I think you'll find that the lodgement slips have

run out in the dispenser on the high table,' he said, in a voice he hoped would be recognised as both firm *and* helpful.

'Yes, of course, Mr Winter. I'll see to it right away.'

On Thursday evening, as he was preparing to leave the bank, Peter Lannigan rang him on the internal phone at the Foreign Exchange counter. The cashier opened the wooden flap and invited him round to take the call.

'Yes, sir?'

'Oh, Horace, I'm glad I caught you before you left. I wonder if you've got a moment. I'd like to see you in my office, if it suits?'

'Of course, I'll be right up.'

Horace wound his way between the desks and chairs of the main office, then punched the security code that opened the door to the stairs and the main vault area. The manager's office door was ajar. He pushed it open. Peter Lannigan was standing at the window with his back to the room. Over his left shoulder Horace could see Capel Street Bridge. The room smelled of polish. He spotted the Minor All-Ireland medal in a small frame supported by a cardboard edge that folded out from behind the picture. Lannigan had been a wing-back. This *should* have been *my* office, Horace thought. He felt a surge of animosity, which triggered another headache. They were becoming more frequent, and often came on in a flash without any warning.

He stood like a schoolboy in front of the desk, waiting for the bank manager to turn and face him. After what seemed to Horace to be a delay that bridged the gap between assertiveness and rudeness, Peter Lannigan pivoted on his shiny patent leather shoes.

'Everybody appreciates what you've done for this branch, Horace. The time you've spent here and your dedication to the customers. This bank has been your life, really, hasn't it?'

'Yes, Peter, it certainly has. And that's why—'

'Why you're finding it so hard to let go?' The manager finished his sentence, but not in the way Horace had intended.

'No, not really. I mean …'

On the desk between them was one of those sharp pointy things you used to get access to the contents of envelopes. He couldn't think what it was called. Horace felt the pain rush to his forehead, then recede. Lannigan's lecture on longevity of service continued.

'And, of course, it's bound to be difficult. But I'm afraid I'm going to have to ask you not to continue visiting the bank like this, Horace. It's not good for the rest of the staff. I'm sure you can appreciate that it's not fair on Sennan. Particularly not fair on him.'

Horace remembered the illustration of a particular moth in the *Beginner's Guide* and could picture the exact page on which it occurred. There was no doubt about it, he thought, as he gazed through the fog of unkind words at the three long red stripes on Lannigan's tie: the Transparent Burnet. Horace had ticked him off in the book years earlier, but it was always reassuring to have the original identification confirmed by subsequent sightings.

Horace looked directly into the torrent of admonition and couldn't see the point of it. He wasn't doing any harm. It wounded him to be spoken to like this. How could helping be harmful? This was as much *his* bank as theirs – in fact, more his in many ways. He'd spent all of his working life in this building, serving, assisting. The word 'assistant' embossed itself on his mind in large, high, thick golden letters.

I shall continue to wonder how I can ever be expected to fill the shoes of Horace Winter. Sennan Callaghan's voice haunted him as he made his way back down the stairs.

When Horace Winter attended at the bank on Friday morning, he found a letter addressed to him, waiting on the table and supported by the lodgement rack. Because he was retired, the letter was in effect personal correspondence and therefore Horace instructed himself not to open it during business hours. So, there it remained, propped up for all to see, until he left the bank and took the bus home. A teenage couple, in love with each other, he assumed, sat in the seat ahead of him, the boy's arm draped across the girl's shoulders providing a blue backdrop as Horace read the letter.

Dear Horace,
Your many years of valuable service to this bank are greatly appreciated. However, your actions over the past few weeks, in attending the branch during opening hours and annoying customers who have come to transact business, are unacceptable. As I explained during our meeting yesterday, your presence has been detrimental

*to staff morale, and has made the job of your
successor, Mr Callaghan, particularly difficult.
I appreciate that we all have to come to terms
with the new set-up at the branch, but you are
not helping matters.*

*It is with profound regret therefore that I
must insist that any further dealings you have
with this branch be by correspondence only.
As your own personal accounts are with the
Ranelagh branch, there should be no need for
you to attend again at Ormond Quay.*

Wishing you a long and happy retirement,

` *Peter Lannigan, Manager (Branch)*
Bank of Leinster Savings and Loan
Ormond Quay

On Sunday, Horace listened to a drama on the radio.
It was the story of two old farmers discussing their
trepidation at a recent spate of attacks in rural areas.
They also spoke about nursing homes as they leaned
on a gate in a country laneway. The play was really
about loneliness, Horace thought.

He carried a box of empty milk cartons to the bin
in the small yard outside the back door. At the bottom
of the box, he found an empty glass marmalade jar,

which prompted him to make a search for a glass object from his childhood that he'd almost completely forgotten about. He searched in the garage, which was more of a concrete shed, because there was no access to it except through the back garden. Afterwards he searched the house, in cupboards and alcoves and in the attic (by standing on a chair on the landing). Finally, just when he'd convinced himself it must have been thrown out, he made one last sweep of the garage and found it hidden behind half-empty pots of emulsion paints at the back of a woodworm-ridden crate the lawnmower leaned against when it was tired.

It was the killing jar.

CHAPTER FIVE

'A butterfly has a narrow waist.'

Butterflies and Moths: A Beginner's Guide

As he entered the house that evening, Horace noticed the telephone on the hall table, the receiver in its cradle. It never rang. No one contacted him by phone. Few enough people contacted him by letter, apart from the pension company and gutter cleaners. He looked at the black Bakelite telephone and felt utterly alone in the world. He had devoted his entire life to the bank and to his mother. What passed for activity in his life might, he surmised, attract the ridicule of others. It was a monotonous existence, bordered by an iron railing and a solid garden wall. On the fringes of this existence lay the corpse of a car he no longer drove, and a faceless institution that would now be sending him a pension cheque each month. Surely there was more than this.

As he turned off the tap in the en-suite, after brushing his teeth that night, Horace heard a voice in his head: *In the beginning there was water.*

He remembered a holiday where he was on a beach with both his parents. 'Come on in, Horace,' his father had shouted, coaxing, as he walked waist-deep into the sea and beckoned Horace towards him. Horace had looked at his mother and would never forget the expression of fear and sadness that had invaded her face, like tea soaking into a dipped biscuit. Horace had turned and run and run and run along the sand away from himself.

The truth was he'd been scared of the water and, even now, and as embarrassing as it was for a man of his age, he could never quite shake the dread. It seemed to him an acquired cowardice, not something he'd always had, but he couldn't remember when it had started. It still came to him in nightmares, the ease with which a body could go under, pulled down as the water closed over your head. He'd always refused to take baths. Even the feel of water on his hands sometimes terrified him, being, as it was, the possible beginning of something overwhelming.

He hadn't coped well with the loss of his father. He knew that. Boys needed their dads, and when they couldn't have them, there would always be a gap that simply could not be filled. He found it difficult to think about death. Big people were supposed to look after little people, weren't they? That was how the thing worked. Small people were supposed to grow up and learn to mind other small people in turn. Horace had no children and he wondered if that was because he'd lost his dad too early in the process ever to be able to take up the role himself. You were only given responsibilities when you'd shown you could be trusted. He knew that from working in the bank. Nobody was handed a branch to manage on their first day, just to see how they got on. And some people never progressed beyond assistant manager. Horace knew that too.

Over the days that followed, Horace went back to reading the bank manager's letter. Words from it cantered around his thoughts and even invaded his dreams: 'annoying customers'; 'detrimental to staff morale'; all further dealings 'by correspondence only'. He was both upset and bewildered by the language, the tone, the contents, the import and the innuendo condensed into the typed missive that was patently designed to swat him from the bank's premises, like a bluebottle. He mused as to how closely the Pallid Monkey moth as well as the Transparent Burnet, resembled Lannigan: *The caterpillar of that species is covered in long woolly fur which conceals poisonous stinging bristles.* But the colouring was not quite right and his original identification remained unshaken.

Horace reviewed the events of the previous week and calculated, as objectively as he could, the perceived detriment to staff morale as a consequence of his actions. He could see no possible way in which his being at the branch, and the unpaid assistance he rendered to customers he'd known for years, could be harmful. He admitted, somewhat reluctantly, that one of the main motivating forces behind his continued attendance at the bank was a vague hope that he might be re-employed, even in some part-time capacity. All the same, the slur on his character contained in the letter could not go unanswered. He would go back to the bank and demand a meeting with Lannigan. He would set out his intentions clearly, and when the manager had apologised for his letter, Horace would then suggest a part-time role for himself, maybe on an unpaid basis, in exchange for his own promise not to complain to Head Office about Lannigan. Desperate times call for desperate measures, he thought, as he turned off the lights and made his way up to bed. As he passed the series of framed and preserved moths and butterflies on the wall by the stairs, he wondered if it were only possible for the Zodiac moth and the Duke of Burgundy Fritillary to be seen side by side when they were dead. They inhabited completely different environments: one flew exclusively at night while the other was only ever seen in daylight. Perhaps death was the only true common denominator of living things. He had acquired the specimens secretly and had only put up the displays on the day after his mother's funeral.

Horace went back to the bank the following week. The manager refused to speak directly to him. Each day, upon his arrival, he found an identical copy of the offending correspondence lurking in an envelope addressed to him. All that changed was the date on the letter.

On the fourth Monday after his retirement, Horace arrived at the bank on Ormond Quay as it opened for business. As the doors folded back, he noticed a man he had never seen before, standing in the doorway behind Jimmy the junior clerk. The man wore a sickly brown suit and only one of his shoes had been polished. He blocked the way, almost deliberately, one might say, and then he spoke. 'Mr Horace Winter?' His voice was coarse, like grainy grey battleship paint.

'Yes.'

'This is for you,' the man said, taking a long envelope from his inside pocket and tapping Horace's arm as he handed it over.

'What is it?' Horace asked as he twisted it in his hands.

'An Equity Civil Bill, Notice of Motion, and grounding affidavit. The hearing of the injunction is tomorrow.'

Horace made as if to enter the branch but the man continued to impede his path.

'Excuse me, please,' Horace said.

'Of course,' the man said, smiling slyly as he stepped aside to allow Horace in.

On the far side of the river, an ambulance raced down the quay past the Clarence Hotel. It was the noise of the siren that caused Horace to turn and look. For a moment, he thought it might have been one of those cars in which the police travel. He struggled to find the word. It wouldn't come. This had been happening lately, more and more often.

To his surprise, the girl from across the road called in again a few weeks after they'd first met. 'Just to check on you,' she said. He was glad to see her.

She busied herself around the diamond-tiled kitchen as though she'd been there before. He saw hands, pale and soft but also worn from hard work, lift saucers; the ones his mother had carried in from the front room all those years ago. She had a slim figure and moved easily. Around the movements there was warmth, a bright shade of living, as if the old house was tasting life again after so many months and years of gloom. Horace wished she was his daughter or his niece; someone who came from the same place as him, someone who might visit him from time to time. It was so astonishing, really, that she should turn up like that. Amazing that she'd remember him at all, after just one little incident.

He watched her as she poured boiling water into the teapot and he saw her face revealed as the steam rose and cleared, like a shivering mirage on a hot tarred road in summer. For absolutely no reason, she laughed; a happy, self-contained laugh. Her face lit up the day around her. Horace felt kindness transferred between them in *his* direction.

'So, you're retired now? That must be great for you, all that freedom, the time to do whatever you want. What plans do you have?'

'I've not really thought about it like that,' Horace said. 'You know what I thought?'

'No. What?'

'I thought they'd change their mind. The bank, I mean. I thought they'd realise they couldn't get along without me. But, of course, they didn't. I think they're better off without me.' Horace told her about the letter from the manager, although he hadn't dreamed of doing so. He told her, too, of how he felt useless now that he was retired.

'You're looking at it in completely the wrong way, Horace,' Amanda said, when he'd finished.

'What do you mean?'

'I mean,' she said, pouring him another cup of tea, 'that you're being a glass-half-empty person when you should be a glass-half-full person. The world is your oyster. You can do what you want, go wherever you like, travel, meet people, do things. Your life is only beginning when you retire. It's full of endless possibilities. The only difficult decision is choosing where to begin.'

CHAPTER SIX

Dark Green Fritillary (*Argynnis aglaja*):
average wing span 63mm; loves thistles

Winter Moth (*Operophtera brumata*)

'All rise.'

The courtroom was packed to overflowing with dozens of young barristers in their pristine tabs and winged collars. The women wore a kind of ribbed bib. Horace was amazed at how fresh-faced everybody was.

'They're all "junior juniors",' his solicitor, Emma Kelly, whispered.

Horace's face must have betrayed his thoughts. His mother had once spoken of her hopes that he might become a lawyer. He wondered how she would have reacted to his being up in court as a defendant — although he knew perfectly well how she would have taken the news. It would have confirmed her view of him as a failure.

The judge sat down when the rest of the people in the courtroom had got to their feet. Horace detected a smirk on his face, which hinted at a creeping contempt for everyone else. A small, hassled-looking man sat at a desk below the level of the bench, and began to call out numbers and names from a list he had to lift and squint at to read properly.

'Fitzgerald and Gannon, Barry and LCD Educational Institute, Murphy and De Braam ...' As the list was being read out, people popped up and down all over the room, rather like that children's game where the object is to hit the targets with a rubber mallet before they retreat into their slots. Horace was amazed that no one was called to give evidence. Everything was dealt with on paper, it seemed. Various matters were adjourned for all kinds of reasons: 'Can't prove service' or 'Let it stand, Judge' or 'By consent, two weeks' or 'Strike out, reserve costs'. These were the snippets that filled Horace's ears. Just as it seemed he would have to wait forever he heard his name called.

'The governor of the Bank of Leinster and Winter.' Someone stood up and said something he didn't catch. Then the nervous man, who had been reading the list, spoke.

'Is there any appearance by, or on behalf of, Horace Winter?'

Immediately Horace got to his feet. His solicitor rose, too, and addressed the court. 'I appear on behalf of the defendant, Judge.' Horace sat down again.

A barrister, who was evidently appearing on behalf of the bank, proceeded to read out a statement from Peter Lannigan. It was written in a mix of formal and informal language, and later Horace remembered being struck by the phrase, 'I say and believe that ...'

The gist of the statement was quite clear: the bank did not want Horace Winter to return to the Ormond Quay branch ever again for as long as he lived. Horace had already read the affidavit but had imagined that any evidence given against him would have to be in person. He felt a chill down his spine when he heard the contents of Peter Lannigan's letter to him being read out in open court, as again the words 'detrimental' and 'annoying' resounded in his ears.

'Yes, Mr O'Reilly?' the judge said to the barrister representing the bank, inviting an ally into a war that was already won.

'The bank requires a sworn undertaking from Mr Winter. Failing that, I would ask your lordship to grant an injunction.'

'Miss Kelly?' The judge's eyes narrowed. Horace looked up at his lawyer. In her expression, he saw the question she had very presciently discussed with him at their long consultation the previous day. He was old enough to recognise the signs of utter futility when he saw them. He nodded sadly in response.

'Yes, Judge. I am in a position to give that undertaking on behalf of my client.'

'Very well, Miss Kelly. I note your undertaking on behalf of your client that he will not approach or enter the Bank of Leinster branch on Ormond Quay again.'

'Judge, I am instructed to insist on a sworn undertaking from the defendant himself.' O'Reilly had the bit between his teeth, there was no doubt about it.

Horace felt the eyes of the entire world upon him.

The judge leaned forward into the case and wordlessly whipped Horace, despite the distance between them. Horace took the stand and affirmed, then promised to stay away from the bank for ever.

'As a result of your client's undertaking, Miss Kelly,' the judge said, 'I will make no order as to costs. I take it you will make clear to him what will happen if he goes back on his word?'

'I will, Judge.' Emma bowed as she spoke. They were the last words Horace heard in the courtroom as his head was suddenly filled with a loud buzzing and an excruciating attack of pain. As he took the last step down from the witness box, he pitched headlong and collapsed on the floor of the Dublin Circuit Court.

*

As he was pushed in a wheelchair down the East Wing of the hospital, Horace was transported back to the day his Leaving Certificate results had arrived. At St Columba's there had been rumblings and mumblings of greatness to be achieved in the exams ahead. Everyone was expected to do well because, in the 1950s, that was the Holy Grail of education in Ireland. No one could get out of childhood successfully without it. In 1959, it lay in front of Horace and his classmates like the bridge to be built on the River Kwai. All thoughts of happy lives, international travel, wedded bliss and undeserved wealth were stayed until the prime piece of the puzzle was tucked securely under your arm.

Horace had always done quite well in examinations. He worked hard and covered most, if not all, of each course. The diary to his schooldays had been page after page after page of timetables for study, plotting the destruction of the paper in the study hall at school, while the Department of Education boffins convened in the war-room in Merrion Square to scheme and counter-scheme their ambitions into practice. It was a war. There was no doubt in the wide earthly world about that.

Horace had loved the drama of the conflict. He had prepared his defences and strategies meticulously. The word 'meticulous' came, he knew, from the Latin *metus*, meaning 'fear'. It was fear, he supposed, in the broader sense, fear of failure, which had driven him to fill dozens of copybooks with the 'grand aim'. After that, came the whittling away, over months, at each subject: subduing geography and trigonometry, and even Latin itself, over the run-in to the invasion, so that each subject would do as it was told on the day and behave as it should.

A drawing room lay to the rear of the house, opposite the kitchen, but Horace was not allowed in there, it was where his mother went to think. Horace had not yet turned seventeen. His mother had been waiting in the sitting room at the front of the house with the envelope when he'd returned from a day at the seaside with cousins. She was seated in an armchair with a bundle of knitting on her lap. To one side lay a card-table upon which three empty teacups sat: testimony to the long wait she had endured for his return. The letter was addressed to Horace, so there was never a question of her opening it on his behalf.

'It's an offence under the Post and Telegraph Act,' his father had said once, when a neighbour had delivered a letter, which they'd received in error and had opened.

Horace had picked up the envelope uneasily. He could still hear the chunky, noisy clatter of crows or magpies relayed down the chimney into the sitting-room grate. He'd slid his finger into the space the glue had missed. A look from his mother had reminded him of what he was about so he went to the drawer in the bookcase and took out the letter-opener. The silver point had slit the paper's throat and spilled the future out.

Horace had read the results like a telegram from the Western Front announcing news that no one had wanted to receive. Most subjects had survived quite easily, others were wounded, but not fatally so, but it was the proud and solitary 'F', opposite 'English', that had torn his world apart. This subject had not come home from the war: it had died in vain on the battlefield.

Horace's hands had simply risen and fled to his sides unwittingly mimicking crucifixion. The Department of Education bombshell and its envelope, now unsupported, hurried to the floor and buried themselves in the fading glory of the royal blue carpet. A fail in English meant that the candidate had failed to matriculate. If you didn't pass English, Irish and maths, you might as well not have sat the exams at all. Repeating the Leaving Certificate in the following year was unthinkable and most schools forbade it.

Both of them had stared at the back of the results, until Horace's mother had bent and picked up the letter and the envelope. Mrs Winter had scanned the page, but already knew from her son's expression that shock rather than surprise would follow a perusal of its contents. Horace had almost expected his mother to use the fire tongs to dispose of the missive, but she didn't. She had stood there, silently and furiously reading the results to herself, wearing a look of contempt on her narrow face. Horace had known for quite some time that his mother did not like him very much, but this was a fatal blow to his chances of ever recapturing her approval, let alone her affections.

They had stayed motionless for a considerable period of time, bathed in the awful silence that surrounds such horror. Horace had wished that his father were alive: he knew that he at least would have been able to see some pathway through the tragedy to the other side. But, of course, he was not there: he had died of disappointment a number of years earlier. Horace remembered seeing the skies outside begin to darken as his mother had put the letter back into the envelope and turned to the bookcase wherein she had deposited the offending correspondence between the pages of a book she had consigned for eternity to its berth on the shelves. She retrieved her knitting from her armchair and placed it carefully in her knitting basket on the windowsill. Slowly, deliberately and coldly, she had gathered the saucers and cups. As she had made her way to the door she had stopped, and the cups had chinged a little as she halted. Mrs Winter had turned towards her useless son with a look of rancid disappointment. 'The bank,' she'd said. 'There's nothing else for it.' The matter was never spoken of again.

In the waiting room, outside the X-ray department at Beaumont Hospital, Horace slumped on a grey plastic chair. A lady and a child sat across the room. The small girl was only three or four, Horace supposed, yet she was as quiet as a mouse. It was actually the adult who couldn't sit still. The woman kept getting up and wandering around, to the low table of *Hello!* magazines and back to the chair, checking her handbag, then opening and closing a small compact she took from her pocket without looking into the mirror.

'Horace Winter?' A nurse had poked her head round the door and shouted his name.

'That's me,' Horace said unnecessarily, and noticed that his left hand was shaking. Horace stood up but actually felt like he was still sitting. He was aware of other people around him but, for a moment, they lost their faces and were a bit blurry. It all cleared up though and he made his way after the nurse, who had come back in to the waiting room to find him again. He followed her down a short passageway and in to the consulting rooms.

The consultant took an X-ray from a huge green folder and pushed it up under the edge of the illuminated box on the wall. He was dressed in a suit that was a slightly brighter shade of grey than the day itself. 'Have you had any nausea?' he asked.

'Nausea?' Horace repeated.

'Yes, a feeling of sickness in your stomach, like you're about to vomit.'

Horace *had* felt like that but wasn't sure when it had been. 'A little bit,' he replied

'Yes, yes, that's quite normal. You may also notice a difficulty with word-finding. That's where, say, for example, you want to say "knife" but can't think of it so you get circumlocution and you might say instead "the thing you cut with". Have you noticed anything like that?'

'No,' said Horace. 'Knife, knife ... I'm pretty clear about what that is.' He remembered another word, 'circumadjacent'. It came from the Latin, and meant 'lying near' or 'abounding'. The hue of the consultant's suit reminded him of the markings on the Winter moth. Horace thought of how the tiniest choices and events could sometimes have the most far-reaching consequences. He recalled the time he'd admitted the wrong people into the bank. He thought about his mother. Sometimes the shadow on the X-ray looked like the outstretched wings of the Dark Green Fritillary in flight. The butterfly effect, he thought.

'We're going to start you on a course of corticosteroids. That should reduce swelling in the brain areas around the tumour. Now, there are other things we can look at as the condition progresses – radiotherapy and possibly even surgery – but, given where it is, I'd rather try everything else first and see how we get on.'

'How *we* get on?' Horace volleyed the statement back across the net as a question.

'Yes,' the other man said, with a smile. 'We've got to tackle this thing together. There are new developments in treatment and therapy every couple of months, and success rates are going up all the time.'

Horace thought a little. 'I got an F in English in the Leaving,' he confessed. He saw, or thought he did, a look of shock come over the man's features. Perhaps they'll refuse to treat me now, he thought.

'Don't worry, Mr Winter, we'll do everything we can to make you well again.' The doctor carried an array of different-coloured pens in his breast pocket. Horace wondered whether he changed colours depending on the severity of each prognosis.

'Have you any questions, Mr Winter? I'll do my very best, of course, to address any concerns you might have at this time.'

'Can I go home now?' Horace asked. He knew this was important but his mind felt foggy. He couldn't concentrate on what the man wanted him to concentrate on. He just wanted to be away from all of this, at home in his own bed with the blankets pulled over his head.

'I'm afraid not,' the consultant said. 'I'd like to admit you to our oncology unit right away and carry out further tests. We should be able to start the treatment in a couple of days or so and monitor you at the same time.'

'May I borrow some pyjamas?'

'Absolutely,' said the consultant. 'In fact, you may even be allowed to keep them when you leave.'

★

'This place is like a morgue, Horace,' Amanda said. 'You need to liven it up a bit.' As she spoke she held up a box of Christmas lights in each hand. 'The tree is still in the boot of your car. Get your coat on and give me a hand with it. It's massive.'

Horace had forgotten he'd bought a tree.

Together they manoeuvred the giant plant into the hall and struggled to get it the right way round so it would fit through the drawing-room door without snapping. They found an old log basket in the garage and wedged the tree into it with a mixture of briquettes and brute force. Horace – and the woman he hadn't known until a few weeks earlier – looped the chains of lights around and under its branches.

'Hey, Horace, have you got any decorations?'

In the spare room, or perhaps more properly, Horace thought, in *one* of the spare rooms, a box of ornaments lay at the bottom of a cupboard, smelling of mothballs. Horace liked the smell of mothballs.

Later, together, on their hands and knees by the warmth of the fire in the grate, Horace and Amanda sifted through the Winter family's decorations. They found turtle doves on a perch and Santa Claus on a sleigh, and dozens of glittery balls and lanterns, and the golden apple that had been his father's favourite.

'Never eat golden apples, Horace,' his father would say, with a chuckle, 'or you'll end up with silver teeth.' He would immediately dissolve into peals of uncontrolled mirth each time he delivered the line. Mrs Winter never found the joke in it.

The fire in the drawing room was still quite alive. The tree lights didn't work at first, but then Amanda crawled under the branches and pushed the plug fully into the socket. It was Grafton Street in his own house, Horace thought. He couldn't recall the last time there had been a Christmas tree at number fifty-seven Edenvale Road. He couldn't picture a time when there had been a tree and there had been just his mother and himself at home for Christmas, although perhaps he was wrong about that. They sat on the small settee, watching the run and blink of the coloured lights illuminate the decorations, then condemn them to shade. Horace wished they could have had one of those figures for the top, the ones with wings.

They sat together as the fire crackled and Christmas Eve edged towards Christmas Day.

CHAPTER SEVEN

Death's-head Hawkmoth (*Acherontia atropos*):
this species has a mark on its thorax that
resembles a skull

Zephyr Blue (*Plebejus pylaon*): perhaps the
most beautiful of all butterflies

What had prompted him to come here, to
Donnybrook rugby ground? He should be at
home in bed, writing down reminders of how often
to take his pills, and thinking about Life and Death,
but instead he was here. A letter had arrived a day or
so earlier calling Horace for jury duty. He wondered

if he would still be alive when the date came around in two months' time.

The air filled for a time with the delighted screams of a child and then, overlapping that, the awkward shriek of a rook or raven. From inside their wrought-iron gates, held together with thick black paint, and up their red-tiled paths, the citizens of nearby Eglinton Road celebrated Sunday. Through an open window, the sound of vacuuming had damaged the integrity of the day as Horace walked by, and then it had been quiet once more. Horace now looked at his feet, felt the beginnings of a headache, then wished it gone, and it was. He had been taking medication for three weeks now. He could not recall any of the journey on foot from Ranelagh to here, although it had only been a few mintues earlier.

An enormous blue metal gate shut the world out of the rugby ground. Horace placed his hands against it, as if he were about to be searched. The metal was warm. He wondered how he would survive if he didn't go home but instead waited at the entrance until they opened up to admit supporters to the game in three weeks' time. He saw a flashing display-board, which herded its digital letters from left to right. 'Donnybrook Travel …' it read '… Sending Dreamers on Dream Holidays.' He wondered who on earth would have come up with such a slogan. He watched the message run around a few laps of the display and tried to picture the other side of the screen. Did the letters appear on the back or was it all just a trick of the computer and internet age where you could be anything you said you were?

There were two turnstiles. One was open. Horace could see a man on a tractor mowing the pitch. He knew that someone had to press a pedal to let you in by the turnstile, but there was no one in the booth. He stood at the narrow entrance and looked in at the place where, just over fifty years earlier, he had run onto the pitch. The other side had scored a drop-goal to take a two-point lead with only a few minutes remaining. Horace could see the past now, through the turnstile, as a wave of images, like old newsreel replayed with shocking clarity.

The ball had been put into the scrum by Newbridge, but Columba's had taken it with a strike against the head. As their pack had begun to recede, against the superior strength of the Newbridge scrum, the Columba's wing-forward had broken his bind and picked up the ball from between his feet. He had made a break on the blind side, away from the

obvious support, which lay to the open side. A graceful
runner, he'd turned to shoulder the first defender and
to sidestep neatly between two others, who had tried
to converge on him. It had been beautiful to watch
and Horace's heart had soared as the clock moved to
seventy-nine minutes. The number seven had made
thirty yards before he was tackled. Quick ball from
the base of the ruck, and the Newbridge defenders
had been scrambling in a drift to plug the gaps.

The Columba's backs had begun the decisive
move. That had been the moment their lives had been
ambling towards since they'd first togged out. As he
fell, the inside centre had turned and pushed the pass
from his chest with both hands. The outside centre
had caught the ball, then handed off the penultimate
defender.

Horace had heard the crowd baying all around him.
The Newbridge full-back had been tall and rangy,
like a Gaelic footballer from a bygone era. Horace had
waited on the wing – in the wings – for the operatic
roar of his own destiny to call him into the fray. He'd
chanced a glance up into the stand and met his father's
eye for an instant.

What had been needed in that moment was nerve
and perfect hands. The Columba's outside centre,

Alan Dodd, would pass to Horace. He had to. It was coming, coming, any second now ... Horace had checked his run ever so slightly so that the pass, when it finally came, would not be tainted with illegality. He could already see the pass before it happened.

But Alan Dodd had not passed the ball. He'd kept his head deliberately averted from Horace the whole time. It had only been in the split second before he'd been smashed to the ground by the full-back, before the ball was lost, and with it the game, that he'd bothered to turn and shoot a look at the boy to whom he'd refused to pass. It was a look Horace had never forgotten. It was a look that reeked of contempt. It was a look that had been seen by every single person on the stand side of Donnybrook rugby ground at that moment, including Horace's father. It was a look that conveyed a judgement of unworthiness from the giver of the glance to its recipient and to the rest of the world who watched. In that glance, the other boy had told Horace that he was a failure, a washout, someone who did not deserve to exist and would henceforth merely be ignored. Horace had felt the judgement seep into his soul.

In the here and now, a full half-century later, the memory of it still had the power to jolt him, like a shock from an electric kettle. Horace had seen such utter disdain and contempt in the eyes of his school classmate that, even now, he recalled with perfect simulation the feeling of failure it had engendered within him.

There had been no sound from the whistle when the referee put it to his mouth, only raised arms and unbelieving smiles on the faces of fifteen boys from Newbridge College in the County of Kildare. In the crowd of spectators, Horace's father had stood out from the hundreds of others around him as he'd risen to leave the stadium before the teams had vacated the pitch and approached the presentation table.

It had all been merely a prelude to the most awful thing that had ever happened. As the Columba's players had hunkered down in tears, or stood with hands on hips, shaking their heads in disbelief, there had been a sudden flurry of activity near the exit from the stand. A man in a long grey coat had climbed up onto the roof of the team dug-out. He'd calmed the crowd with his hands and then asked, 'If there's a doctor here could he please make himself known to the stewards at once? A man has just collapsed.'

Without having to make any enquiry at all, Horace had known instinctively that the man they had been talking about was his father. He had run across the pitch to the edge of the crowd that had gathered around the man lying on the steps. It had been an eerie experience, because the crowd had seemed to sense the connection between the man's collapse and the boy's failure to be given a pass that would have won the match for Columba's; they had parted and allowed the boy through to see his disappointed father. Robert Winter had lain on the cold concrete steps. Someone had rolled up a coat and put it under his head. Someone else had loosened his collar and taken off his tie.

A small man had arrived, carrying a black leather bag held closed by an enormous silver clip. He had taken out a stethoscope and placed the earpieces in his ears before inserting the other end through an opening in Horace's father's shirt. The entire crowd had seemed to hold its breath as the doctor listened for life. There had been none to be found. Horace had remembered touching one of his father's hands and, finding it warm, expected him to speak and to resume living. But the simple fact had been that his father was dead, and it had been Horace's fault. Robert Winter had died from disappointment, from the knowledge that his son was unworthy of bearing his name. Between the moment of his father's death and the funeral a week later, Horace and his mother had lived in near-silence. Horace had known that she, too, blamed him for his father's death.

'Why did he have to go and watch that bloody game?' she had asked. It was the only thing she said to Horace all that week, and that said it all. Horace knew at that point that he would probably never do anything right in his entire life, not as far as his mother was concerned. He had ruined everything.

He had a very vivid memory of his father's face as it had been when Horace was a child. But somehow he felt that they had missed out on a large chunk of each other's lives. Although he'd spent some time alone with his father, they had essentially failed to connect when Robert Winter was entering middle age and Horace was in his early teens. It was as though every time one of them was in, the other was out. A little, he thought, like those old comedies on the stage where two people were actually the same person so that a third party could encounter only one of them at any time. And now, fifty years after his father's death, Horace was beginning to see him at last in the form he might have taken in the part of Horace's life that he had missed out on: between the rugby cup final and

now. It was a bit like seeing someone every day at the
bank for years but not really studying that person's
face. Then, one day, you'd find yourself somewhere
else, he thought. You could be in a post office buying
a stamp, and the same person you'd seen every day
might walk in, at that moment of your life and theirs,
and they would look to you entirely different. You
could feel as though you were seeing them for the
first time, ever, as though each time they'd called to
visit you before, you'd been out (or had simply not
answered the door). He wondered about the water
on the day of the landings. Had it been cold, even
though it was June? Had there been sharks in the sea
near Sword Beach that summer? Horace wondered
if his father had shared his fear of water. He realised
that his father would have been armed. Did he have
to shoot anyone during the war? He had asked him
once but had not received an answer. How could you
get through a war without killing anyone? Was there
a question on the application form to join Customs
at Dublin Port that required disclosure about how
Corporal Robert Winter had got on in France? 'There
won't be any shooting in this job, Mr Winter,' they
might have said at the interview. Horace left and took
a taxi home.

On the wall in Edenvale Road, to the left of the fireplace in the sitting room, hung a photograph of his father in uniform somewhere in France during the war. He was sitting on a low wall with two comrades. Their bodies partially obscured a road sign at about waist height in the background. Horace took the photograph down from its hook and stared into it.

He was conscious that his father had rarely spoken about his time in the army. He knew that Robert Winter had joined the British army in 1939 when war had broken out. Horace's parents had lived in Devon after they'd married, and his mother had nursed in London during the Blitz. Horace had been born in Devon but they'd moved to Ireland in 1947 when he was only five years old. All he remembered about Otterton were the thatched roofs of the houses and a snippet of a song by some Morris dancers that sounded like 'A Wicky Wick Wack Wack Woo'. He had no idea if that was a genuine memory or just a dream he'd once had.

Before they'd come to Ireland, his father had secured a position as a customs officer at Dublin Port. He learned that this had been partly due to family connections on his mother's side. She was originally from County Meath but had emigrated to England in the 1930s to train as a nurse. It was the death of her own father some years after their return that had resulted in her inheriting fifty-seven Edenvale Road. Horace barely remembered his grandparents. It was a mystery to him as to whether they'd been butterflies or moths. He tried to picture them in his head but could only generate a scene from his childhood in which he was being chased by a cow in a meadow full of dandelions. Life was funny like that.

On the back of the photograph, he read the names of his father's companions: 'Fred Alexander and Migsie Spring'. Was one of them the fallen comrade his father had mourned? With the aid of an atlas and an old encyclopaedia, Horace had worked out that the road sign behind the three men was for a place called Ouistreham. It sounded like a Dutch name to Horace, but there it was on the map, in France. '2nd Batt E Yorkshires' was written in brackets beneath the men's names. Horace knew that his father had landed in Normandy on D-Day but could not even say upon which beach he had been, or how many beaches in total had hosted the landings.

'Sword Beach,' Amanda announced, when she ducked in later that week to visit.

Horace was flattered to see her. He didn't tell her about Beaumont Hospital, about the things the doctor had said and the pills he'd been given. He had answered the door wearing his slippers, but she didn't seem to notice, or if she did, she gave no sign of being offended by it. He enjoyed her company enormously. She was easy to be with, easy to talk to. She was almost certainly a Zephyr Blue, one of the most spectacular species of butterfly. It was also one of the rarest. In fact, for a moment, he almost wondered whether she might be a Mazarine Blue, but of course they had been extinct since 1877. No, on reflection, she was almost certainly a Zephyr Blue.

Now *there* was a species he'd never thought he'd get to see in his lifetime. They were sun-loving, and tended to prefer upland habitats. They were normally seen between May and July and were not usually found outside Greece. Horace remembered that his categorisation of people in this way was not an exact science, and what it captured more than anything else was the essence of the person. She was most certainly a butterfly and, without doubt, a sun-lover. A Zephyr Blue seemed the closest he could find for now. She gladdened his heart and made him feel young again.

'I'm pretty sure it was Sword Beach your dad landed on. I looked it up on Wikipedia.'

Horace hated computers and thought them more likely to prise people apart rather than bring them closer together.

'I can't believe you worked in a bank for two hundred years and still don't really know how to use your PC,' she said. They sat at the kitchen table and Amanda pointed at some sheets of paper spread between them. 'Can you believe it, Horace? There are ads on the radio for "one hundred and five per cent mortgages".' It's bananas.'

Various maps and pictures were contained in the conglomeration of information on the table. Horace got up and put the kettle on, then remembered he'd forgotten to buy the biscuits she liked, the ones with the chocolate fringes that overlapped the actual biscuits.

'Okay, Horace, here's the story. There were five beaches in the landings: Sword, Juno, Omaha, Utah and Gold. They were pretty much divided up in terms of nationality. So, for example, Juno was where the Canadians landed, Utah was nearly all American and Sword was where the Brits went ashore. You see those kind of square things? They were called LCIs, Landing

Craft Infantry. Your dad would most likely have disembarked from one. Earlier in the day, the Allies had shelled the German positions, then paratroopers were dropped a bit inland to try to secure the bridges and the canals. The infantry landed, almost thirty thousand of them, and only six hundred and thirty casualties resulted.'

Horace studied the maps and put his finger on the dot beside the name 'Ouistreham'. 'What's this?' he asked, as his finger found the word 'Queen' on the map of the beach.

'That's a section of the beach, Horace. It says here …' she rustled through the stapled pages '… that the beach was split in four and they called each portion by a code name. The others were 'Peter', 'Roger' and 'Oboe'.'

Horace remembered that, when he'd been a child, his father had played a wind instrument. Flute or maybe even oboe, he couldn't quite recall, but he'd certainly heard it being played when he was very small, perhaps before he could even walk. He'd been lying down somewhere and the sound of the melody had come at him from a corner of the house he couldn't see. How did he know it had been his father?

'I just know, that's all,' he said aloud to himself.

As he and Amanda sat there, on that Saturday afternoon, Horace was aware of his father in a completely different way.

'You really miss him, don't you?' Amanda said, as they gathered up the various bits of paper.

'Yes. Yes, I do,' Horace replied.

'You think you let your father down, don't you, Horace?'

His father had been gone far too long from Horace's life for Horace to make him proud now. He did not reply.

'So, Horace?'

'Yes?'

'What *are* you going to do with all of your time now that you're retired? You must have *hobbies* – everybody has a hobby. What do you like to do in your spare time?'

'Lepidopterology, I suppose.'

'Oh, how wonderful!' she exclaimed. 'Butterflies and moths. This probably isn't the best time of year to see them. Do you have a collection?'

'Yes!' Horace was delighted. 'I have several species in small glass mountings on the stairs and on the landing. I have some books and there's even an old net knocking around somewhere, although I couldn't lay my hand on it the other day when I went looking. Did you know there's a butterfly farm somewhere in County Kildare?'

He made them tea. He produced a small plastic bottle from the pocket of his suit and shook it before placing it on the table. He twisted the cap and spilled the tablets out onto his hand. He scooped them all except one back into the container, then popped the remaining one into his mouth and gulped some tea to sluice it down his throat.

'What are those for?' Amanda asked, nodding in the direction of the plastic cylinder of horse tablets.

'Headaches and nausea,' Horace replied. 'A bit of a brain tumour, actually. It's right in here.' He tapped the front of his head and felt for a second as though he was pointing at the exact spot where it lived.

'Does it hurt?' she asked gently.

He watched her stare at her own cup of tea, and realised that the last visitor to his house had been the Church of Ireland minister who'd called to see him about a month after his mother had died. 'Sometimes it does.'

'You know, tons of people recover from it, have remission. Sometimes they get cured mysteriously when everyone else has given up hope for them. Sometimes the scientists even find a cure by accident when they're trying to make something else.'

Horace started, but it began to dawn on him that most of what she said was true. He felt a little better than he had for a very long time, and she was the reason. The tumour might be in his head but surely it was what was in his heart that mattered most?

Amanda left to go to work. Horace thought about death. He imagined the world as a gigantic chessboard where everyone stood on their own square and could move only in a particular way, depending on what they were. But when Death came looking for companionship, what happened then? He imagined each square as a trapdoor springing downwards, making the occupant of that grid-point disappear. What dictated the order in which the traps were sprung? Maybe the trapdoor was in your own head sometimes, growing or receding, depending on the size of the tablet you took.

Horace knocked the electricity bill off the sideboard in the hall while he was writing a cheque. It fell off and, as it settled on the floor, its last swish carried it under the large piece of furniture from which it had fallen. When Horace eventually managed to move the sideboard to retrieve the bill, he found his old butterfly net, jammed against the wall. It was a little squashed and had no handle, almost as if someone had deliberately hidden it there.

CHAPTER EIGHT

Black-veined White (*Aporia crataegi*): thought
to be extinct in Britain and Ireland since 1926

Niobe Fritillary (*Argynnis niobe*)

Orange Tip (Anthocharis cardamines): a
butterfly that flits along flowery verges and
meadows

Iron Prominent (*Notodonta dromedarius*)

Swallowtail Moth (*Ourapteryx sambucaria*)

Horace continued to take his tablets. He'd
returned to the Oncology Unit for check-ups
twice since his initial visit. Progress was being made:
the growth had begun to recede under the assault of

modern medicine. Horace's headaches were a little less frequent but a lot less severe, and the nausea had not reappeared for weeks.

'You're not going to find them sitting here moping in your front room,' Amanda said one evening. She'd dropped in for a cup of tea.

'Not going to find what?' Horace asked.

'You know, the Brown Fibber or the Heavy Breathing moth, or whatever the ones you need to find are called.'

'There's no such species as the Brown Fibber,' Horace said, in an exasperated voice.

'Well, whatever they're called, you won't find them here,' Amanda said, with a shy smirk. 'Look outside, it's pitch dark.'

'So?'

'So, moths come out at night, don't they?'

'That's true, although, of course some species do fly during the day. For example the Silver Y is often found feeding by day on clover, teasel and red valerian around dusk or even earlier.'

'Get your coat, then, Horace,' Amanda said.

'Why?'

'We're going out.'

'Where to?' Horace asked.

'To the bright lights moths are attracted to at night, Horace. That's where to.'

'Legs and Lizards' was an unusual name for a nightclub, Horace thought, as he and Amanda queued on the pavement outside the Leeson Street establishment. Moths and butterflies crowded the narrow stairs down to the entrance. There were plenty of Red Admirals and quite a few Brimstone moths in the line of people waiting to get into the club. It was Friday night in Dublin and the common species were out in force. In the company directly ahead of Horace and Amanda, a man was nibbling the shoulder and neck of a young girl in a green coat. They looked quite alike and Horace noticed that they both had dark brown hair. *In late summer the caterpillar will move down to the trunk of whatever tree it has been feeding on and burrow under any moss growing on the bark.*

The Scalloped Hazel was quite a common variety of moth but this was the first one Horace had seen closely enough to identify for sure. He felt that the outing had already been a success.

'Twenty euro, bud,' the man on the door said, when Horace's turn came.

'Twenty each or twenty for two?' Horace asked.

'Twenty for one,' the large man said.

Horace handed over two twenties – 'Thanks,' the man said – and they entered the small hall behind the doorman.

The noise hit Horace full force in the face after the thick door into the club had been opened for them by a second man in a tuxedo. It was like a pneumatic drill and his ears pounded with the beat of the music.

'It's very loud, isn't it?' he said to Amanda.

'Yes, great!' she replied.

Inside the club there were hundreds of people, all crammed up against each other. Horace wasn't sure if they were dancing or if that was happening farther back in the room, somewhere he couldn't yet see. The lights were brilliant; like paint being thrown around the room, then separated and mixed and separated again.

'I'll get some drinks,' Amanda shouted into his ear. 'What would you like?'

'Milk,' Horace said.

'Fine. See you over at one of those tables in a minute.'

Amanda moved effortlessly across the room through the dancers or onlookers or whatever they were. Horace inched his way through hordes of angry-faced people. At first it was difficult to see much of anything, but as his eyes became accustomed to the measly ration of useful light, he began to identify possible species from their movements and attire. A Niobe Fritillary was dancing by herself at the edge of the crowd. Horace sensed that she was already the subject of the attention of various other butterflies, and he was right. A Black-veined White was hovering nearby with a pint of Guinness in her hand, pretending to be looking for someone while an Orange Tip stood motionless in front of her, staring at her feet. Orange Tips were cannibalistic, although you would hardly have guessed it from his stance. While those three butterflies were engaged in their varying degrees of playing hard to get, Horace noticed a movement into the scene from behind the roped-off VIP area. A *Notodonta dromedarius*, or Iron Prominent moth, was (characteristically) almost invisible, with its dark grey wings melting nearly seamlessly into the fabric of the wall covering. Without notice, it swooped in a movement of near-violence low to the ground between the chattering male butterflies. Within seconds, it was devouring the hapless Niobe.

'Do you need to use the loo?' Amanda asked. She had not bought them any drinks. Horace guessed his expression must have appeared pained. The mere suggestion, however, prompted an immediate necessity and he rose from the red-cushioned settee to seek out the Men's.

In the toilets of Legs and Lizards, a lone occupant stood with his back to Horace. The man was hunched and jittering over the counter to the right of the basins. Horace used the facilities, but it was not until he approached the taps that he saw what the man was up to. He was chopping a small pile of sherbet with a red credit card and dividing it into thin lines. Horace watched as he produced a crisp banknote from his inside pocket and began to roll it up. It was at that point that the man noticed Horace. 'Want some?' he asked, in a voice that seemed to belong to someone bigger.

'No, thanks,' said Horace. 'It gives me fizzy rash on my tongue.'

'Jaysus,' the man exclaimed. 'Do you eat the bleedin' stuff?'

'I used to,' Horace replied, remembering lollipops and liquorice.

Just then the door opened and a large man in a dress-suit entered. The man at the counter tried to gather the sherbet into an envelope. Horace finished washing his hands, then approached the dryer and pressed the large silver button. With a *whooooosh* the entire heap of sherbet blew across the basin area and into the air, like a desert storm. The man who had been about to eat it turned from the mirror. Horace saw that his suit jacket was covered with sherbet-y dandruff. He pointed two fingers in a V at Horace and promptly ran out past the latest arrival.

'That's the Swallowtail moth for you,' Horace remarked, as he dried his hands under the electric blower. 'Always on the move. Never stays in one place but is unmistakable at night due to its fast flight.'

*

In the summer of 1958, Horace had met the love of his life in Rosslare. An ice-cream van had caught fire on the promenade. Its owner managed to escape through the hatch from which he handed out the cones and choc ices. He stood only a few feet away from his vehicle as it was crowned by a halo of fire and smoke. A fire engine arrived from Wexford Town, much too late to do any more than cover the charred wreck with seawater, pumped by hand from the incoming tide.

As the crowd of onlookers in bathing suits began to disperse, Horace noticed a girl looking at him across the dip in the middle of the fire engine. She waved at him as he returned her gaze. Horace's feet felt heavy and light at the same time. He wanted to walk around to see her but, by the time he had, she was gone. He looked for her but could see no sign, so he continued on his way.

The following day he was walking along the sand dunes near the golf course when she jumped out from behind some marram grass and said, 'Boo.' She wore a red and white polka-dot dress, and held her sandals in one hand.

'Scared you, didn't I?' she said, with a grin.

'No,' said Horace, defensively.

'Why did you jump, then?'

'I didn't.'

'Look at the tracks you made when you landed.'

Horace looked down at his feet and by the time he looked up again she had disappeared. He heard a whistle so he followed it, and that was how they met. Her name was Rose Burke. Her father had rented a caravan near the beach at Rosslare in a campsite called Strand View. She was from some small village in County Galway.

'We spend the whole summer here, until it's time to go back to school.'

That had been in early August, and for the next ten days they were inseparable. They walked for hours along the sand and up the grassy hills at the end of the beach to where they could lie on their stomachs and watch the fishing boats creep home in the late evening. They built a campfire among the dunes one night and roasted apples on pointy sticks. Out beyond them, in the seaside holiday empires, people lived lives that Rose and Horace did not care about.

'My mammy says Protestants never tell lies,' she said to him one afternoon, as they stared out to sea from behind a wall of wet sand they'd built using a square plastic bucket and a yellow spade.

'I lie to my mother all the time,' he replied.

'Maybe she's been fibbing to you, and you're not really a Protestant,' she said, with a laugh.

He turned towards her and their hands touched on the hot sand between them. The warmth of the sun lay around them. He heard her breathing. Curlews were yodelling in the dunes behind them, and the sky was as blue as it had ever been before for anybody else, for any other boy and girl, for any other first kiss.

Those days had melted into a sovereign of happiness in Horace's heart and in his memory. It was a magical time, when he was suddenly, and for the only time ever, absolutely free. It was as though someone had left a gate open on the edge of his life: Horace had bolted through the gap like a horse with a real chance in the Curragh.

And then he'd lost her.

CHAPTER NINE

Purple Emperor (*Apatura iris*): very elusive; found near tall oak trees; occasionally may be observed at ground level near carrion

Essential equipment for collecting: a net, a killing bottle and a setting board.

'Round Hall, court number two,' the summons said.

'All rise,' said a voice, so they did.

'Good morning, ladies and gentlemen,' the judge said. He was a large man with a face that looked to be of the no-nonsense type. A Purple Emperor, thought Horace.

'... as soon as your name is called,' the judge continued. 'Now, I want to make clear that both the prosecution and the defence may object to a certain number of jurors selected without giving any reasons. Similarly, if any of you believes that, for any reason, you should not be empanelled as a juror to try this case, please bring it to my attention when your name is called. I refer here to circumstances in which you might for example know one of the witnesses, be a neighbour of the accused, have gone to school with one of the gardaí in the case or have any connection, however minor, with the case you are selected to try.'

'The DPP and Thomas Hackett.' A voice from somewhere between Horace and the judge called the case.

'Thomas Anthony Hackett, you are charged as set out in the indictment that on the fourth day of September two thousand and six at Sycamore Street Apartments in the City of Dublin you did murder one Zosia Krasnopolska contrary to common law. How do you plead?'

The first voice spoke again. Horace could not see any of the speakers. He began to feel faint. His dizziness had come on quite unexpectedly. They were called one by one to the jury box and sworn in. From time to time, an objection was raised and that person stood aside.

Horace made his way into the jury box and stood for a moment, looking out at a sea of strange faces.

'I, Horace Boythorn Winter, do solemnly swear and affirm that I shall well and truly try this case and a true verdict give according to the evidence.'

'No objection for the prosecution,' said a tall barrister with a Cork accent.

'No objection for the defence.'

Horace sat down. For the second time in his life, he found himself in a courtroom. He could imagine his mother's reaction if she'd been alive: 'First a defendant, then a juror. Maybe you'll eventually come back as a barrister.'

The jury room was quite large. It had a huge oak table in the middle and comfortable chairs with leather seats arranged around it. There were no windows to the outside world but, rather, a long, frosted pane high up on an internal wall that seemed to give out onto a corridor that was also well within the internal anatomy of the Four Courts complex. Horace looked at his teammates. He made it eight butterflies and three moths. He concentrated on the faces and colour of the other jurors as a discussion began on how best to select someone to be their spokesperson.

'Maybe we should draw lots or something like that,' said the female Moorland Clouded Yellow.

'What about asking people whether they'd like their names to go forward?' That sounded like a good idea to Horace. He could feel himself smiling in support.

'There's no need to embarrass anyone about this,' said a thick Dublin-accented Sword-grass moth. 'I'm prepared to put *myself* forward as a *compromise* candidate. I know a little bit about life *and* the law.' He gave a chuckle, and Horace thought he saw a glance pass between the other two moths in the room.

'How about a show of hands?'

'Okay so,' echoed the Sword-grass. 'That's settled, then.'

That morning, the jury were shown photographs of the murder scene. The assistant state pathologist gave his evidence. 'The deceased was subjected to a sustained and prolonged regime of torture prior to the final act of strangulation.'

'Hooker Hacked and Strangled' was emblazoned across the *Daily Mirror*'s front page. At home that evening, Horace was sitting in the front sitting room when Amanda visited. He had been very troubled about what he could and couldn't discuss with her concerning the case.

She put his mind at ease right away. 'It's a very important duty you've got to carry out, Horace. I think I know which case you're involved in, and you're probably not supposed to talk about it with anyone. I won't ask you anything until it's all over.'

'Thank you, Amanda,' Horace said with relief. He knew that if he did have any problems with the case, Amanda would surely know what to do. But he wouldn't discuss it with her now. Not while the trial was continuing and they were still talking about 'ligature marks' and 'multiple cuts to the torso and other regions'.

The technical evidence took days and days to go through in the crowded air-conditioned courtroom.

The succession of witnesses proved the chain of evidence, (including the preservation of the jump leads used to strangle the victim), and dozens and dozens of phone messages and records from an answering service the Polish girl had used. One entire morning was wasted when the jury had to retire to their room and wait for three hours while the legal teams argued about the admissibility of a statement.

'Mr Clotworth, could you tell his lordship what you were doing on the fourth of September 2006?' the prosecuting senior counsel asked the latest witness. It was day six of the trial. The witness was a small rotund man in his fifties. He struck Horace as being rather like the type of bank customer who regularly arrives late on a Friday afternoon, just as the bank is about to close, and makes cash lodgements while simultaneously seeking large amounts of small-coin change.

'Yes, Your Honour. I was just opening my shop in Dame Street.'

'What kind of shop is that?' asked the judge.

'A newsagent's, Your Honour.' The witness

garbled his way towards the answer. A slight tinge of purple iridescence showed on the Emperor's face as he rolled his eyes but made no further comment.

'I was just opening the bales of newspapers when the man came into the shop to buy something.'

'What man?' asked the prosecution counsel.

'That man there,' said the witness, pointing across the courtroom at the man sitting between two prison officers on the front bench at right angles to the press box.

'I think you're pointing at someone in the court, here present today?' the prosecutor prodded. Although there had been no background noise until now, the silence seemed to Horace to go up a notch as every butterfly and moth in the room controlled its wings so that the moment would not be disturbed.

'Yes, that man over there,' said the witness. 'Mr Hackett.'

'The accused?' asked counsel, unnecessarily, for extra effect.

'Yes,' agreed the witness. 'The accused.' The information soaked through the room, like water into a sponge laid lightly on the still surface of a full bath.

'How can you be sure?'

'Because after the murder happened, all of the local shops held on to their CCTV footage from the day of the killing, and that man was in the footage from my shop.'

'Did the accused purchase anything in your shop?'

'Yes,' the shopkeeper answered. 'A large box of Saxa salt.'

'I think that the video footage from your shop proved inconclusive to the gardaí in trying to identify the person concerned?'

'Yes. One of the cameras wasn't working that morning so he could only be seen side-on at the till. There are better cameras now that my—'

'And that person wore a hood?' The prosecutor deflected the witness back onto the tracks.

'Yes.'

'So, Mr Clotworth, how can you be so sure that the person who bought the box of salt from your shop that morning was the accused?'

'Well, I served him myself, and I'm pretty good at remembering faces.'

Horace thought that one moth might look very like another, even with a box of salt under its wing.

'Had you ever seen the man before that morning?'

'No.'

'Did you ever see him again?'

'Apart from the line-up in the garda station?'

'Yes, apart from that.'

Mr Clotworth shifted uneasily in the witness box and moved himself forward a little so that his nose struck the microphone that grew out of the small shelf in front of him. The rude noise reverberated around the room and a release of laughter rose for a moment before the silence recast itself over the multitude assembled. 'Yes. At least, I'm fairly sure I saw him again.'

'When?'

'On the same day.'

'The day Miss Krasnopolska was killed?'

'Yes.'

'Can you tell us about that, Mr Clotworth?'

Horace felt the wings of the Sooty Copper digging into his side as the jury edged along their seats so that they were as close to the witness as they could physically be.

Mr Clotworth continued: 'Every evening at five I drop the *Evening Herald* over to Mrs Keelin in one oh three.'

'What did you see?'

'I saw a man standing near the Olympia on the corner of Crane Lane.'

'What man?'

'Yer man there.'

'The accused?'

'Yes.'

'What was he doing?'

'He was standing on the corner looking around as if he was being followed or something.'

'What do you mean by that, Mr Clotworth?'

'Well, he was nervous, like. I thought it was unusual.'

'You thought what was unusual?'

'Well, he was looking around and, at the same time, trying to rub something off his hand into his sleeve. He kept rubbing his wrist and his hand with the sleeve of his jacket.'

'Did you notice anything else about him that appeared out of the ordinary to you, Mr Clotworth?' the prosecution senior counsel asked.

'The only other thing that struck me was that as he just stood on the corner wiping his hand or rubbing it, he looked back over his shoulder a couple of times and then he suddenly started walking away quickly.

That was the last I saw of him until the line-up in the garda station.'

'I think this is an appropriate time to rise for lunch,' said the judge.

The final witness for the prosecution gave evidence on day eight of the murder trial.

'Sergeant O'Shea, could you tell the court how you came to arrest and question Mr Hackett in connection with this murder investigation?'

Although the barrister asked him the question the garda addressed his answers to the Purple Emperor.

'Yes, Judge. Well, the investigation had almost come to a dead end, you might say, until one member from Pearse Street arrested the accused in connection with a separate investigation, something quite unconnected with these matters here.'

'Could you tell us when that was, Sergeant?'

'Yes, Judge.' The garda looked at his notebook. 'On the nineteenth of November 2007, a call was received at Pearse Street Garda Station that an alarm had been activated in a leather-goods shop in Wicklow Street. A suspect was apprehended at the scene. The suspect in that incident was Mr Thomas Hackett, who had been out shopping with his young son. He had attempted to steal a wallet. That set off the security alarm when the accused was leaving the premises. He was arrested and taken to Pearse Street station and when he was fingerprinted that profile was uploaded to the garda database.'

Horace contemplated the enormity of this disclosure. *He* was the person responsible for the arrest of Thomas Hackett. But for his own wrong action in the leather-goods shop, there was little chance that the man would be on trial at all. Was he guilty?

What would Horace have done if he'd heard the man's voice at the arraignment and recognised it as that of the Spurge Hawk-moth he'd encountered in Grafton Street violently abusing his son because of some spilled football cards? What would he have said to the judge, to the Purple Emperor, as he'd approached him and whispered in his ear? What reason could he have given for his own unsuitability to be part of the jury, this jury, *any* jury? *I'm guilty of setting this man up by knocking a wallet with a security tag into his bag. I framed him for a robbery he did not commit because I was angry with him over the way he treated his son.* Would the judge have had *Horace* locked up?

The Polish girl was already dead when the man was

belting his son and dragging him down past Brown Thomas's by the hair. This was horror squared. Now Horace felt entirely responsible for whatever happened to the Polish girl's memory from this point on.

The defence called no witnesses, not even the accused. The closing speeches of both sides and the judge's charge to the jury took almost a full day. Then, suddenly, the trial was almost over and all that remained was for the jury to do its job. That would be tomorrow. Horace gathered his coat and hat and opened the door of the jury room, as the other butterflies and moths made small-talk with each other and did not seem in any rush to leave.

A female garda stood outside the door. 'Are you all right?' she asked.

'Yes, I'm fine. I'm just going home,' Horace replied.

'Oh, I'm sorry, sir, but that's not possible,' the garda said.

'Why ever not?'

'The jury is now sequestered as it's in the process of deliberation. You'll be sent to a hotel tonight and guarded by myself and Garda Garvey until you reach a verdict.'

'But what about my pyjamas?' Horace had asked the obvious question in the circumstances.

'I'll send someone out to Dunnes for you. You're not allowed to have contact with anyone apart from the jury until your work is done.'

Horace asked her to make sure the person they sent out to Dunnes Stores bought blue pyjamas for him. It was the only colour he could sleep in.

'I want to call this meeting to order,' the Sword-grass said, as he banged a lighter on the table. The rest of the jurors fell silent. 'What we have to do now is make the most important decision not only in our lives but also in the life [he pronounced it 'loyfe'] of that man out there.' He pointed at the wall of the room as he concluded this remark. 'There is a fellow human being out there, handcuffed to two prison officers, wondering if he's going to spend the rest of his bleeding life in Mountjoy Prison.'

'I think you've lost sight of the victim,' said Mr Apollo. 'We're talking about the death of a person here.'

'We all know that,' said Miss Geranium Argus. 'The question we have to answer is, did Thomas Hackett do it?'

'*Did* he do it?' The Knapweed Fritillary unleashed a cackle.

'I'm with you, on that, Emer,' said the Chalk Hill Blue. 'The guy is a bloody psychopath or a sociopath or whatever they call it.'

'What about the evidence?' asked the Pale Tussock, her pink tail just ever so slightly pinker on that Friday morning.

'What *about* it?' said the Grizzled Skipper, angrily.

'Okay,' said the Sword-grass, raising his arms in mock surrender. 'Let's go through the evidence bit by bit, then see where we are for a vote on it.' The afternoon dripped past minute by minute, until the clink of cups and saucers broke the conversations and speculations into little pieces, which seemed so much more remote after Jaffa cakes.

'Are you all right?' said the Sooty Copper. 'Horace, are you all right?'

'Yes, yes, I'm fine,' Horace said, but he wasn't.

'Somebody give him a glass of water,' said the Gatekeeper.

'Stand back now, give him room to breathe. He's

just fainted. I'd say it's dee-hi-dray-shun,' said the
Sword-grass, in a poisonous voice.

'You should have told myself or Garda McGuinness
last night and we'd have driven you home to get them.'
Horace was in the passenger seat of a squad car. It eased
carefully through the parked-car haven of Ranelagh's
weary redbrick roads. A jangle to their right as the Luas
tram passed by.

When he arrived at number fifty-seven Edenvale
Road, the house was warm, the evening sunlight fading
through the kitchen window. Horace came down the
stairs holding the L'Oréal zipper bag his mother had
kept her own medication in near the end. He'd packed
an extra pair of socks and underpants, a clean shirt and
his shaving things in a heavy-duty Spar bag, the kind
they give you if you buy more than one large milk.
The pyjamas the gardaí had bought for him had been
blue, but had 'Relax, don't do it' written across the
front. He had his own pyjamas in the Spar bag.

He thoughr about the poor girl's family. Someone
on the jury had pointed them out to him during the
trial. He recalled their faces, two haggard butterflies, a
Hermit and a Rock Grayling, with a translator sitting
beside them, interpreting the horror of their daughter's

death for them. Regardless of the language used, Horace thought, they will never really understand. Would Hackett kill someone else if he was allowed to walk free? Horace was suddenly back on Grafton Street, under the Christmas lights, listening to the Spurge Hawk-moth lambast his young son over the spilled football cards. He recalled the slap, the foul language, the absence of love, the dragging by the hair. He, Hackett, knew he'd been seen near the crime scene. Had his eyes locked with the shopkeeper's in that half a jiffy? Horace recalled again the man's violent treatment of his son, then thought of the box of salt, the jump leads, cuts filled to the brim with Saxa. How could one human being torture another like that?

'Because some moths love to tear the wings off butterflies, is that it?' Horace said aloud, without meaning to.

'Pardon?' said the garda. They passed Sycamore Street where the girl had lived and died. A few yards later, they passed the newsagent's. It was closed. Horace had thought it stayed open until eleven every night.

The Purple Emperor had told them that their decision had to be unanimous but the Geranium Argus had informed them differently. 'Every half-baked bar-stool lawyer or law student in the country knows that after a particular period of time the trial judge will tell a jury that a majority verdict is acceptable.' The pieces of paper were distributed and everyone retreated behind a cupped wing to cast their vote.

Horace knew that he should have told the judge, as soon as he'd realised it, that he had been the cause of Thomas Hackett's arrest. And what about the son of the accused, Max? What if Hackett were actually innocent of the entire crime and he was sent to jail wrongly? His son would be taken into care. And what if he were acquitted but he was *actually* guilty: would he harm his son?

The Sword-grass stacked the votes in three piles.

'What's the result?' the Knapweed Fritillary asked excitedly.

'The result is, guilty nine votes, not guilty two votes.' He scanned the faces. 'And one person has written "abstain" on their voting paper.

'It doesn't really matter, does it?' said the Grizzled Skipper. 'Even if there was one more vote on either side it wouldn't change things. It has to be unanimous.' Butterflies and moths nodded at this observation: the Grizzled Skipper was right. It wouldn't make a hoot of a difference.

It was almost five o'clock when the usher told them that the judge had asked them to return to court. The Purple Emperor spoke solemnly: 'Ladies and gentlemen of the jury, I understand from your foreman that you have been unable to arrive at a verdict upon which you are all agreed. In those circumstances, I can now inform you that the court will allow you to deliver a majority verdict. In the event that you cannot do so after a further period of time, I will address you on that issue in due course. I should say also that if clarification is required on any point regarding the evidence or the exhibits, I will be glad to provide that clarification for you. The only other matter of which you need to be aware, of course, is that a majority verdict in the case of murder means a verdict on which at least ten of you are agreed.'

'All rise,' said the usher.

Saturday dawned sunny over the capital. There was a March chill outside but the streets of Dublin were warmed by the excitement of rugby fans traipsing the streets in advance of the match. A large contingent of Ireland supporters sat at another table in the hotel dining room. They wore jerseys and the battle-scars of a hard night's drinking. One of them left a newspaper behind on a chair. The Chalk Hill Blue swooped on it and began the crossword immediately.

A good night's sleep had convinced Horace more than ever that the right thing to do was to hold his nerve and continue with his abstention. At worst, there would have to be a retrial with a different jury. *That* would be the perfect solution. On the bus to the Four Courts, the Chalk Hill Blue sat behind Horace.

'What was the name of the man who owned the newsagent's?'

'Mr Clotworth,' Horace replied.

'No, no, his first name.'

'I don't know.'

'Was it Mervyn?'

'I don't know. Why?'

'I'll tell you when we get to the jury room.'

As they hung their coats on the stand, and stood around in knots of two and three, Horace noticed that the Sword-grass and the Geranium Argus were deep in conversation.

The Sooty Copper read aloud: '"Died, Clotworth,

Mervyn, suddenly, at home. To the inexpressible grief of his wife Janis and son Harold. Funeral service today, Saturday, at 11.30 St Michan's Church of Ireland, Church Street, Dublin 7.""

'Do you think it's the same guy who owned the newsagent's?' the Apollo asked.

'I'd say so,' said Horace. 'The shop was shut at tea-time yesterday when I was being brought back with my tablets.'

'It's got to be him, then,' said the Pale Tussock.

'We don't know that for sure,' said the Gatekeeper.

'Horace saw the shop shut yesterday. It's got to be the same guy. I mean how many people can there be in the world called Clotworth?'

As a consequence of this remark, there was a moment of levity, but it passed quickly.

'What does it matter? What difference does it make? The case is over – well, all the evidence has been heard.' This observation from the Sooty Copper seemed sensible.

'Don't you see?' said the Grizzled Skipper. 'It makes a huge difference. If it is the same guy and we don't bring in a majority decision, then this bollix, Hackett, will get away with it scot-free.'

'But if we can't bring in a decision, won't they

simply have a retrial? With a new jury?' The Holly Blue was, as always, the voice of reason.

'Not if the only eyewitness has died,' said the Pale Tussock, sadly. 'It's now or never. There can never be a retrial without the witness.'

'That's none of our business,' said the Sword-grass. 'Let's just go out and tell them we can't bring in a ten to two verdict, and go home.'

The Sword-grass was growing in confidence now and Horace watched as he made his move, his Dublin accent getting fatter with every word.

'So what if Clotworth died? That bloody Polish slut has taken up two whole weeks of our lives, and I don't know about the rest of you, but I have a job to get back to and a bleeding life to get on with.'

Horace felt a volcano of anger begin somewhere below his knees and start to work its way up through his legs and into his torso. He had been wrestling with his own conscience, worrying about whether he should even be on the jury. 'You idiot,' he said to himself, 'catch a grip. You're always thinking about life passing you by, about curling up in a ball and hiding on a model battleship. Well, now it's time to make your voice heard. The manner of the arrest was just a coincidence.'

Horace still had a right – no, a *duty* – to weigh right and wrong. Come on, Horace, moth or mouse?

'Let's have one more vote,' he suggested. 'Just to be sure.'

After the guilty verdict, the accused's barrister made some remarks on his client's behalf. He spoke of how he was a single parent and how he hoped to be able to make things up to his son at some point in the future. The Purple Emperor noted the not-guilty plea and the 'apparent absence of either empathy or remorse', and imposed the mandatory sentence of life imprisonment on Thomas Anthony Hackett. The jurors were exempted from jury service for life.

As Horace stood up to leave the court, he saw the girl's parents embrace each other in tears. Horace was rooted to the spot. In another part of the room, a lady wearing the insignia of the Health Service Executive sat side by side with a young boy. The child had a blue zipper hoodie, which was open and revealed that he wore a red football shirt underneath it. He sat stock still, staring ahead of him, then suddenly glanced across the room at Horace. Horace remembered holding out his hands, full of football cards, to him many months earlier. He wondered if the boy remembered who he was. The child turned away, to look in the direction in which his father had disappeared, and began to cry silently. The social worker put her arm around his shoulders.

Horace remained in the courtroom until an usher came in. 'I'm locking up now, sir. I'm afraid you'll have to leave.'

Horace collected his coat and bag from the jury room. Everyone else had gone. He sat on the front steps of the Four Courts and watched the river go by. He did not understand why he felt as he did. What was the reason for his unhappiness? Hadn't they done the right thing? Wasn't it the right verdict? Eventually, he got the bus home to Ranelagh. He went into Birchall's pub and ordered the 'early bird': chicken chasseur. He delayed going home because somehow he felt the need to try to resolve his feelings while he was still part of a world that ended at his own front door.

A television on the wall of the lounge bar was showing the news. It carried the conviction of Thomas Hackett as its lead story. Horace couldn't stop thinking about Max. First, he had been cast adrift without a mother he had never known (she

had died of cancer when he was less than a year old).
Now, he was irrevocably alone, without a father.
Horace felt entirely responsible for this turn of events
in the boy's life. From the moment he'd nudged the
wallet with the security tag until the point where
he'd changed his vote from 'abstain', Horace Winter
had become the architect and cause of that innocent
child's misfortune. But for Horace's intervention,
in the shop and in the jury room, Thomas Hackett
would now be free and his son would not be in state
care.

CHAPTER TEN

'The importance of keeping an accurate account of sightings cannot be overstated, future generations may come to rely on it.'

Butterflies and Moths: A Beginner's Guide

Yellow Horned moth (*Achlya flavicornis*)

In the front room, Horace closed *A Dictionary of the Second World War* (by Wheal & Pope) and gathered the rest of the papers into a pile. He deposited them in the largest of the drawers in the bookcase.

'You've got tons of books, Horace,' Amanda said,

as she came into the room carrying two mugs of tea.
'Do you read a lot?'

'Not really,' he said.

'Well, what was the last book you read?'

'*The Bride of Lammermoor* by Sir Walter Scott,'
Horace replied.

'Is it a horror story?'

'Sort of,' he said, with a little smile playing at his
mouth's edges.

She began to look at the books in closer detail.
Horace thought of an incident in that room nearly
half a century earlier.

'Start at that end,' he instructed. 'I'm pretty sure
it's still here.'

'What's still here?' Amanda asked.

'My Leaving Certificate results.'

'You're joking? Here? In one of these books?'

'Yes,' Horace said. 'My mother was too ashamed
even to look at them again, she was so disgusted.'

Amanda regarded Horace with an expression he
felt contained a mix of pity and amazement. After a
moment's hesitation, she began at the other end of the
bookcase with *Kidnapped* by Robert Louis Stevenson.
Horace did likewise, beginning with *A Complete
Course of Meteorology* by L. F. Kaemtz. He held it by

the spine with one hand while the other flicked the pages into a fan.

Later, they sat in armchairs side by side and read the document that had determined the course of Horace Winter's life. It had lain, for all of that time, pressed between the pages of a memoir by Lady Fortescue entitled *There's Rosemary, There's Rue*. The results had slept within the body of the June 1941 Fifth Impression, published by William Blackwood and Sons Ltd, of Edinburgh and London. Horace recoiled in shock at the title of the work: could it be that his life had, even then, been mapped out for ever and a day by the hand of Fate? He simply didn't know.

It was his greatest regret that the very language he'd spoken from birth had proved to be his downfall in the Leaving Certificate. Even now, decades later, the harsh slap of it came leaping back across the intervening years. He'd spent too long on the poetry question and hadn't left himself much time to write the essay. He knew that his preoccupation with his own experiences had bogged him down in the poetry section. 'An analysis of the themes of loss in the poetry of Milton and Emily Dickinson' had been too much of a temptation. If he had been honest about it, Horace Winter had found and lost Paradise in Rosslare, County Wexford, about a year earlier.

Mr Almond, their teacher, had always warned them not to neglect the essay. 'It's a proven fact, lads, about English in the Leaving Cert, that if you do not pass the essay you cannot pass the exam.'

'You did pretty well in most subjects,' Amanda said helpfully.

'Hmm,' replied Horace.

'You could always sit the English paper again now, if you feel *that* badly about it.'

'Could I? At *my* age? Surely you'd have to be at school to sit the Leaving Certificate.'

'Not at all, Horace. You just pay a fee to the Department of Education for whatever subjects you want to do, and off you go.'

'I spent too long on the poetry section. I didn't have enough time for the essay,' Horace said, with a shake of his head.

'Haven't you plenty of time now?' she asked.

'I suppose so. I suppose so.'

★

There was an article in the Weekend section of *The Irish Times* about the detention of young offenders in various institutions around the country. Horace was frightened by the revelation that, from time to time, by virtue of the lack of proper residential care facilities, some teenagers and even younger people might be housed in those places. He felt sickened to think that Max might effectively end up in a prison, despite having done no wrong. 'Such facilities are dangerously understaffed,' the article concluded, 'and are regarded by many social commentators and child-welfare activists alike to be utterly unsuitable to promote the aim of rehabilitation or to tackle the increasing rate of recidivism.' Horace read and reread the article until his eyes hurt almost as much as his heart did.

Horace visited Emma Kelly to be sure she'd received his cheque for her fee.

'And the hospital? I take it everything was fine?'

'More than fine,' Horace said.

'Well, goodbye, then, Horace. Take care.' They'd shaken hands.

'May I ask you something?' Horace said, as he was about to leave his solicitor's office.

'Of course.'

'I was just wondering about someone,' he began. 'A child whose father has been sent to prison, what would happen to that child? Where would they go?'

'It all depends, really. Usually nothing changes if the other parent is still—'

'The mother is dead,' Horace said.

'Well, I suppose the extended family would probably come into play.'

'How do you mean?'

'Oh, you know, an aunt or uncle or grandparent might step in and take over the care of the child, unless Social Services or the HSE had become involved.'

Horace cast his mind back to the scene in the courtroom and the lady sitting beside Max as the sentencing occurred. He told Emma Kelly what he'd seen.

'It sounds to me as if the child will be in care until the father is released from prison, then. The child shouldn't have been in the courtroom at all.'

'Why would they have allowed that to happen?' Horace asked.

'Sometimes the defence feels that it could influence the jury or the judge on either the verdict or the sentence. What was the charge?'

'Murder,' Horace replied. 'He was sentenced to life.'

'How old is the child?' Emma asked.

'I'm not sure,' Horace said. 'Maybe ten or twelve years old.'

'He'll be well grown-up when his father gets out of prison, by the sound of it, Horace. Do you know the family?'

'No, no,' Horace replied. 'I just wondered what would happen to him, that's all.'

'Well, from what you say, the child seems to have been already taken into care by the HSE. Under the legislation, they are the primary carer when an order is made, but given the length of the sentence, my guess is they'll look for a suitable foster family to take care of him.'

'And until then,' Horace asked, 'where would he be put up or kept?'

'Some state facility, I suppose,' Horace's solicitor said. 'It's really not my area.'

'Nor mine,' Horace said as he opened the door to leave.

★

'Are you married, Mr Winter?' the lady in the HSE child-welfare section asked, as she continued to tick various boxes on a form in front of her, which Horace couldn't read upside-down. She wore a pair of rather sinister horn-rimmed glasses.

'No,' he replied.

'Any children?'

'I beg your pardon?' Horace said.

'Do you have any children of your own?' the lady continued.

'No.'

'Are you working currently?'

'I'm retired,' he replied.

'Have you had any experience of looking after children of *any* age?'

Horace froze. What was the answer to that question? He hadn't managed to look after Rose Burke very well. 'No,' he said eventually.

'I take it you are at least in good health, Mr Winter?'

'Yes,' Horace replied. 'I'm in fairly good shape, apart from the cancer.'

'Cancer?' the lady said in alarm, staring at him incredulously.

'Just a little touch of it,' he responded. 'It's almost completely under control.'

The interview lasted for another twenty

minutes, and then the lady glanced through the vast questionnaire. She now knew that Horace lived alone, had an illness he was being treated for, owned a car he drove 'occasionally', and she also knew his mother's maiden name and that Horace had never owned a pet – he'd decided to say nothing about killing butterflies.

'That's all fine, then,' she said, as she scanned to the bottom of the form and turned it around so that Horace could sign his name. 'Now, have *you* any questions, Mr Winter?' she asked finally.

'When will I know if my application has been successful?' he asked.

The lady looked at him over her spectacles as though she were going to say something funny, but did not. 'Well, first of all we need some documentation before the application is deemed complete.'

'What do you need?' Horace asked.

'Just a few things. A copy of your passport, driving licence, garda vetting, bank statements, household bills, pension details, certificate of health and competency from your general practitioner, statutory declaration in relation to your home ownership, and once that's all sent in, the application will go into the system and you could expect an initial decision probably within the next six months or so, all going well.'

'So about six months, then?' Horace asked. 'Seems like a long time.'

'Oh,' said the Yellow Horned moth, 'that's just the first stage. If you're accepted, phase two begins.'

'Phase two?' Horace said.

'Oh, yes,' she continued. 'There's mandatory child-welfare training. It's quite intensive. That course is for anyone who is not already a parent. In addition, there are basic training modules in health and safety, nutrition and first aid. After that it's straight on to the PMP, the provisional mentoring programme. All going well, you could expect to be allocated a child on a weekend fostering basis, usually one weekend in four, within two years of the final application being receipted and stamped.'

'But what happens to the boy until then?' Horace asked.

'What boy?' She seemed surprised by the question.

Horace realised he'd said too much. He racked his brain for a suitable answer. 'The boy who needs minding,' he said eventually.

'I don't follow,' she said, a little crossly. 'All

children covered by the Act have that care provided by the state. Are you suggesting you're aware of a situation concerning a child at risk that requires intervention?'

'No, no, nothing like that,' Horace said tiredly. 'I was just wondering, that's all.'

'Hmm,' said the lady. 'Now, there's one more thing I should say to you. I'm not sure if you're aware but we give priority to people in their twenties and thirties.'

'Aren't they a little old to need fostering?' Horace asked.

'Thank you, Mr Winter,' the lady said, lifting her glasses onto her forehead. 'We'll be in touch.'

Horace didn't believe her, not for a second.

He had another mission to attend to that day. He'd arrived in Newbridge on the one o'clock train and had eaten his lunch of sandwiches while sitting on a bench on the terraced school lawn that overlooked the weir. The river scene was broken only by a solid concrete bridge, supported on steel pillars sunk into the riverbed. The aluminium rails encasing this modern viaduct were like the clean teeth of a comb.

Newbridge College was an impressive school to look at. Its quadrangle had the River Liffey on one side and the rest gathered around the space north of the river, as mourners might surround a freshly dug grave without intruding on the resting place of its neighbour. It exuded a sense of calm, and whether that ambience was enhanced by the river or entirely due to it was unclear. What Horace did note, however, was that the sound of water was everywhere. *In the beginning, there was water.*

At the reception desk, a lady sat at a computer and punched words into the keyboard. Perhaps she's doing a search on the web, Horace thought. Maybe she's looking at my father's beach. Or her own father's beach. Oboe, Roger, Queen, deny me thrice?

'I wondered if I could see some old photographs,' Horace said to her, when she'd slid back the window.

'I beg your pardon?' she said, with a push of spectacles back up her nose.

'Photographs,' Horace repeated. 'I wondered if I could see some.'

The lady gave him an odd look and shrugged her shoulders. 'Photographs?' she asked.

'Yes.'

'Perhaps I can help,' a man's voice said, beside him.

Horace turned to see a white-robed gentleman

with a Sam Browne belt. 'I'm Father Jordan,' the man said, extending his hand. 'I teach English here.'

In the school library, the priest unlocked a bookcase cabinet and took out a large and heavy scrapbook. He set it down on the librarian's table and began to turn the pages. 'Newbridge haven't a won Senior or Junior Cup since 1970.'

The pages were filled with newspaper clippings and showed the faces and jerseys of heroes, many of whom must now be deceased. The black and white playing shirts of Newbridge College were timeless in a way, and the photographs might have been taken recently, except that the opposition colours would have been vividly obvious in an era of digital cameras and electronic mail. 'Here we are,' Father Jordan announced.

He held the extremes of both pages down and swivelled the scrapbook around to let Horace see. In the centre of the right-hand page, there was a scene of jubilation as the Newbridge captain held the Junior Cup over his head and was engulfed by his teammates. Clippings on other pages contained reports of the match. Horace tried to read some of the accounts but the words did not seem to be in the right order. The montage of an old day in 1957 began to move in Horace's eyes. He saw the scrummage form and the ball shoot out on Columba's side. The scrum-half waited to take and pass.

As the kindly Dominican closed the book, the tail end of a clipping peeped out from inside its cover. He opened it again and took out the yellowing remnant. 'The *Irish Press*, 9 February 1957' was scrawled on the back of the extract, across an advertisement for 'Angelus Grand and Upright Pianos'. As the priest turned over the clipping, the face of an angry fifteen-year-old second centre greeted him and Horace. In the foreground of the photograph was the oval-laced conveyance of schoolboy dreams. It lay out of the spilled reach of Alan Dodd and had come to rest in a parallel with the studded boots that were all that was visible of the Newbridge full-back, who had pulled off the match-saving tackle just before the final whistle blew. In the top right-hand corner of the same photograph, the third-choice left-winger stood with disbelief etched on his face. It was the last time he had played rugby. He had drifted almost like an automaton through those last two years at St Columba's. The weight of lost love and the confusion of becoming an adult had made him simply want the whole process to be over as quickly as possible. No wonder he'd failed English in the Leaving Certificate. The butterfly effect again? Horace wondered.

On the library returns desk, Horace noticed a novel he'd read once in his teenage days. It was *The Bride of Lammermoor* by Sir Walter Scott. He remembered little of it now, except that one of the characters, Lord Ravenswood, dies in a fit of fury directed at the man whom he regards as the author of his ruin. It was a memory from his days at school, perhaps even the year of the cup final. Horace couldn't remember any other books he'd read at that time. In the bank, he'd read hundreds of reports and balance sheets each week and, in a way, that had cured him of the desire to read for pleasure. He'd sometimes flicked through books that customers had left in the bank by accident, but he'd never taken any home.

'But that's rubbish, Horace,' Amanda said, later that evening, when he told her of his expedition to Newbridge College and the story of Alan Dodd. 'It wasn't your fault that that boy didn't pass the ball to you. And your father did *not* die of disappointment.'

'But *why* didn't he pass?' Horace asked her. 'That's the thing that bothers me. In that split second, he gave me such a look you couldn't imagine. As if – as if he knew something about me that I didn't know myself. Almost as if there were a book of final judgment somewhere and he'd managed to look at the entry beside my name instead of his own and there, in bold letters, was the word "moth".'

Amanda was busy tidying his bookshelves: the gap where the book holding his Leaving Cert had been seemed to bother her. 'There's something else here,' she said, as she was about to replace the volume.

'Hmm?'

'Look,' she said, holding a single folded sheet of blue notepaper towards him.

Horace didn't react until Amanda stuck it under his nose and it tickled him. 'What?' he said, rather crossly. He took the page from her. He unfolded the paper and, as he did, he noticed that one edge seemed to have been yellowed by exposure to sunlight. This document had lain between two slim volumes just to the right of the book in which his Leaving Cert results had slept for half a century. Outside, a rook landed on the window-ledge and crackled and croaked before taking off again.

Horace instantly recognised his father's handwriting. It was quite a shock, a bit like hearing the voice of someone who had last spoken to you decades and decades ago. In the top right-hand corner was their address: '57 Edenvale Road, Ranelagh, Dublin, Ireland'. The address of the person to whom the letter was written was 'c/o The Falcon Inn, Arncliffe, Yorkshire, England'. Horace read the letter:

Dear Migsie,
Sorry.
Yours,
Corporal Robert Winter.
PS

CHAPTER ELEVEN

Goat moth (*Cossus cossus*): the smell exuded by
this moth is said to resemble that of a billy-goat

Grayling (*Hipparchia semele*)

There was nothing written after 'PS'. What
Horace noticed next, and most significantly, was
the date: '7 Feb 1957'. His face filled with horror.

'What's wrong, Horace?' Amanda asked.

He turned the letter around and handed it to her
to read.

'It's quite short and to the point,' she remarked.

'The date,' Horace spluttered. 'Do you see the date?'

'Yes. What about it?'

'It's the day before the Junior Cup final. My father wrote this letter on the day before he died. He mustn't have got the chance to finish it or couldn't find a stamp or something. For whatever reason, he never posted it.'

'But what does it mean, Horace?' Amanda asked. 'What was he sorry for? Why was he apologising?'

Horace shook his head. 'I don't know. I just cannot imagine what he was saying sorry for. I mean, he wouldn't have seen Migsie Spring for years. Not since the war, probably. In fact, I often wondered whether either Migsie Spring or Fred Alexander might have died in the war. Dad rarely spoke about that time in his life. To be honest, I don't know anything about what happened to him in the war, apart from the fact that he landed in Normandy on D-Day.'

'You know the name of his regiment,' Amanda encouraged.

'Do I?'

'Yes, silly. It's on the back of the photograph over there on the wall.'

'"Second Battalion East Yorkshires,' Horace read, from the faded backing of the photo frame.

'Well?' Amanda asked.

'Well what?' Horace responded.

'What are you going to do about it?'

'About the letter?'

'Yes, about the letter. Are you going to find an envelope and a stamp and finally post the thing?' Amanda asked.

'Absolutely not,' retorted Horace. 'Who knows if the man is still alive? Even if he were, he'd be very old now. A pub is hardly the kind of place he'd still be living.'

'You could always telephone and see,' Amanda suggested.

Horace digested this proposal for a moment or two. He hadn't been to England since they'd moved to Ireland when he was a young boy. He had often thought about it, though, frequently even seeing it in his dreams. He had idealised the place, he supposed, the *thwock* of cricket ball and bat on the village green, that sort of thing. It was the country of his birth yet he knew next to nothing about it for real. He knew that he was ill and that he might not have much time left within which to explore the present *or* the past. This was an opportunity that cried out to be grasped with both hands, a chance to find out more about his father. But Horace hated the telephone.

Horace knew that this was a call to arms. He didn't know what for. He didn't know what his life had been for. But he wanted, more than anything, to make something right. He had made a mess of Max's life, though he was trying to fix that, and now this, a question from the past crying out for an answer. If you could die knowing you had made one wrong thing right, that should be enough, shouldn't it?

'I'll track him down and deliver the letter myself, by hand. If Migsie Spring's not alive, then to someone in his family. *That*'s what I'll do,' Horace said decisively.

The hospital had altered his medication, giving him one of the new tablets to take there and then. He now had nine pills a day instead of six. Horace stared at the toast that had just popped. He wanted to reach out and grab it but was not altogether clear about the sensation he should expect. Would it be very hot or very cold? He waited a little longer, then began to look for the marmalade. When he finally retrieved the toast, it was cold, just as he had expected it to be. He looked down at the reply he'd received a day earlier from the Ministry of Defence in London. The words answering his enquiry stood out like a raised platform in the centre of the page: 'Our records show that Cpl Matthew 'Migsie' Spring was discharged from the 2nd Batt East Yorks in late July 1945. We regret to say that we have no further information.'

'What about seeing if he's listed in the telephone directory on the internet?' Amanda suggested.

'We can try,' Horace replied. And they did.

Find People UK was just one of many sites they came across offering search facilities to trace people. This particular site turned up a list of 1,411 people in the UK named 'Spring' with the initial 'M'. They were spread all over the place, including the Channel Islands and Scotland, but most were in London and Manchester. A refined search for 'Matthew Spring', yielded fifty-three results, again spread all over the country, but with a proviso that almost the same number again carried only the initial 'M' and were thus possible Matthews as well.

Max Hackett's address, it turned out, was a lot easier to come by. The media had mentioned more than once that Thomas Hackett lived in Tallaght and there was only one such Thomas Hackett in the phone book. Horace was surprised when he arrived at the place, having travelled on the Luas tram using his old-age travel pass: it was a quiet and not at all rundown part of the city, on the very outskirts, near the foothills of the Dublin Mountains.

It was late afternoon. He walked up the crazy paving to the front door of number 893 and rang the doorbell. The sound echoed throughout what appeared to be an empty house. He was not sure whom he had expected to find.

'They're not home, mister,' a child's voice said, behind him. Horace turned. A group of five boys and three girls were standing in a row on the pavement outside the garden wall. Their leader, who had spoken, carried an Arsenal football under his left arm. His hair was bleached blond and his young face was almost entirely covered with freckles. Horace noticed that two of the boys were black and appeared to be identical twins. The ringleader spoke again: 'The dad's in the Joy and the mum's in Shanganagh.'

Horace knew that Shanganagh was an enormous cemetery for Roman Catholics. 'The Joy' was short for Mountjoy Prison.

'I was looking for Max,' Horace said. 'That's who I wanted to see.'

'You from the papers or the telly?' one of the girls asked. Horace shook his head, wondering what he should say next.

'Are you from the court?' another of the girls asked.

Horace was relieved at the question. He did not want to tell lies: that was something he had never done. 'Yes. Yes, I am,' he said.

'He doesn't live here any more,' the largest child said. 'He hasn't been in school for ages, but ...'

'But he's still making his confirmation with us on Sunday week in St Mary's,' said one of the twins.

'Do you want us to give him a message, mister?' the freckled boy asked.

'No,' Horace said. 'That's fine.'

Horace stood outside Lyng's Haberdashery on the main street in Naas and looked up at the traditional ornate shop front. This is more like it, he thought. This is exactly the type of establishment where he might find suitable clothes for Max. He had already visited almost two dozen shops that stocked children's clothes, but most of them seemed to be offering poor-quality articles made in far-flung places, most likely the product of child labour. It was Amanda who had suggested he look farther afield.

'You don't need any of that designer stuff, Horace. What about trying some decent-sized country market town, one of those places where they still have *real* shops, you know, the kind of places that sell buttons and zips?'

Naas was perfect. It had the mix of new and traditional that Horace felt represented the best of both. He'd parked his car outside Lawlor's Hotel, then wandered around the town for half an hour before he'd stumbled upon the place he wanted. He opened the door into the shop and stepped back into a bygone era; a traditional outfitter's that reeked of old-fashioned values and timeless elegance. He was the only customer and he couldn't see any counter assistants. As the door closed, a bell sounded somewhere and another door, at the rear of the premises, opened. Horace caught a glimpse of a sitting room before someone he assumed to be Mr Lyng emerged into the body of the shop.

'Good afternoon, sir,' the man greeted Horace.

Horace knew from both his tone and appearance that he must be the owner. The man was almost a mirror-image of himself in terms of stature and age. He wore a three-piece black suit, with a red handkerchief folded into a triangle protruding from the breast pocket of the jacket. He was almost completely bald and wore half-glasses, which enabled Horace to see the squirrel-grey eyes through which the proprietor probably viewed with horror the fast-disappearing world of good manners and bespoke clothing. Horace knew that he was dealing with a Goat moth, but instead of being wary of the other man, he sensed that he had once been a butterfly, possibly a Grayling. It shocked Horace to think that hardship, ill-fortune or bitter experience might have brought about such a change in a person. It was the first time he had ever admitted the possibility that such a fundamental change might occur in a someone's life. Until then, people had always been clearly either a butterfly or a moth. He wondered whether his own experiences on the jury and in other parts of his life might have prompted this accommodation within him. He wondered, too, whether people might not all have a little of both inside them. That would explain why good people sometimes did bad things and might also account for the ability of people you might mistrust to confound you pleasantly.

'How may I be of assistance?' the moth asked.

As the man spoke, Horace was suddenly overcome

with a feeling about or, rather, *for* the place. Some extra part of him concluded that he was standing in premises built by butterflies but now staffed by moths. 'I'm looking for a set of clothes for a boy who is going to make his confirmation,' Horace said awkwardly.

'Do you have the young man with you?' the Goat asked, looking past Horace to the door.

'I'm afraid not,' Horace replied.

'But you have his measurements?'

'Erm, no. Well, he's about this height,' Horace said, indicating his best guess with an outstretched hand. 'You see, I'm trying to buy an outfit for him as a gift. I don't want to spoil the surprise.'

'Ah,' said the Goat. 'I see. A surprise? Do you have something in mind, a particular style? Most young men wear a blazer and slacks for Confirmation.'

Horace thought for a moment. 'Something bright,' he said. 'This young man needs cheering up.'

The moth began to smile as though the notion of cheering someone up had cheered *him* up. 'Do you have a budget?' he asked slyly.

'Not at all,' Horace said, without really thinking.

'I'm sure you'll be able to find exactly what you're

looking for here,' the man said, with an even broader smile.

Less than an hour later, Horace emerged into the Naas afternoon, carrying a large swish paper bag that contained his purchases.

At home in Edenvale Road, he laid out the clothes on the settee to show Amanda. The bright oak-leaf green blazer with matching trousers and polka-dot bow-tie were perfectly complemented by the scarlet shirt with its ruffed cuffs and sleeves. The shoes were size six but with a 'little room for compromise' as the Goat moth had said.

'Absolutely perfect,' Amanda said.

'Do you think he'll like them?' Horace asked.

Amanda held up the blazer in one hand and the trousers below it in the other and dangled them over the shoes. 'How could he fail to?' she said. 'They're bright and fresh and cheerful. They'll definitely revive his spirits.'

'And all for less than six hundred euro.' Horace repeated the Goat moth's final words to him.

On the following morning, Horace went to the

post office and sent the entire wonderful rig-out to 'Max Hackett, c/o Children in Care Section, HSE'. He put extra stamps on the parcel so that it would get there quickly.

That afternoon, Horace Winter visited the Natural History Museum on Merrion Square, his favourite place in Dublin. There, surrounded by glass cases full of the preserved remains of animals and fish – butterflies and moths too – he felt at ease. There was a calm about this old place. At its very centre, reptiles and birds kept as silent as clouds. It was a speck on a dot on a blob seen from space but, within these walls, Horace Winter felt like the king of a wonderful universe where the grey wolf sat side by side with the hare and the vole, animals it might have eaten in different circumstances. Here, butterflies, moths and rare species of spider lived in glass for ever, under brown leather flaps, and the skeleton of a whale hung above the entire taxidermied lot, like their Creator. It was a place where, in Horace's experience, nothing could go wrong – or ever had. In an oblique way, it reminded him of the bank's customers. They were as diverse a bunch as these quiet beings. They, too, ranged from the tiniest pieces of coral to great hulking beasts that devoured all in their path. In his dealings with many thousands of people over several dozen years, Horace felt he had learned a little about the human condition. He knew from the way people looked at you, or did not, how badly they needed whatever amount they requested. He'd observed all shapes, sizes and manner of mortals, but yet felt that people, by and large, fitted into one of two discernible categories: butterflies or moths.

Before he had been given the book, Horace had sometimes expressed interest in the subject to his father, but had only done so because of the occasional invitation it prompted to accompany his dad on one of his 'fieldy trips', as he called them. In truth, it was the opportunity to spend time alone with his father that initially drew Horace to the subject but, more than that, it was what Rose Burke had said to him on the beach, combined with the shooting dead of the young bank-raider, that had eventually led Horace to engage in the practice of evaluating people in this way.

Horace circumnavigated the narrow top level of the museum and, stopping for a moment, he looked down − over the collection of Common Flies − at two boys trying to remove the elephant's tusk from its display table on the ground floor. They were schoolchildren, about Max's age, he supposed, and yet for a short time they might have been fully grown men, adult poachers in a pocket of the world where ivory was everything. They eased the huge item across the shiny surface to where the point swung out over the edge of the dusty wood it lay upon. One boy, wearing a red tank-top sweater, shorts and sandals, wrapped his arms around the curved end and began to lift it slowly. His accomplice slid two hands along the underside until they met the junction of table and tusk, about two thirds of the way down. Horace could see the guard on the other side of the room beginning to walk briskly around the ferrets and stoats to a point at which he would have a view of the unfolding drama.

Horace wondered what the boys intended to do with the tusk. Were they planning to steal it unnoticed, or was it simply an exercise in mischief or curiosity? It mattered little because, almost at the exact time the museum employee spotted the prank and shouted, 'Hey!' across the room, the tusk swivelled completely on its axis and fell from the display table. The heavy end, which had once been attached to the elephant, was lured like a magnetised trinket to the sandalled left foot of the boy in the red tank-top. His screams filled the old museum and came as close as anything could have, in a hundred years or so, to waking the inmates from their formaldehyde-scented slumber. Before the tusk finally fell intact onto its side on the faded tiles of the Natural History Museum, it rested for a split second on the mauled foot where it mingled with crushed sinew, bone and creeping, drizzling blood. It looked much the same, perhaps, as it had decades earlier, in Africa, when some hunter had wrenched it out of its owner's head.

Horace was reminded of an old movie he'd once seen about Tarzan. In it, there was a place to which elephants made their way when they were close to death. It was called the Elephants' Graveyard. Horace wondered what humans did when they sensed their own time was near. Two of the elephants in the black and white film had been together for years and had made the journey to the graveyard at the same time. He thought about the bank robber who had been shot by the man from Special Branch all those years ago and of how his chest had been blown apart and of how the policeman's face was covered with blood but how none of it was his own.

On the side of the display case nearest to the top of the stairs, the one containing spiders, someone had scrawled in blue biro: *Death comes to at least 72% of us.*

Horace wondered what it must be like to die. He then pondered what it would have been like to be married. Married and promoted.

CHAPTER TWELVE

Spurge Hawk-moth: the offspring of this
species reach maturity more quickly than is
common with others of the Sphingidae family

S unday dawned purple and grey over the city. In
the street outside Horace's home and also, for
the most part, everywhere he drove that morning,
curtains were still closed and people slept on. He had
planned the route on an Esso garage map the night
before. Amanda was helping to prepare the gardens
at Airfield House in Dundrum so Horace drove past
Milltown, then turned left after Alexandra College

and headed for the suspension bridge. Amanda was waiting for him on the footpath beside the traffic lights. Horace stopped to allow her to get in. Behind him, irate drivers beeped their horns.

They drove on, past some beautiful houses. A balding, kind-faced man went by in the opposite direction, dragged along by an enormous dog, which looked more like a medium-sized bear.

The church car park was vast but was filling up quickly with cars when Horace indicated right and turned in off the main road. He parked between a blue minibus with a Galway registration and a white van with a sign painted on the side, which said 'Momentum Support Services'. By the time it was five to the hour, the entire car park was full. Others, latecomers, had to park on the street and even in the grounds of the Tesco opposite, in defiance of signs that said: 'Customer Parking Only'.

Horace had never been at a Roman Catholic service before. He and Amanda worked their way around the edge of the vast modern glass and concrete edifice until they found a spot against a side wall in an alcove. From there, they had a side-on view of the main altar. The church was packed with children and parents, all dressed to the hilt. For the most part, the boys wore blazers and slacks, as the shop assistant had predicted, while the multifarious colours of the girls' dresses surprised Horace, who had expected them to be wearing white. He scanned the faces in the crowd, hoping to spot Max, but could not. It became clear early on through a series of announcements that pupils from seven different schools were making their Confirmation, in the same ceremony. Almost three hundred children were involved.

After some initial prayers, the process began. One by one, the children's names were called out for each different school, and, as they were, each class filed up in turn to be blessed by the bishop. Horace listened carefully to a litany of Jacks, Hannahs, Chloës, Emmas, Michaels, Charlies, Zoës, Ruths, Patricks, Alans and Deirdres, and even some more unusual names, such as Lavina, Bethany, Tiffany, Zebo and Wivinie. As each child stepped forward, so, too, did a parent or guardian as sponsor. Horace wondered who would stand for Max and decided to step forward and offer his own services as a sponsor if Max was unaccompanied.

Finally, he heard the name 'Maxwell Ignatius Hackett' called out. Horace stepped to his right and craned his neck to get a better view. When no one came forward, the announcer repeated the name, 'Maxwell

Ignatius Hackett.' When there was no response, the man with the microphone moved on to the next name. Horace hoped the child was not unwell.

'Perhaps the suit you sent didn't fit him,' Amanda said, on the way home.

'I wondered about that too,' Horace said. 'The other thing I suppose that could have happened is that maybe they wouldn't allow his father out to act as sponsor so they might have to wait until another day or find someone else to stand in.'

'It's quite a mystery,' Amanda said. 'Quite a mystery indeed.'

On Monday morning the mystery was solved. Horace strolled down into Ranelagh village to buy a newspaper.

'Die, Scumbag, Die', read the headline in the *Sun*. *The Irish Times* was a little more delicate: 'Murderer Hackett on Life-support Following Attack in Mountjoy'.

Horace woke in the middle of the night, shivering. He sat on the edge of his bed and felt for his slippers with his feet. *What* had he done now? It had never in a million moments entered his head that his actions and choices could lead to *this*: an attack with boiling water and knives fashioned from razorblades and toothbrushes. It was like a film, a ruthless, barbaric, heathen medley of cause and effect, which was in fact not a film at all but rather a living, organic Gehenna in which he, Horace Winter, retired assistant manager of the Ormond Quay branch, was the bloody ringmaster. From the moment he had heard an echo of his own past, in the plaintive voice of a child on a crowded street, these events had lined up in the future, like dominoes waiting to be nudged. How could it have come to this?

He thought about Maxwell Ignatius Hackett, now visited by even more horror when he already had mountains of ill-fortune and adversity to contend with. Horace had to find him, talk to him, comfort him, if possible, but above all protect him, somehow make everything all right. But how? How could anyone go back into the knots of things past and undo them?

He tried to remember what it was like to be a child, to imagine himself into the boy's shoes. How must he be feeling? It was an impossible task, being a child that was, when everything that was thrown at you always seemed bigger and more overwhelming than anything you could either dream up or throw back. He went downstairs to wait for the day and to wait for more news.

He thought about the letter his father had written to Migsie Spring and suddenly at least partially understood how such an obligation to apologise might arise in the course of a lifetime.

Horace rambled around Blessington Street Basin park on his way to the Mater Hospital. He had decided to try to meet the boy. At first, he had considered going to the school Max attended but a mixture of feelings prevented him doing so. First, he knew from the children outside the Hackett family home that Max did not attend school every day. Allied to that was a concern he had about being noticed by a large number of people, which might make seeing Max all the more difficult. Also, Horace had read about a particular type of person who sometimes waited outside schools or playgrounds to do children harm; he did not want to risk being mistaken for one. He thought about Thomas Hackett, now lying in a hospital bed with wires and tubes keeping him alive, and quivered with regret at the knowledge that it was his action which had brought about that situation.

He thought about the ruined Confirmation Day. He felt sure that Max would be brought to visit his father from time to time. Horace crumpled up the wrapper of his breakfast sandwich and left the park just as a flock of eight Brent geese landed on the green water of the lake.

He walked up the steps into the public part of the old hospital. The corridors had about them an odour of disinfectant and kindness. Reflected in the faces of the people who passed him was a concern he associated only with *other* people, with people who were not ill themselves. It was a sort of safe concern, he mused, a little like the fear of losing something that belonged to someone else.

He followed signs for the Intensive Care Unit, suddenly wondering if his assumption was correct, querying whether this was where Thomas Hackett would have been brought after his attack. But logic told him he was right: the hospital was just across the road from the prison. Where else would they bring him?

On the top floor, Horace stepped out of the lift. Down away to his left, he saw a uniformed garda sitting on a chair beside a sign that said 'ICU'. Horace looked for a suitable place to begin his wait. Across from the lifts, a set of double doors was open and revealed a waiting area for Eye Laser Surgery. He decided to wait there as it would give him a clear view of anyone exiting the lifts. If he were challenged, he could always say he was waiting for someone. That, at least, was true. He presumed that if Max was being brought to the hospital to see his father, it would be during normal business hours: someone would have to accompany him to get him there from school or wherever he was being kept.

For two days, Horace sat in the Eye Laser Surgery waiting area. He was on the *qui vive* in his vigil, treating the task with an attentiveness he hadn't really called upon since his retirement had begun. By the end of the second day, he was tired and had scorching neuralgia, which he somehow managed to ignore until he left the hospital at tea-time.

During the two days he waited, watching the everyday business of illness and repair unfold around him, he became acutely attuned to the noises of gurneys, wheelchairs and canteen trolleys as they invaded and retreated from the square area over which he kept watch. In that patch, the two enormous lifts yawned and mouthed silently at him many hundreds of times as they collected and deposited sick and well people and carried them uncomplainingly up and down.

From time to time, he was approached by hospital staff who asked him whether he was all right. At about lunchtime, Horace went down to the hospital shop and bought a novel, *The Blue Olive* by Mary Honan. As he made his way through the hospital with the book in his hand he passed a sign saying 'Mortuary' and the thought struck him that everybody's life is a novel in which the hero dies.

Horace soon realised that the simple act of bringing a book with him and placing it open on his lap deterred most people from intruding. He brought a packed lunch with him each day and, on the occasions when he needed to use the toilet, he did so as quickly as possible, fairly certain that he could not be so unlucky as to miss the visit of the boy in that short time.

On the third day, Horace arrived at the hospital at half past eight in the morning. As he came out of the lift, he saw that the garda was out of his seat outside the ICU and was anxiously looking up and down the corridor. The other lift door opened just as Horace walked across to the waiting area and he heard Max's voice before he saw him. 'I hate it! I hate the people there! I want to go home to my own house.'

Horace glanced over his shoulder and saw that Max was accompanied by a man in a suit, who looked a little like one of the policemen you saw in old black and white television dramas.

'Frostfield Abbey's not the worst place you could be, you know,' the man said with a grin, as he pointed to his left and directed the child towards the Intensive Care Unit. 'At least the food's pretty good and you've got your own room.'

'I want to go home, to my *own* house,' Max said again, as they walked towards the place where his father was being kept alive.

Horace sat in a chair that gave him a view all the way down the corridor.

'Tuck in your shirt,' the man said to Max, as they reached the uniformed policeman. 'You want to look your best for your dad.'

'He can't see me,' Max said sullenly, and left his shirt-tail hanging out.

After Max had gone through the door into the ICU, the man came out and chatted with the garda for a moment or two before getting back into the lift and leaving the floor. Horace did not know how he was going to engineer a meeting with Max, given the presence of the policeman. He did not know how long the visit would last or how soon it might be before the other man returned to bring Max away. As he continued to keep an eye on the entire corridor, the policeman sitting on the chair suddenly got up again and started walking briskly towards him. Horace felt sure he'd been rumbled. But how? He was unsure about how to react and, for a second, even considered running to the lifts and pressing both buttons in the hope that he could escape. As the man came closer, Horace took the book out of his pocket and pretended to be reading, although the book was upside-down. He suddenly felt like a spy from a film. He felt himself go redder and redder in the face as the feet approached. Remarkably, the man walked past him and headed around the corner to where the toilets were.

Horace hurried down the corridor past the water-cooler. As he reached the door, he hoped it wouldn't be locked. It wasn't. He entered the Intensive Care Unit and found himself immediately in a small room with two further doors leading from it. Through one, he could see a reception desk and behind that a vast ward area with about a dozen beds, all full. There were machines everywhere, just like in the movies. Five or six doctors and nurses moved about on his horizon, but he could not see Max among them. He knew that he would be escorted out of the hospital by security personnel if he was found wandering around in there. Horace pushed the other door open and walked through.

Here, individually numbered rooms lay on either side of the narrow L-shaped passageway. Horace moved along as quietly as he could. Through the door of the second room on his right, he spotted Max. Beyond the boy, in the centre of the room, Thomas Hackett lay supine on a hospital bed. A thick oxygen pipe had been placed down his throat and was held there with a bandage that striped each side of his face. Two tubes protruded from his right arm. High above the patient, bags of fluid waited to drip into him through the plastic tubes. On the right-hand side of the bed, a screen showed a set of green blipped peaks, which flashed across like a display on a Wall Street trader's monitor. Another display on a machine at the opposite side of the bed showed readings that might have been blood pressure. Thomas Hackett was unconscious but his face wore an expression of distress rather than calm, his brow furrowed like that of a much older man. Horace stepped into the room and the boy turned around. He had been crying and the front of his shirt was stained wet.

'I know you,' he said. 'You were in the court that day. What are you doing here?'

'I came to visit someone,' Horace replied.

'Someone who's sick?' Max asked.

'Someone who needs help,' Horace said. He was afraid that Max might be angry and associate him with the result of the court case, but the child was measured and his tone was not unfriendly.

'I remembered after,' the boy said.

'Remembered what?'

'The cards. You were the only person who helped me to pick up my cards when I dropped them and my dad got really ...' He searched for a word.

'Yes,' Horace said. 'I tried but didn't manage to get them all.'

'At least you tried,' the boy said. 'You did your best.'

'I suppose so,' Horace replied. 'What's the place you're staying in now like? Have you made new friends?'

'It's a bleedin' awful gaff. They lock you in your

room at night and if you wake up and need to use the jacks you have to press a buzzer on the wall so they'll come and get you.' The boy's face was sad and Horace was sad *for* him.

'And the others, what are they like?'

'The other boys?'

'Yes. Are they friendly?'

'Not really,' Max said, averting his eyes from Horace's gaze. 'Most of them are much bigger than me. Some of them have even started shaving.'

Horace put a hand to his own face. 'But the people who look after you, the ones in charge, they're all right, aren't they?' he asked desperately.

'Yeah,' the child said, shrugging his shoulders. 'I suppose.'

Horace looked at the boy, his shirt hanging out and his heart on his sleeve. He wanted to be able to offer more than football-card salvation. He wondered whether or not Max had received the suit he'd sent to him in the post, but didn't want to ask. Had it been too big or perhaps too small? Perhaps that didn't matter. What mattered now was that the child was unhappy and his father was on a life-support machine just a few feet away.

'What size shoes do you wear?' he asked, as a

compromise. As he looked down at the boy's feet he saw an embroidered butterfly on one of the upturned trouser hems. He didn't recognise the species. Perhaps it's a sign of some sort, Horace thought.

'I'm a size seven and a half,' said the child. There was a comfortable silence between them, of the kind Horace recalled enjoying with his own father. The silence was ended by a question from the child. 'Are you an angel?'

Horace was jolted by the words. 'What made you ask that?'

'Well, Mrs Gill says that if you're ever in trouble, and you pray hard enough, God will send an angel.'

'Are *you* in trouble, Max?' Horace already knew the answer. He watched the boy's face as it took on the fear and helplessness of an abandoned soul.

The child turned back towards his father, then returned his gaze to Horace amid the hum of the life-support machine and the timid ambient lighting of the Intensive Care Unit. 'You know the three-wishes thing?' he said.

Horace felt a lump in his throat the size of an Easter egg. 'Yes,' he said. 'Yes, I do, the usual three wishes, yes.'

'Well, I only want one,' Max Hackett continued.

'OK?' Horace said, not knowing what else he *could* say.

'I want to go home,' Max said. 'I just want me and my dad to be able to go home.'

The boy turned quietly to his comatose father and Horace slipped out into the corridor.

CHAPTER THIRTEEN

'The transformation is complex and wonderful.
In the pupa, the caterpillar disintegrates into
dense fluid and then reconstitutes as either a
butterfly or moth. Eventually the process is
completed and the insect crawls triumphantly
out into the world. Shortly afterwards, the
butterfly or moth is ready to take flight.'

Butterflies and Moths: A Beginner's Guide

The cogs were turning in Horace's brain about
what he could do for Max. One wish didn't seem
so much to ask for and Horace felt it should surely be
achievable. While he pondered it, he readied himself

for an outing. He checked his pockets for his travel pass, then set off for Dún Laoghaire. He caught the bus across the road from the newsagent/deli run by the Large Oakblue. The bus trundled off.

Dún Laoghaire shimmered, and the dozens of boats moored in the harbour bobbed and swayed in the breeze. The air was filled with the clacking of steel wire cables on aluminium and wooden masts. Horace walked up the sloped road from the seafront to the village. For no reason at all, he crossed the road to the Roman Catholic church and went inside. It was a modern building, full of light and sharp edges. A couple of people sat or knelt at various points around the interior. On the wall was a huge painting of the Last Supper. Horace wondered whether the artist had painted the faces from his imagination or if the guests at the meal were based on real people he had known. He liked the art in the church: it made the place feel calm and worthwhile. Horace wished he could believe in God, but knew that he did not. He was unshakeably of the conviction that when his own last day came, it would be the end. It made him feel sad. He just had to deliver the letter. What else was there to be done?

The Royal British Legion Club was a large, terraced three-storey over basement house in Crosthwaite

Terrace. He rang the doorbell. A small man with a round face and a green suit answered the door. 'Can I help you?' he asked.

'I'm trying to find some information about someone who was in the British army during the last war,' Horace answered. The man smiled. Horace stood on the front step, unsure of what to say or do next. He heard a whistling sound and the man reached an index-finger nail into his left ear. The whistling stopped.

'Ah, that's better,' he said, with a grin. 'Now. How can I help you?' Horace told him again and the man invited him to step in. 'I'm not very good with computers and all that malarkey,' he said, 'but you're in luck. There's a lady who comes in two mornings a week to help us with our accounts. I'm sure she'll be able to do the needful.'

The pair walked up a flight of blue-carpeted stairs. On the wall, to either side, there were regimental insignia and emblems of various squadrons. They reached a landing where an office door was ajar.

'Mrs Meehan?' the man called, as he knocked gently and pushed it open fully.

'Yes, Mr Borthwick?' A lady in a black leather office chair swivelled around to face them. Horace's heart fell, then soared. It was his former secretary from the bank, Sarah Carolan. He saw immediately from her expression that she was delighted to see him too. She rose and came across the short distance to embrace him. 'Excuse the bump,' she said, rubbing the curve of her advanced pregnancy tenderly. 'How have you been, Mr Winter? How is your retirement going?'

Horace looked at her hand and saw a wedding band and, glancing at her face, understood that she was happier now than she had ever been. 'Oh, I'm – I'm fine,' he said. 'Absolutely fine. I'm just, well, just getting on with it, with being retired and all of that. And you? How are *you*?' he asked, trying not to stare at her tummy.

'Well, as you can see,' she said, laughing, 'I'm all married and ready to pop any day now. I left the bank just after Christmas, took a package, the usual. Everyone says the economy's about to collapse so I thought, Why not get out before it all goes pear-shaped? I help out here for a few hours every week.'

Mr Borthwick spoke. 'I didn't realise you two knew each other. I was just telling this gentleman that you might be able to do a search for him of our database. He is doing some research.'

'Oh, how exciting,' Sarah said. 'Are you writing a book, Mr Winter?'

'No,' Horace said. 'I'm just trying to trace someone so that I can deliver a letter to him.' At that moment, he caught her gaze and followed it down the lapel of his jacket and into the centre of his tie where, as usual, he was wearing the gift with which she'd presented him on the day of his retirement. Horace cast aside all thoughts of what might have been, or of his successor at the bank, or any regrets or misgivings he might once have had, and for one of the very few times in his life, he allowed himself simply to be content. Although it was not really his turn to speak next, he did so. 'Please call me Horace.'

She smiled, then stood back a little and responded with kindness. 'So, Horace. What's the name of the person you're trying to find?'

'Spring,' Horace said, 'Corporal Matthew Spring of the Second Battalion East Yorkshires.'

'Let's have a look then, shall we?' she said, turning back to engage with the almighty computer.

The search yielded little of any use. Sarah searched through dozens of records relating to the East Yorkshires and, apart from one reunion in the early 1950s, there was no sign of Corporal Matthew 'Migsie' Spring.

'It was absolutely lovely to meet you again,' Horace said to her, as she walked him to the front door.

'You too, Mr Win— I mean Horace,' Sarah Meehan (née Carolan) said, with a broad smile. 'I'm glad I left the bank. It was never quite the same after you retired.'

'So you're Mrs Meehan now?' Horace asked a little awkwardly. No one in the branch had had that surname. He wondered who had been lucky enough to win Sarah Carolan's heart.

'Yes, I am,' she said, fingering her wedding and engagement rings. 'Seamus is a musician, he arranges and composes for stage shows. He's from the West originally, but we're living in Kilcoole. They used to film *Glenroe* there, you know.'

Her comment about the bank not being the same after he'd retired lifted Horace's spirits to unscaled heights and he left for home feeling much happier about everything, despite drawing a blank in his search for Migsie Spring.

On Monday morning, Horace gathered up all of his bits and pieces of researched information and decided that it was time to begin to deal with reality rather than theory. He drove to the warehouse in the Ballymount industrial estate and ventured into the Radio-controlled Models Wholesale and Retail Outlet.

'Have you ever flown a plane before?' a cheery sales assistant in a pilot's uniform asked him.

'No, never,' Horace replied.

'Have you used a simulator?'

'No, I haven't. You see, I'm not really very good with computers and all that so I—'

'Perfect,' said the man, with a smile. 'Most people who come in here with some experience on simulators think they're ready to fly jumbo jets next. I think you're better off starting from scratch with the real thing. Did you have any particular model in mind?'

Horace thought for a moment and remembered an advertisement he'd seen on the internet. He fumbled in his sheaf of papers and showed it to the man.

'Ah, yes, the Mark 7,' the man announced. 'That would be an ideal starting point for you, or at least something like it. Those bi-wings are much easier to control and they tend to be more resistant to crash damage than most of the other starter models. The wings and other pieces come apart easily on impact so you just put them back together and off you go again. They're also generally much less expensive. How does one of them sound for a start?'

'Absolutely fine,' Horace said, as he wondered whether he was utterly insane to even contemplate learning to fly a radio-controlled plane. He followed the sales assistant down a vast aisle between shelves and shelves of model kits for planes, ships, helicopters and cars. Eventually they reached a beginners section and the man chose a model from a shelf with a large sign above it, which read 'ARF'.

Approved Retirement Fund, thought Horace.

'Almost ready to fly,' said the man. 'This is the SlowBipe,' he said, tapping the box and showing Horace the picture of the plane. 'Everything you need to get airborne is in here, and they're easy to assemble. If you've got a bit of time, I can bring you around to the hangar at the back and show you one or two similar models and let you have a go.'

And so Horace's apprenticeship began, in a vast high-ceilinged granary-like building where an assault terrain was laid out on the ground for radio-controlled tanks and motorbikes, and where three runway landing strips were in constant use by a variety of children and adults who were almost ready to fly.

'You've got two control sticks,' the man instructed. 'The one on the right for most small planes is the throttle. That controls your power. The other goes left to right and that enables you to turn the plane, either on the ground or in the air. Later on, when you've got the hang of it, you can move on to bigger planes. They have only two control sticks as well, but they also manipulate other things, like wing flaps and ailerons. You don't have to worry about any of that with this model.'

The model Horace had bought was highly unusual. It looked almost like a catamaran boat rather than an aircraft. It had an awkward high tail fixing and a double set of wings.

His flying lesson continued. 'This model is so light that it can be launched by hand. Just switch it on and give it a little throw, like a paper plane.'

Horace was given an hour-long lesson in which, to his absolute shock, he managed to fly the plane by himself. 'What happens if I just let go of the controls?' he asked the instructor, as the plane shook from side to side in the air at a height of about thirty feet.

'Try it and see.' Horace released the dual sticks from his grip and the plane righted itself and continued flying level with the ground. With careful instructions from the man, Horace then managed to land the plane almost smoothly.

'You'll get the hang of it. Just practise a bit,' said the man, as he escorted Horace to the checkout so that he could pay. Horace wondered whether it would be very different when he tried to fly the plane outside.

When he arrived home, Horace proceeded to assemble the model plane from the kit. It was remarkably easy to follow the step-by-step guide and diagram, and within twenty minutes or so, the plane was ready to take its maiden flight. He checked the batteries in both the plane and the control transmitter, and decided to begin practising in the back garden. The SlowBipe could indeed be launched by hand and Horace switched on the transmitter, then the plane itself and gently launched it down the garden at a height of about four feet. Everything went well until he realised that it was going to collide with the shed unless he could turn it around and fly it back up the garden towards him. He pushed the control lever to the left, but there was insufficient time and room for the manoeuvre so the brand new model aircraft lodged in the laburnum hedge and the bottom wings collapsed.

Amanda appeared through the side gate as Horace

was rebuilding the plane. None of the pieces had broken. 'How are you getting on?' She laughed.

Horace looked up. 'I think I've got a very long way to go before I'll be ready to proceed with my ...' He stopped himself before he'd uttered the word 'plan'.

'Why don't you practise in a bigger space?' she suggested. 'Herbert Park would be ideal.'

Over the next few weeks, Horace spent at least the morning or afternoon of each day, depending on the weather conditions and his illness, learning all he could about how to fly his aeroplane. He learned about testing the wind direction by throwing some wisps of grass into the air and also, more importantly, how to determine the strength of the wind by tying a ribbon to the end of the transmitter antenna. When it was secured, the trick was to hold the control panel flat to the ground, so the aerial was lying horizontal, and then to see how the ribbon behaved. If it blew parallel to the ground, it was too windy to fly the plane.

In a way, landing it was the trickiest part, but all of the videos Horace had watched on YouTube had advised him to take off *and* land into the wind.

Horace felt that the SlowBipe could be landed with the wind behind it, but had an inkling that the bigger models probably could not. When he returned to the Ballymount industrial estate two weeks later, he spoke to the same salesman.

'Are you really sure you're ready for the Spitfire?' the man asked.

'I think so,' Horace replied. 'I'd like to work my way up to more challenging models.'

'Oooh-*kay*, you're the boss,' the man said, 'but be careful when you're turning. Don't be too heavy on the tail flaps or the rudder.'

As he drove home, Horace glanced in the rear-view mirror at the Spitfire in its box on the back seat. He imagined what it must have been like as a German pilot to see a Spitfire on your tail.

Herbert Park proved to be the Spitfire's graveyard on the second day Horace practised with it. The take-off had been perfected and Horace now knew to advance the throttle quite slowly to full power before delicately using the elevator flaps at the back to make the Spitfire leave the ground fluently. It was very different from the bi-plane: it was heavier and faster but, consequently, more difficult to manoeuvre. Any heavy-handed use of the control sticks caused a greatly exaggerated response from the aircraft. As Horace took the fighter plane in a high circle around the park, he decided to make it fly in a figure-of-eight over the pond before bringing it round to land between two vast beds of roses. Everything was fine on the first part of the exercise, but, as Horace's thumb used the right-hand control stick to move the ailerons to make the turn, he overdid it and, at the same time, nudged the stick back so that the Spitfire immediately went into a downward spiral. He tried frantically to get the plane to pull out of the spinning dive but was helpless to do anything but watch in alarm as the hero of the Battle of Britain plunged into the pond and sank sluggishly from sight as the fuselage filled with water. It was an expensive lesson to learn. Horace did not despair but resolved to make the experience of the crash contribute to an even greater determination on his part that the mission should succeed.

About three weeks into his training, Horace decided that it was time to embark on a reconnaissance trip to see the lie of the land. Armed with an Ordnance Survey map of Wicklow, his father's lepidopteran binoculars and a packed lunch of egg and watercress sandwiches, he set off. The countryside behind Bray Head provided the best chance from which to spy on the Departments of Justice and Health establishment known officially as 'Frostfield Abbey Residential and Correctional Juvenile Facility'. Horace discovered that he could get quite a good view of the entire campus by parking on the seaward side of the main Dublin–Wexford motorway and walking up the Coillte forestry road into the woods on the back of a small mountain called Fagan's Hill.

In a tiny clearing in the woods, a couple of hundred yards from the main track, he gained an uninterrupted view across the busy road to the place where Max Hackett was being held in the company of convicted juveniles, while his father was still a prisoner and in hospital. Horace wondered whether the state would ever find a suitable foster family for the child. If they didn't, Max might be doomed to spend another six years in Frostfield Abbey.

Horace spread a travel rug at the base of a large Scots pine and sat, waited and watched. The former Augustinian abbey was set amid acres of open grassland and the occasional clump of trees. It was surrounded by a twelve-foot-high stone perimeter wall topped by rotating metal bars covered with blades and razor wire. Behind it lay steep hills, which eventually became the Wicklow Mountains. To the southern side the facility was bounded by a vast meadow of as yet uncut grass.

Each afternoon that week, Horace assiduously kept watch on Frostfield Abbey through his father's binoculars for a couple of hours and took notes. He discovered that, at approximately a quarter past five each evening, the 'residents' of the facility were allowed out into the grounds for a half-hour's recreation. Roughly twenty boys were being held there and, although it was difficult to tell at that distance through binoculars, Horace felt they all seemed much older than Max.

On the third day on which he watched the place, Horace brought with him high-powered binoculars he'd bought in the Dublin Camera Shop that morning. This time he saw Max clearly, standing apart from the football game in which the rest of the boys took part. Horace saw now for sure that the others were far bigger, older and tougher than the small child with size seven-and-a-half feet who had missed his Confirmation. As the others shouldered and shoved each other in their search for goals, Max went for a walk around the abbey's grounds. He took a route behind the old building, then reappeared and walked down the main avenue until, halfway along, he reached a large shed with a green corrugated-iron roof; the type of shed where rollers and mowers might be kept. Turning off at the shed, Max then walked directly across the open grass away from the main avenue and rejoined the perimeter path on the other side, then made his way back to arrive at the recreation yard, just as the exercise period ended. In all of that time, the child had spoken to no one and met no one.

As Horace continued to keep the place under surveillance over the next few days, he saw that Max walked exactly the same route each evening while the others played football or lounged in groups and smoked. The two staff members who supervised the recreation period never bothered with him and simply let Max occupy the time by himself.

Horace decided to take all of the decisions about this venture himself and not to bring Amanda into his confidence about his plan to help Max escape from the clutches of the HSE. She had understood the need for discretion when Horace had served on the jury and so he presumed that she would never press him for answers about his activities concerning his sudden interest in aviation.

On his visits to Herbert Park to practise flying

his planes, he had glimpsed Amanda once or twice in the distance but their paths had not crossed. If he continued to use Herbert Park, they would inevitably meet at some point and she might ultimately ask him some awkward question. He was determined not to involve her even by association in his daring plan in case it went horribly wrong and he got into trouble.

As the plan began to take shape and became more serious, he realised he needed somewhere else to train for his own D-Day, just as his father had prepared for Normandy on the beaches of Slapton Sands in Devon. He was also going to need a bigger aircraft than a Spitfire.

CHAPTER FOURTEEN

'The courtship rituals of butterflies
and moths are many and varied.'

Butterflies and Moths: A Beginner's Guide

'Do you ever think about dying?' Rose Burke
asked, during one of those magical days among
the sand dunes as they lay on their backs and squinted
up at the sun.

'Not really,' Horace replied. 'My dad was in the
war and I'm glad he got back safely. He died eighteen
months ago, but I think that the longer we can live
for, the better that will be.'

Rose Burke giggled and turned onto her side to look at him. 'You're funny, Horace,' she said. 'A real ticket.'

She was a real ticket herself, and she took Horace by the hand and led him into a different world that August. It was a place where he began to understand that he could really start to believe in himself, in what he was and what he might do or where he could go with his own share of life and time. It gave him a warm feeling to connect her in his heart with his dad's memory through the discussion they'd had about butterflies and moths.

'You're very different from anyone else I've ever met,' he said to her, as they walked grandly past the penny arcade on the promenade, holding hands like grown-ups.

'I should certainly hope so,' she said, with a laugh, as she squeezed his hand in hers. He squeezed back.

One afternoon, they'd taken the train from Rosslare to Wexford Town.

'Don't we have to buy a ticket?'

'Don't be silly, Horace. Tickets are for people with lots of money. We're not that kind of people. The train's going to Wexford anyway. What's a couple of extra passengers?'

They crossed the tracks in a field beside the station and then crept up the line and along the side of the carriages, hidden from the ticket office and the platform by the heaving train itself. Horace realised why the Red Indians called it an 'iron horse'.

'C'mon, Horace,' she prompted, as the station master blew the whistle. She climbed up onto his shoulders, opened the door of a carriage and scrambled in. Horace stretched one hand up and she grabbed it, pulling him onto the floor of the compartment. The train began to move.

'Hurry up, Horace.'

'I'm hurrying as much as I can,' he said breathlessly, as the train edged away from the platform at Rosslare station. His legs dangled for a short time and he felt for a brief moment that he might fall back onto the tracks. Her hands grabbed the collar of his shirt, dragging him in from the afternoon to the comfort of the former Great Southern Railways' finest rolling stock. No one disturbed them to check for tickets or anything else on the short journey to Wexford, and Horace and Rose just sat side by side looking at each other or out at the sea and the golf course passing by. They kissed, and suddenly it was more than just a kiss, and Horace began to feel strange and awkward and exhilarated all at the same time. Rose's hands caressed his face. She kissed his eyes and his cheeks and his mouth and led his hands to other parts of her they hadn't touched before.

In Wexford, they walked the streets as though they both now lived in each other's hearts. Horace felt that something very important was happening to him that August. He had moved from somewhere he'd been to another place altogether, and yet he was still essentially the same. The difference was Rose Burke. He recalled the return trip from Wexford. This time they had gone to the ticket office, but the man behind the glass had only charged them for one. Horace was very happy about that: it seemed to signify that whatever was happening to them was visible to other people, this change and the love they had together.

'He's got to be a butterfly,' Rose said, with a smile and a squeeze of Horace's hand as they boarded the train. Horace knew exactly what she meant.

A young couple had come into their carriage on the way back and sat down opposite them. The man was carrying a small white coffin and he held it on his lap for the short duration of the journey. The lady was crying while the man's eyes filled with tears, though none fell. The train, the last of the day, was crowded and there had been nowhere else for the grieving couple to sit. Rose and Horace held hands tightly and Horace wondered what it would be like to be a father himself, to be responsible for a wife and a child. He'd looked at the oblong deal box on the man's lap.

Horace had rarely wondered about his appearance, but when he did, he sometimes imagined that he looked increasingly like the faded photograph of his own father taken in Donegal in the summer of 1950. In that picture, the boy and the man stood side by side. The boy seemed to be kicking at a pebble – or something – at his feet. He remembered little about that holiday apart from a visit to a funfair. He recalled holding his father's hand as they'd made their way through the throng of people who crowded the event. He thought he could remember music, but wasn't sure. The *snap* of air rifles peppering balloons was the only sound he could faithfully bring to mind.

He could feel, even now, so much later, the fear he had had at that moment that if he let go of his dad's hand, he would be lost for ever. He remembered his father's face in profile against the sky as he edged sideways through the crowd and never lost sight of his son. Horace could not imagine his own face from that same scene. What was increasingly clear to him, though, was the way in which people's image of themselves was so often at variance with the reality. When he'd been in his twenties, he'd always believed that he was quite ugly. There had been little enough in the way of independent evidence to confirm this, but nonetheless that was how Horace had felt. Now, in his sixties, he was more assured of himself but perhaps that was only because, deep down, he no longer believed that it mattered what he looked like. He'd met many people who were clearly self-conscious about their appearance when he, at least, had thought them beautiful.

At St Luke's Hospital, Horace was admitted for a course of radiotherapy. He had to attend for five days each week for six weeks. Each treatment session took fifteen minutes.

'It's like a zapper gun,' a porter said to him, as Horace was being fitted with a lead apron, which itself was encased in the kind of plastic covering that you found on bus seats. 'What they do is direct the beam onto the tumour and they give it a lash for a few minutes at a time. It shrinks the thing – as long as it doesn't miss the target of course!'

The man laughed in bursts of snorts at his own observations while Horace lay on the raised table in the centre of the room and watched the blinking lights through sunglasses like Amanda's. He couldn't feel a thing, not there and then anyhow. Later, near the end of the third day of treatment, he vomited in the car park as he got into his car. He'd been told not to drive.

'All right there, Mr Winter?' A nurse, with a watch that seemed to have stopped pinned to her breast pocket, held his arm on day twelve or thirteen and brought him to the Gents where he could be sick in comfort. He had painkillers and anti-nausea pills, but they didn't seem to be much good at fighting either ailment. He thought about the whole issue of butterflies and moths; the fail-safe mechanism he'd developed for trying to understand people. Guiltily, however, he admitted to himself now, in the unsentimental surroundings of the men's toilets, that he'd never had the courage to ask the butterfly/ moth question about those closest to him. He had never determined the species of his parents. In his heart, Horace knew that he'd been skirting the issue for years. Decades. He vomited once more.

During the fourth week of the treatment, Amanda accompanied him to St Luke's and back. 'Sure it's no bother at all, Horace,' she'd said. 'I'm off for the rest of the week, next Monday and Tuesday as well. Why don't we go somewhere for a day-trip when you're feeling up to it?'

'Where do you suggest, Amanda?' Horace sat in the back seat of a cab with her while the windscreen wipers cleared water, front and back, from the glass outside. His flying plans had been quite disrupted by the treatment.

The zapper did its sniper work. There the lighting was subdued and apologetic.

Week six. Horace felt extremely tired and decrepit. He wished he could sleep for longer periods than he was currently managing each night. He had begun to dream, too, and sometimes the dreams were of such a vivid and disturbing nature that he recollected them precisely when he woke.

In one, he'd been in a small village, perhaps it was Otterton, and it was snowing. A bright orange car, the type that had doors that opened out and upwards like wings, tried to run him over but instead wound up in a ditch. A man emerged from the driver's seat and confronted Horace. He was more aggressive than a customer at the bank would ever have been, whatever the error on the part of the branch. He reminded Horace of a cousin of his, whom he hadn't seen for decades. He had red hair and a face like the boy in the ancient John Hinde postcard, the one of the boy and girl loading turf onto a creel on the back of a donkey. The snow began to ease off as the confrontation progressed and the man handed Horace a paper bag, then drove off. In the bag was a red tartan shirt.

'Give it to *them*. They've been looking for a clue for ages,' was all of the man's diatribe Horace could remember.

Later on in the dream, Horace was standing in a village square outside a pharmacy. A little girl, whom Horace thought might be his daughter, went into a drapery shop and emerged wearing the red tartan shirt. Horace lost sight of her for a time while Christmas shoppers obscured her from him, and, in the dream, he was filled with a fear that someone had stolen her.

That morning, after he'd got up, he turned on the radio downstairs and noticed a clump of hair in the kitchen sink. His treatment had ended.

In the mirror in the hall, he'd become someone else altogether. He did not know who. That night, before retiring to bed, Horace ventured downstairs in his favourite blue pyjamas and rechecked that the front and back doors were locked. On his way up again, he paused on the landing outside the main bathroom and put his ear to the door before checking that it, too, was locked. Horace hadn't been into that bathroom for a very long time. Something about it made him sad, and afraid.

Amanda had taught him how to turn on the PC and begin a search on the web.

The Germans had not known in the summer of 1944 where or when the Allies might try to land. There had been rumours for almost a year and yet nothing had come of them. They had anticipated, however, that the invasion might occur along the Normandy coast and in particular on the Cotentin peninsula. They had dug ditches and planted mines and fortified the beaches with mortars and machine-gun posts. Inland, just beyond the Orne river, was a heavy gun battery, but more menacing still was the presence of the 21st Panzer Division.

He found more information on yet another website:

Sword was the farthest east of the beaches and was close to the city of Caen, the major German stronghold in the region. Despite the presence of 155mm guns only twenty miles away at Le Havre, Sword was the most lightly defended of the five beaches on 6 June 1944. Paratroopers, who had landed inland near the village of Ranville, joined the soldiers who disembarked on the beach. That evening the 192nd Panzer Grenadier Regiment counter-attacked, and some of the tanks actually reached Sword Beach. Many of these armoured monsters were destroyed by British air attacks. About fifty Panzers attacked the British-held positions. One company even made it through to the coast at Lion-sur-Mer. As the Germans began to reinforce the intact defences, more than two hundred gliders, of the 6th Air

Landing Brigade, flew over the Panzer Grenadier positions. Believing they would be cut off, the Germans abandoned their defence. The day ended with 28,845 British troops ashore.

Corporal Robert Winter and his compatriots, Fred Alexander and Migsie Spring, were among them.

Horace wondered what the place looked like now, sixty-odd years later. He had been less than two years old when D-Day had happened, and now there was an invasion of another sort going on inside his head. There was no air support, no gliders to fly overhead and make the invader turn back towards the town of Caen. His pain and nausea had been horrendous for a time but he'd noticed since the course of treatment had ended that he had more energy than before, and that the pain and sickness had all but gone away. Maybe the invasion *was* being repelled. His almost daily visits to St Luke's were over now, for a time at least.

He thought he probably had enough material from which to discern his mother's butterfly/moth identity: she had lived and breathed and walked about upstairs in his life until quite recently. Her presence was still all about the house in Edenvale Road; it even lingered in his car. But where could he

go to find his father? And what species was Robert
Winter? Horace hoped that his father would not
turn out to be a moth. He wondered what it might
be like to visit Sword Beach.

'Go for it, Horace,' Amanda's response had been.
'You only have one life.'

CHAPTER FIFTEEN

Grey Dagger (*Acronicta psi*)

White Letter Hairstreak (*Satyrium w-album*)

The television in his mother's room was playing, but Horace did not remember having switched it on. He'd heard it on the way back from the downstairs bathroom where, for the first time in his life since he'd needed to, he hadn't shaved. 'Let the hair grow where it will,' he said, to the stranger in the mirror.

He stood on the landing and watched the TV screen through the open doorway, as ghosts flew in and out of the scenes where an old man called Ebenezer lay on a four-poster bed and worried about how much money he had and the cost of candles. Horace knew that his mother was dead and that even if he knocked on the door and walked into the room, she would not be there. He knocked and said, 'Mother?' in a whisper, before turning off the TV set and wiping a handful of mouse-grey dust from the top of the tall pile of television schedules that stood alone in the middle of the room. He'd stopped collecting them on the final weekend before he'd retired, although he hadn't watched television for a very long time now, not since the day she'd died.

Horace knew that not all of his feelings about his mother were positive. He knew that sometimes she had said unkind things to him and to his father. He wondered what his life might have been like if his mother had been someone else. He wondered whether she had hidden the butterfly net behind the sideboard. He was certain that the reason she had thrown out his butterfly and moth collection was because of her anger and disappointment with him over his exam results. It wasn't a professional collection — no entomological pins or expensive boards — but it had been *his*. For all its faults, in fact, it had been pretty damn good. He'd started another collection but had hidden it from her in the garage where she never trespassed. He'd been afraid to bring it out into the open until after she'd died. What did that say about her, about either of them?

She knew about Rose Burke, too, he was pretty certain of that. On the day after she'd admitted binning his collection, she had made a veiled remark at tea-time about Catholics. 'Marry your own, Horace. That's all I'll say to you about that. There's no point in having a large family. One or two children is more than enough for anyone.'

His mother's illness had resulted in a cessation of her attendance at church services, but Horace was never quite sure whether it was an impairment of a physical or spiritual nature that had caused the change. 'Religion is the glue that binds civilised society together, Horace,' she had often said to him. Horace suspected that her own devotion to the exercise of her faith had been partly driven by the desire to kick against what she called 'Rome-mantic Ireland'. He recollected her steadfast refusal to attend the funerals of acquaintances of either Christian hue. 'Funerals are for dead people. They have to attend. We do not. I hope that people say their goodbyes to me when I am still able to hear them.'

Death seemed to embolden Mrs Winter – at least, the death of others did. Horace was drawn sometimes to the library of photographs in the drawer in the front room. There he could see, in the sepia and shadow echoes of his past, that she had grown stronger than ever after the death of her husband. She stared out from the later photographs defiantly, taking on the world and defeating it by use of her limited resources: a widow's pension from the state, and a battleship-worth of determination to survive.

Just before he got into bed that night, Horace opened page seventy-four of *A Beginner's Guide*. And there she was, as he'd always known somehow she would be, her wings greyish at the fore, and hind wings suffused with brown, Fig. IV in black and white: a Grey Dagger moth. He took the pencil in his hand and allowed it to hover over the page and the diagram, the memory and reality of almost the entirety of his life with her. Horace thought about his Leaving Cert results and his butterfly collection and his father, and many more things he'd tried to forget. He read aloud from the text: '"The cocoon in which it pupates is reinforced with a distinctive bark. Prevalent along the east coast of Ireland, this species is particularly noted for its dislike of its own offspring."'

And finally, after six and a half decades of his own life and an Atlantic Ocean's worth of not wanting to believe it, he put a cross on the illustration and wrote the word 'Mother' underneath it. Horace felt his temples with his hands as an excruciating pain within his head threatened to render him unconscious.

The next day, Horace sat in front of the fire in the sitting room on his own, surrounded by maps of France and the fragments of his research into D-Day. He had begun to think seriously about travelling to the place where his father had landed with so many thousands of other soldiers on 6 June 1944.

Horace had never ventured outside Ireland since first coming to Dublin as a child after the war. He had a passport, just in case, but he had never needed to use it. Some species of butterfly were indigenous to certain countries and were not widely observed elsewhere. The Small Blue, for example, was to be found in most parts of Europe, except southern Spain, the Netherlands and parts of Scandinavia. In

Britain and Ireland it tended to live in tiny isolated colonies.

That morning he had woken with a ferocious headache. It was directly behind his left eye and he'd thought it might never pass. He'd imagined one of those toys, the ones with the multicoloured sides that twisted so that the smaller squares (which made up each side) could be mixed up together and rearranged in patterns you couldn't quite get hold of. All of those moving squares were piled on top of each other. Inside his eye, it was as though someone was trying to right the colours but could not because Horace was in the way. This direction and that, the squares had turned on an axis and were unscrambled and back-filled until they made no sense any more. It was then that he'd first noticed that the pain had almost stopped.

But Horace knew he couldn't afford to sit in bed any longer. He had a mission to fulfil, the particular business of a wish to grant. He knew that there was no point in trying to send Max something in the post that might help him to escape, such as a disguise or a file baked in a cake or a wax mould of a key. He didn't know if the Confirmation suit had been delivered to him, but even if it had, what chance was there that items designed to help him escape would ever reach

Max? Similarly, Horace had also discounted the possibility of digging a tunnel under the perimeter wall or of using a grappling hook or a rope ladder to effect the rescue himself. He was simply too old for any of that. It *had* crossed his mind to try to help Max escape during one of his visits to the hospital, but he'd discounted that on the dual grounds of the unpredictability of the boy's visits and the presence of both the garda and the care worker. No, from the moment he had carried out a search on the world wide web, after he'd heard Max identify the place where he was being held, Horace had concluded that the only way in was from the air. His flying training had continued whenever he was able, between the headaches and the hospital visits and the days when he simply couldn't bring himself to leave the house. The detention authorities would not be expecting such an approach, and from his reconnaissance trips he knew there were no air defences in the entire facility. He had graduated from fighter planes and was now learning to fly bombers.

'There's a gardening trade fair on in Cork the week after next,' Amanda said that weekend, as they had Sunday lunch together. 'I think I'll go.'

'That's a great idea,' Horace said, as he avoided

eating the rest of his vegetables and sensed the beginnings of a headache.

'Are you all right, Horace?' she asked.

'Yes, yes, I'm fine,' he said. He knew now that he might have to bring D-Day forward. He could feel his illness resurrecting inside his head. There were other preparations to be made too.

The sculptor and artist Rowan Gillespie's workshop was at the end of a leafy lane near Blackrock village. Horace had read an interview with him in the Weekend section of *The Irish Times* some months earlier. He'd managed to track him down by using the telephone directory at the post office in Ranelagh.

'It's a very unusual design,' the sculptor said, when Horace showed him the drawing he'd done of exactly what he needed him to make. The design consisted of a three-dimensional rectangular frame. A central bar bisected the underside of the brace and from it protruded two large springs. He had chosen this particular artist because he had his own foundry. 'And you want two of them, is that right?'

'Yes,' said Horace. 'And I'd like them to be cast in

aluminium or whatever would allow them to be as light as possible but still very strong.'

'Do you want the spring portions to be rigid or flexible?' the sculptor asked. He was a fresh-faced, honest outdoors type and Horace knew at once that he was a White-letter Hairstreak butterfly.

'Oh, definitely flexible,' Horace said. 'I want them to be as springy as possible.'

'Hmm,' said the sculptor, as he scratched his cheek. 'I could try to make the spring in wax, then use the lost wax process to pour it with an aluminium bronze alloy. That would probably get the weight down a fair bit. We could temper it by plunging the cast while it's about six hundred degrees in cold water. That would probably give it some spring. It might only spring a few times and then it would probably snap.'

'But it *would* be springy *and* light?' Horace asked anxiously.

'Yes, it would probably be both of those things,' the Hairstreak answered. 'May I ask what they're for?'

'Of course,' Horace replied. 'They're Angel Springboxes. Designed to make the wearer's wish come true.'

The sculptor looked at Horace with a strange

expression for a few moments, then smiled broadly. 'Very few people understand modern art like we do, Mr ...'

'Winter,' he replied. 'Horace Winter.'

'Well, Horace, I'm delighted to meet you and I'd be more than happy to do your casting for you. Are those measurements exactly what you want?' He pointed at Horace's spidery handwriting in the margins of the blueprint.

'Exactly what I want,' Horace said. 'As long as the four springs are all the same size you could make them a little larger if you think they'll still hold.'

'No problem,' said Rowan Gillespie. 'Have you ever had a solo exhibition? I'm trying to remember if I've seen your work before. Did we meet at a dinner in IMMA?'

'How long will it take you to make them?' Horace asked, ignoring both of the man's questions.

'How soon do you need them?'

'Within a week or so,' Horace replied.

'Can do,' said the sculptor. 'Would you like to have a look around the foundry and the workshop?'

The other items Horace decided to add to the escape package were a lot easier to source. He'd bought a pair of size seven and a half running shoes in a sports shop and had used them to work out the measurements of the rectangular frame he'd commissioned the sculptor to cast. The other things he included were: a student rail and bus ticket combined, valid for a year; a large bar of Bournville chocolate; a modern edition of his treasured *Butterflies and Moths: A Beginner's Guide* and a twenty-euro note. He put the ticket and the cash into a plastic coin-bag and left it, with the chocolate bar and the book, on the kitchen work surface near the weighing scales.

Horace had decided that the butterfly on the boy's trousers was indeed an omen. It was a signal to him that it was time for him to pass on his interest in butterflies and moths to a boy who was almost the same age he had been when his father had given the book to him. If he had fostered the boy he would have given a copy to him at some stage. For Horace, this act of handing on his passion for butterflies and moths to the next generation was, he felt, the closest he might ever get to being a parent. Even if the boy decided not to escape, he would at least have something important and vital to read.

During the week, while he waited for the sculptor to cast the Angel Springboxes, Horace went to the local library and borrowed a DVD about D-Day. He watched the black and white footage of the adapted bombers pulling the Horsa gliders and he planned his next move.

By day Horace honed his skills as a pilot. He had now moved on to even more difficult terrain in his quest for the kind of conditions he could expect to face when the mission proper occurred. On Sandymount Strand, in plain sight of Joyce's Martello tower, Horace made the final adjustments to the Halifax bomber's wing fixings with a small wrench. Then he was happy that it was ready to fly. Two petrol engines were needed to get the bomber off the ground because of its size and weight. It had four propellers, a pair on each wing. Horace had identified the drop zone for his mission, but had yet to find a suitable place from which the bomber could take off. Before he returned to County Wicklow to scout for an appropriate airstrip, he needed to master the business of controlling the enormous model plane. He would have to know, down to the last few inches, the minimum runway length required for the beast to take off.

On his first day of learning to fly the Halifax, it took him almost two hours to fly the heavy plane along the seashore for four or five hundred yards, then successfully return and land again on the beach near the car park. He had had to use a roof-rack on the Morris Minor to transport the aircraft from Edenvale Road. A tall grey-haired man had stood on the promenade, watching Horace with interest. Horace recognised him from a photograph he'd seen in a newspaper. He thought the man might be a well-known writer.

Unlike the SlowBipe or the Spitfire, the engines of the Halifax had to be started by hand with the use of a cord. When they were running, and all of the propellers were spinning, it took 330 feet of runway from starting to move to actually becoming airborne safely. Horace found that landing it was not as difficult as he had feared. As long as he landed it into the wind and did not touch the elevator stick, but simply reduced throttle, the plane would descend on its own. Ten feet above the ground, Horace knew to cut the throttle altogether and simply raise the nose slightly at the last moment and all three wheels would touch down together.

The range given for the Halifax was more than seven miles. Horace's eyesight was not the best so he was glad to have finally decided on a much larger model. In any event, he thought, none of the smaller planes available would have been up to the task of pulling the load required.

Amanda would be away the following week. Horace looked at the long-range weather forecast and decided that Wednesday would probably be best for Operation Springbox. He knew that he could do nothing to change the circumstances in which Thomas Hackett now found himself, but he had given his word to try to help the boy to get home to his own house. Anywhere would be an improvement for him rather than to continue to be incarcerated in that awful place, full of other boys who *were* criminals. Max had done nothing wrong.

Horace collected the springs and their frames on Monday morning.

'I hope these are what you wanted,' Rowan Gillespie said, as Horace inspected them. He was astonished at how little they weighed.

'They're just right,' he replied. 'Are you sure the springs won't break off easily?'

'Absolutely not,' the sculptor confirmed, testing them with his hands. 'I moulded and cast them separately, then welded them on. Because of that they're actually much stronger at the join than if I'd made them all in one piece. If I can do anything else for you, just let me know.'

'Thank you ever so much,' Horace said, to the

White-letter Hairstreak, as he handed him an envelope containing the agreed fee, which he reckoned wouldn't do much more than cover the cost of the materials.

'Let me know when the exhibition's on,' the man said. 'If you need any other pieces cast, just give me a shout.'

Horace was now sitting in his car. He rolled down the window and gave the man a wave. 'Thanks again,' he said.

He drove out to Wicklow and, once again, parked off the track on Fagan's Hill. He hadn't yet found a suitable place for the take-off. He needed a runway that was long and flat and visible from a vantage point from which he could also see Frostfield Abbey. As he continued on his way, he glanced to his right to see a small country school with a pair of goalposts behind it.

Horace parked his car some distance away and made his way back down the winding road on foot. He slipped into the school grounds through a low, unbolted gate. The place was locked up and all of the staff had gone home. He edged carefully around the side of the buildings and looked over his shoulder to make sure no one was watching from the road. He was met with the sight of an almost completely sheltered tarmac playground immediately behind the main buildings. Beyond it was a grass playing pitch with two sets of goalposts, one of which he'd glimpsed from the road. Horace walked out onto the pitch, which was bounded on the other three sides by a drystone wall. The pitch sloped very obviously from end to end. He would have to use the playground and the width of the pitch in order to keep the runway as straight as possible.

He looked down into the valley below. He saw the motorway and, just beyond, the high surrounding wall of Frostfield Abbey. Even without the binoculars, Horace could also make out the main avenue and the gardening shed with the green corrugated-iron roof, where Max always cut across the large field in the complex during his solitary daily walk. In the still of the June evening, the only sounds that could be heard were the cawing of crows in the trees and the distant and melodic rattle and hum of a tractor and baling machine in the vast meadow that abutted the correctional facility.

Horace practised a bit more with the flying, and when he'd done as much as he could for the day, he went home.

CHAPTER SIXTEEN

'One of the other ways of distinguishing
between butterflies and moths is that
while some butterflies never disclose their
upper wings at rest, moths usually roll or
angle their forewings.'

Butterflies and Moths: A Beginner's Guide

The morning of Operation Springbox arrived
with a little light rain, but it soon cleared.
Horace spent quite some time weighing and
packaging the springboxes, the running shoes, the
bar of chocolate and the money pouch. He bought

a length of clothesline from the hardware store at the Triangle in Ranelagh village and tried to figure out how long it would need to be to enable the Halifax bomber to pull the load successfully. The longer it was, the less likely it would hamper the take-off. Horace tied the aluminium-bronze casts together, using the spare pair of laces he'd got with the running shoes. He attached the shoes tightly to one springbox, each using its own lace. Inside one, he taped the pouch containing the money and the travel ticket. He decided to include the chocolate bar only if he was happy that the package wasn't too heavy. Using the kitchen scales, he determined the total weight as follows:

- Training shoes (combined) (incl. ticket and money), 15.5 oz
- Angel Springboxes (combined), 19 oz
- Chocolate bar, 7.4 oz
- *Butterflies and Moths: A Beginner's Guide*, 15 oz
- Total, 56.9 oz

Horace strapped the plane to his roof-rack, placed the package on the rear seat and set off for the Phoenix Park. He parked on a grass verge behind the Papal

Cross, which marked the site of the Pope's visit in 1979.

Horace assembled his thoughts and his cargo for a trial run. It became immediately apparent that the plane would be unable to take off if it simply dragged the package behind it, regardless of the length of the cable, because as soon as the bundle began to drag along the ground one of the springs lurched sideways and became tangled in the grassy earth of the runway. Horace instantly eased back on the throttle and was relieved to see that the plane still had enough slack clothesline left to enable it to land without being damaged.

Horace had made a second visit to the sculptor's workshop.

'Hydrogen's what you need,' Rowan Gillespie had told him. 'It's a super idea to have the exhibits float above the audience during the exhibition. You just need a few balloons filled with hydrogen and then, obviously, tie the exhibits to something solid on the ground so they don't fly out the window. You wouldn't want that.' The sculptor laughed. 'When you know the total weight, get back to me and I'll fill the balloons for you from this fellah here.' He tapped a tall cylinder with a dial on its top. 'I use it for my blow-torch when I'm cutting glass.'

'Fifty-six point nine ounces,' Horace announced, holding out a bag of party balloons in each hand.

'Eh, right, erm, okay. Just give me a few minutes,' the sculptor said, in a slightly shocked tone. 'How will you carry them home?'

'In the vast boot of my Morris Minor,' Horace replied with a smile.

Under the cockpit of the Halifax, Horace had made a small hole with a screwdriver and fixed a bent piece of carbon fibre so that it protruded, facing forward, from the undercarriage like a capital letter L, with an elongated upward-slanted lower piece. Tied to one end of the length of clothesline was a metal ring and this slipped easily over the hook. Horace reckoned that as long as the cargo package hung behind or even below the bomber, it could not fall off during the trip.

When the plane was over the drop zone, a gentle diving movement would cause the cable to detach when he needed it to.

There was a bus stop directly outside Frostfield

Abbey. Suburban Dublin Bus double-deckers stopped there every fifteen minutes.

When Max had boarded a bus, his ticket would take him home and Horace would have kept his promise.

At the stroke of four fifteen that afternoon, Horace pulled off the road into the tiny car park at the front of the primary school on Fagan's Hill. He carried the plane around to the playground, tested the wind direction and strength, and smiled.

He laid the escape package on the ground and tested the knots to make sure the load was tightly bound together. He attached the clothesline cable to the package, using a triple granny knot, then arranged the remainder of its length in parallel lines of three feet each on the tarmac so that it would pay out gradually as the plane taxied down the runway. Horace tied the balloons in bundles of six while sitting in his car. He got out of the car clutching the balloons and walked cautiously around via the side of the school. Using a series of granny knots, Horace attached the strings to the package. It began to lift from the playground surface.

The only other thing he needed to do now was to go back to the car and retrieve the small lawnmower he had hired from the hardware shop in Ranelagh. He started the mower and cut the upper part of the path across the football field, which the plane would have to travel along. This, he hoped, would neutralise the slope. He stuck one of the flags that marked the pitch at a point outside the runway some twenty paces short of the drystone wall. He then put the lawn mower on the back seat of the Morris Minor.

At precisely a quarter past five, the inmates of Frostfield Abbey spilled out into the recreation area. Through the binoculars, Horace watched the forlorn figure of Max Hackett detach himself from the rest of the boys and begin his ritual walk. The wind was starting to increase slightly as Horace switched on the transmitter. He wrenched the plastic handle and pulled the cord with a contemptuous confidence, provoking the engines into life.

Horace Winter stood with his back to the rear door of the little school and held the control transmitter in position against his chest and adjusted the strap. He looked down the length of the runway. He had calculated that the wheels would have to be off the ground at the very latest by the time the plane reached a point level with the flag. Otherwise it would probably not clear the wall. Horace had one final look through the binoculars and saw that Max was approaching the gardening shed. With the slightest of touches, Horace's left thumb encouraged the throttle to rouse the engines to their monumental task. The cargo had floated to a height of about ten feet.

The huge model aircraft started to move along the tarmac in a direct path towards the gate. Horace barely nudged the throttle and the wheels gathered pace. As the Halifax moved more quickly along the basketball court of the playground, it was at half-speed and the clothesline was now whipping incautiously and extending itself, granting extra altitude to the freakish package of springs and shoes and an under-18 monthly combined bus and rail pass.

The hulking aeronautical colossus gathered courage and momentum as it accelerated and strained violently at the leash. Horace coerced the throttle to its absolute limit. He looked up at the balloons and saw that they were above the roof of the school, their passenger dangling below them, swinging madly in the breeze. The enraged engines now commenced a whine that reverberated above their own roar. The aircraft thumped and palpitated its thunderous way as it sped through the gate.

Smoke began to pour from the propellers as though

the improbability of what was about to happen devastated and disfigured the very laws of physics the plane had been built to obey.

The bomber was now moving so ferociously fast down the runway that Horace feared it might explode under the weight of its own ambition. As the vast metal and plastic hulk headed cantankerously across the playing surface towards the apocalyptic drystone wall marking the boundary of St Bride's National School grounds, Horace abandoned the precision of his own calculations. As the plane raced past the flag, he refused to move the flight stick that controlled the elevator flaps at the rear of the smoking beast. His experience of the past two months in learning to fly planes had imbued him with an instinct as to when the aircraft was ready to leave the ground, and he knew that point was not yet at hand. Something inside urged him to wait a few seconds more, a few yards more, for just an extra ounce of speed and power. When the plane was barely twenty-five feet from the wall, Horace finally flicked the control and closed his eyes.

The Halifax bomber veered up at an angle that was beyond either belief or hope. Up, up, up the veteran and unprepossessing air-animal climbed, screaming, dragging the gift of escape materials behind it across the Wicklow evening sky.

He eased back on the throttle and at the same time dropped the nose of the bomber slightly so that it flew parallel to the ground, which now lay 175 feet below. He watched proudly as the bouquet of hydrogen-filled balloons was pulled compliantly across the N11.

Satisfied that the plane was on course, Horace allowed himself a one-handed glance through the binoculars. He was a little surprised to see that Max was now more than halfway along his circuit of the abbey's grounds. Slowly sweeping the horizon for a suitable new drop zone, Horace saw the farmer on the huge tractor skewering vast round hay-bales and depositing them on a long trailer in the meadow adjacent to the home for delinquent boys. His last view of the Halifax bomber through the lenses reassured him that the engines were no longer smoking. Their hardest work had been done in getting off the ground.

The plane was now over the large grassy plain at the centre of the complex, so he decided that this was an opportunity to bring it over the target area in a wide, sweeping trial run and simultaneously reduce its altitude. Skilfully, gently and with no hint of difficulty, Horace guided the Halifax in a wide arc out over the wall of the abbey's grounds, above the meadow beyond, and then he coaxed the rudder so that the plane made a wide circle and doubled back over the main buildings.

Horace watched as the boy stopped and looked up into the sky above him. He prodded the controls so that the nose of the plane dived earthwards for three seconds, then, just in time to avert a stall, he made it climb once more into the clouds. His concern that the cable might not decouple had been groundless. He watched with electrifying pride as the balloons and the bomber parted ways. The Halifax slowly began its turn eastwards to commence the home run while the balloons stayed behind and now held their booty in the middle of the sky directly above Max Hackett. He took up the binoculars once again and saw that Max was now frantically jumping up and down in the middle of the open space below the balloons. It became clear instantly that the uncoupling had occurred at too great an altitude or else the balloons were beginning to rise even higher. The trailing end of the clothesline was well out of the child's reach. Horace dropped the binoculars and resumed two-handed control of the Halifax. The balloons were being lifted even higher by the air currents. He had only moments to perform a miracle or Max would be trapped forever at Frostfield Abbey.

With desperate skill, he compelled the huge plane into a steep banking manoeuvre, which brought it back over the open expanse of the large field at the heart of the Frostfield Abbey complex. He drove the aircraft directly upwards at the mass of balloons. Through his hands he could feel the straining of the Halifax against the wind as the throttle tried to snub his insistence. The narcissistic engines battered away catatonically.

BOOM! An elephantine explosion of flame and noise ruptured the entire valley across to Fagan's Hill and Giltspur Forest, as the propellers made contact with some of the hydrogen-filled party balloons. The aeroplane blundered onto its side with one entire wing wrathfully ablaze, lurched grotesquely across the sky in a disfigured spin, and, for a moment, Horace thought the fire on the wing might quench, but it did not. He wrenched at the throttle, blindly imploring the rudders, ailerons, elevators and all else within the plane's anatomy to respond to his own terror and somehow to banish the madness of what was happening to some other untouchable, invisible place.

A sudden realisation hit him that absolutely nothing he was doing or could do with the transmitter would make a blind bit of difference to what would inevitably happen. Horace raised the binoculars to his eyes and helplessly watched the fate of the Halifax as it unfolded.

The bomber was now completely out of control and began to spiral deliriously on its side, spitting fire, yet without seeming to lose altitude as quickly as he had expected. He willed the plane to disintegrate in the sky rather than to crash, but Destiny was wearing earmuffs: the unwieldy hunk of burning plastic, resin and rubber suddenly began to descend at a slope, and Horace was almost afraid to keep looking, but he could not take his eyes off the terrific and horrible scene. Inexplicably, the plane stopped falling and continued to burn in midair. Some of the balloon strings had become snagged on one of the propellers on the unburned wing and the result was a parachute-type effect where the balloons were now slowing the fall to earth of the Halifax. Four, still attached to the clothesline, separated from the main bunch. The rescue package now began to descend rapidly to the ground and fell in a heap not twenty feet from where the boy stood rooted to the spot.

Gradually, the plane cleared the line of the perimeter wall and drifted away from Frostfield Abbey. The boy went over and began to examine the package. Horace exhaled in relief. But his entire body began to shake as he saw where the remaining burning torso and limbs of the plane were heading.

'No! No! No! *Look out!*' Horace roared, as he signalled hysterically, waving one hand, to warn the farmer on the tractor of the impending catastrophe. He witnessed the blazing remains of the bomber collide with the enormous cylinder of hay impaled on the hydraulic skewer of the red tractor just as the load was being deposited on the already over-laden trailer. Horace could hardly look as the entire load caught fire and generated a rising mantle of smoke that he imagined could probably be seen from space. The farmer attempted to extricate the vehicle from the inferno before abandoning ship and running up the meadow in an effort to escape. All Horace could hear was a series of detonations as the apocalypse continued relentlessly.

One last look at the grounds of Frostfield Abbey revealed Max clutching the package in his arms and making for the shelter of the high perimeter wall as the inferno raged in the next field.

Gathering his remaining shreds of sense about him, Horace realised that it was time for him to go home. He stumbled to his car. The spider ties, which had once secured the Halifax to the roof-rack, hung limply across the windscreen, like ivy, as he drove, but he was too emotionally damaged even to think of getting out to clear them away. He drove slowly along the narrow, winding country laneway that linked Fagan's Hill, Giltspur Forest and Barchuillia Commons with the rest of the surrounding terrain. At the end of the road, he turned left for Dublin and knew that the sooner he got home to bed the better. As he changed down into second gear before a roundabout he saw two garda squad cars, their blue lights flashing irresistibly, on the far side of the roundabout, escorting a fire engine onto the main road.

CHAPTER SEVENTEEN

Chequered Skipper (*Carterocephalus palaemon*)

Twenty-plume Moth (*Alucita hexadactyla*): sometimes flies on mild winter nights

A couple of days after Operation Springbox, Amanda dropped in on her way to work. Horace was glad he hadn't involved her in the mission: she would only have been worried about him. She'd brought a gift for him. It was an airline ticket to Leeds.

'Why Leeds?' he asked.

'It's in Yorkshire. That's where the letter to Migsie

was addressed, Horace. That's where Migsie Spring lived. Lives, if he's still around. I thought perhaps you could go and find him. Deliver the letter.'

Horace was overwhelmed. He sat for a moment, unable to take it in. He stumbled to his feet and went upstairs for a minute or two, then returned.

'It's just something small,' he said. He gave her the tiny parcel he'd had to rewrap after opening it by mistake. For a little while as he'd wrapped it, he'd lost the power of his right arm. He'd bought it for her birthday, but didn't know when it was. This seemed as good a time as any.

'Oh, Horace, it's beautiful,' Amanda said, as she held the turquoise butterfly brooch between her fingers.

As the plane landed, Horace looked out at the aircraft clustered on the tarmac surrounding the airport buildings. He tried to imagine them as gliders packed with troops, ready to be pulled into the air by heavier aircraft before descending silently to their destination behind enemy lines.

On the train to Settle, Horace watched as the vast sprawl of Leeds drifted past. A lady with a trolley of tea and snacks came down the aisle towards him, at just the instant he needed to use the lavatory. She looked down at Horace's luggage, a small overnight bag with the Tesco logo on it, and smiled.

'All right, love?' she asked.

Horace was embarrassed at her use of the word 'love'. He thought it was not the kind of word that should be used casually. He gathered the bag closer to himself and looked out of the window again: factories, houses, rusting trains, abandoned stations, fields and more factories. The train continued northwards.

Yorkshire was absolutely beautiful. Horace recalled another television series his mum had liked, the one about the vet practice. He remembered snippets of storylines, parts of programmes, fragments of country life depicted on film. Apart from the cars being more modern, the whole area appeared as it had in the series. At the small Gothic-style railway station, Horace saw a minibus with the words 'Layhead Farm Cottages' on the side. There was also a jeep with a trailer full of pigs waiting for someone in the station car park. He felt lost. He took out a small map from the inside pocket of his jacket. He saw that Arncliffe was quite a distance from Settle. It began to rain, so he sheltered on the railway platform and tried to gather his thoughts.

Inside his shirt, hanging from his neck, was a small waterproof pouch in which he carried his father's letter. Since discovering the correspondence, Horace had spent countless hours trying to figure out what his father had been apologising for when he'd written the one-word message to Migsie Spring. He thought about Rose Burke and all the letters he'd written to her with absolutely no reply ever coming back. He regretted having confided in her about himself, certain that the sharing of that information, about his father's death and other things, had made her run away from whatever it was they'd experienced together in those days on the dunes at Rosslare.

'Where are you headed for, mister?' A voice roused him from his thoughts. A farmer in wellington boots stood beside Horace and nodded down in the direction of Horace's map.

'Arncliffe,' Horace said.

'Hop in,' the man said, indicating back over his shoulder with a jerk of his head. 'Hope you don't mind smell of pigs!' The man walked in the direction of the jeep. Horace decided from the man's clothing and demeanour that he was definitely a Chequered

Skipper. The purplish-bronze-black colour was a dead giveaway. Although its haunts are normally woodlands, it can be found almost anywhere that the bugle flower grows. Horace remembered his father stretched out on the concrete steps of the rugby stand. Any hesitation he might have had about accepting a lift in a foreign country, from a total stranger with a trailer-load of pigs, vanished instantly.

It took about twenty minutes to get from the station through the town of Settle and up into the Yorkshire Dales. Horace was jolted from side to side as the jeep climbed high into the countryside with its bullion of squealing pigs. He suddenly realised that this was the part of England his father had come from. Had he ever travelled along this same road?

'Arncliffe,' announced the farmer, bringing the jeep to a halt.

Horace looked out of the window at the vast expanse of moors and hills that made up the landscape. 'Where?' he asked.

The farmer pointed across the wold, away from the direction in which the jeep was facing. In the very far distance, Horace saw the faint outline of what might have been a church. The famer leaned across him and opened the passenger door.

'Thank you for the lift,' Horace said.

'You're welcome,' said the farmer, without the slightest trace of irony or a smile. As Horace began his walk across the Dales he could hear the screeching of the pigs receding into the distance. He set out across the landscape on a narrow road that wound its way across the breathtaking scene in which he now found himself. Although he had been travelling since early that morning, he felt sprightly and positive.

As he began to near the village, the raw, naked beauty of the setting struck him even more, like a punch in the mouth. He had carried out some research in the Royal Dublin Society library and knew from the pictures he'd seen that he should expect to find a quaint and pretty settlement, which nestled around a village green. Despite being forewarned, however, he was still surprised at the scene when he took the last turn in the steep road down into the basement of the Wharfedale valley. The evening sunshine suffused the stone houses and barns as they huddled and faced the grass centrepiece. Away down and over the roofs of the houses, the church of St Oswald stood on the banks of the River Skirfare. He stood in the middle of the last chunk of roadway before the houses began and took it all in. He'd deliberately avoided looking to his right, like a student preparing for an exam who knows that the last piece of chocolate cake will still be waiting in the fridge whenever he is ready to reward himself with it, and then just a glance to see what he knew would be exactly where it was: the Falcon Inn. It was an elegant ivy-covered establishment, more than three hundred years old, with a hanging sign bearing a painting of a falcon.

In the entrance hall, a stuffed fox and an owl tried to outstare each other atop an antique table. Horace glanced suspiciously at them before continuing on into the heart of the ancient hostelry. Facing him was a chest-height bar counter. A lady in a T-shirt, which bore the word 'Hop-Hip' on the front, was busy filling glasses of beer from a porcelain jug. Behind her were three small iron beer kegs with taps. They were arranged so that their bottoms rested on a higher ledge to allow the beer to fall towards the tap end. 'Boltmaker Ale', read the sign behind the bar.

'Can I help you?' she asked Horace.

'I'm looking for Migsie Spring,' he replied.

'The nearest spring to here is yonder at Kettlewell, the only public one any road. If it's just good drinking water you're after, you can use the tap outside, or if you want to fill a small container I can do that for you here.'

'It's a person I'm looking for,' Horace said. He explained all about his father and the letter, and why he'd come to Arncliffe. The lady turned and shouted into the kitchen.

'Bill, there's a bloke here from Ireland and he's looking for someone.'

'Aren't we all?' the man said, with a laugh, as he came out and stood behind the bar with his wife and playfully put his arm around her waist.

'Go on out of that, Bill,' she said, giving a girlish grin and pushing his arm away, but not really. 'This man needs some help tracking down someone from East Yorkshire who was in the war.'

'The Fifth East Yorks?' the man asked.

'No, the Second Battalion,' Horace said. 'My father served with them on D-Day.'

'Sword instead of Gold, then.' The man smiled. 'Let's get you settled in a room and sort you out for food. It's Cribbage Night tonight and there'll be some folk in who might be able to help.'

Horace wondered how much lodgings and food would cost and whether he'd brought enough money.

As if reading his mind, the owner took a room key from a peg on the wall and said, 'You get the army rate because of your dad. Thirty quid B and B and your first pint's on the house.'

Horace rattled the tablets in his pocket and said nothing. Two stuffed magpies sat on a high shelf on the landing. Two for joy, Horace thought as he followed his host along the corridor to his room.

Horace hadn't drunk alcohol for years, apart from the very occasional sip of champagne at receptions he'd wished he hadn't had to attend. The small lounge bar in the hotel that night was jam-packed with people playing cribbage. Horace thought he'd seen a cribbage set somewhere at home, but was unsure. Bill and Ethnea had run the pub for nearly ten years and knew everyone, what they liked to drink and how much. Horace sipped gingerly at a pint of Boltmaker and listened to the happy banter of players and the clink of glasses as people moved table after each round. The scores were kept on a blackboard on the end wall near the fireplace. Over the open fire a huge red deer's head, with antlers, was mounted on the wall. The talk in the pub was the chatter of people who had known each other for a very long time, so the conversation was of new cars and old feuds and fishing, and whose son was away at 'university' and whose daughter was 'walking out' with someone. It smacked of the kind of comradeship he imagined might exist among soldiers, packed together and waiting for the command to invade. It was the type of human interaction that Horace had never experienced, shut away for decades in the bank or living alone amid a collection of butterflies and moths. Bill clinked two glasses and brought silence to the room.

'We have a visitor tonight, come all the way from Dublin.' There were a few 'ohs' and 'ums' and 'ayes' as everyone looked in Horace's direction. 'This young man's father fought in France with the East Yorkshires and, before you all ask, it were the Second East Yorks. Now, his father left a letter for another man who served in the same regiment, and that man's name were Matthew 'Migsie' Spring. The reason this man has come here to Arncliffe is that the address on the letter was this very establishment, the Falcon Inn. So, what all this is leading up to is for me to ask all of you whether any of you here tonight can help this man find the man that his father was looking for to write to but couldn't find. Simple as that.'

There was a murmur around the gathering and a general shaking of heads. In the far corner of the room, an elderly couple sat nursing a half-pint of ale each. As the proprietor finished speaking, the lady raised her hand. The innkeeper held up his own to silence the hum in the room.

Someone nudged Horace from the side. A young man with a red face whispered to him, 'That's Mr and Mrs Doasyouwouldbedoneby,' he said, and chuckled, 'after *The Water-Babies*, like. She does all the speaking for the pair of them.'

'Yes, Gladys?' the innkeeper said.

'He wants to know if you have a photograph.'

The landlord turned to Horace.

'As a matter of fact I do,' Horace said. He reached into the inside pocket of his jacket and took out the picture of his father and his two army colleagues leaning against the sign for Ouistreham. He handed it to Bill. The photograph was passed around the room until practically everyone had had a good look at it. It finally reached the elderly couple. They studied it together, then leaned in so that the old man could whisper something to his wife. After a few moments they sat back a little from each other and Mrs Doasyouwouldbedoneby spoke.

'He recognises the one on the left, the ugly one.'

Horace was unsure as to whether this could be of any use to him at all. Ignoring the inherent insult, he spoke: 'The man on the left is my father, Corporal Robert Winter. How on earth does your husband know him?'

'Eh? Speak up. We can't hear much.'

'The man from Dublin says that the man on the left in the photograph is his own father, Corporal Robert Winter,' Bill roared across the heads of his customers. The rest of the crowd turned to see the reaction of the old pair to this new information. The couple leaned in and conferred. The lady held up the photo and pointed to the man on the left: 'So that man there is your father?' she asked.

'Yes,' Horace said, nodding. 'That's my father on the left.' A quick final pow-wow cleared up the mystery.

'My husband meant the other left. He meant the man on the left of the man in the middle. That's the man he recognises.'

'Migsie Spring?' the landlord asked. The crowd held their breath as one.

'No,' said the old man. 'That's Freddie Alexander. He joined the circus after he were demobbed.'

Hopeless, Horace thought, upon his return to Dublin, as he sat down to butter his cold toast. For all he knew, Matthew Spring might not even be still alive. He thought about his father, writing the letter at the bureau in the front room. What was it that had moved him to write an apology to an army comrade, more than a decade after the war had ended? He imagined his father's final hours, preparing to go and watch his son play in a cup final, choosing the shirt and tie that someone, a stranger, would end up loosening in an attempt to stop his life ebbing away. He recalled the rolled-up coat under his father's head. Who had it belonged to? Had they continued to wear it for years afterwards, knowing someone had breathed his last while his head rested upon it? Corporal Robert Winter, deceased.

He remembered the couple on the train in Rosslare, their oblong deal box.

'Are you okay, Horace?' Rose had asked, as they'd walked hand in hand along the beach at Rosslare after they'd returned on the train.

'Why do children have to die?' he'd asked, looking straight ahead.

'It's just God's way, I suppose,' she'd said in reply. They'd sat on one of the sand dunes late that evening and watched the sun go down behind a church steeple. 'My dad says that no Protestants, atheists or Muslims are going to get to Heaven,' Rose had said suddenly.

'Why not?'

'Dunno. No tickets probably,' she'd said, laughing.

'It doesn't really make sense, does it?' Horace had asked.

'What doesn't?'

'Well, God created an entire world just so He could fill it up with people who are supposed to end up living in Heaven with Him for all eternity when they die. And then He doesn't let most of them into Heaven at all, just because He doesn't ...'

'Doesn't print enough tickets?' she'd offered.

'Yes, something like that. But you'd think that if there *is* a God and He can do *anything*, then He'd either print more tickets or else ...'

'Make fewer people.'

'Yes,' Horace had said. 'Exactly.'

'I like being here with you, Horace,' Rose had

said. 'I feel like I could tell you anything and you'd never tell another living soul.'

'Then tell me something,' Horace had said. 'Something you've never told anyone else.'

'Okay.' She'd cleared her throat with a short, nervous cough. 'One day I was delivering food parcels to the Poor Clares on Nun's Island in Galway with my father, and when he went back out to the car for more, I spotted a biscuit tin of hosts on a table. I took a handful of them and put them into the pocket of my dress. Myself and Monica Lydon ate them at break-time the next day in the boys' bicycle shed.'

'Really?' Horace had said. 'I can't believe that.' He had no idea what 'hosts' were, but they sounded dangerous.

'Well, it's true. My dad would kill me if he ever found out. He's mad keen on the religion. He should have been a nun himself. Your turn now.'

'Hmm?' Horace had said absent-mindedly.

'Your turn, Horace. Tell me something you've never told anyone else ever.'

The heat of the day was receding with the setting sun, and the seaside town was shutting down for the night, with only the sound of a fairground far away on the edge of the settlement competing with the last calls of the curlews in the marram grass farther up the beach.

'I love you,' he'd said.

'I love you too,' she'd said back, without hesitation.

He had begun to worry what his mother would say when she found out he loved someone besides her. But this was *his* life now, he'd thought, and surely he could decide whom to love.

Horace went shopping but was not sure what he had come out intending to buy. He assumed it was milk, but could not remember. He found himself in the city centre. He had never seen a Twenty-plume moth before. He'd read about them, of course, and had once met someone years ago, perhaps at the Natural History Museum, who had claimed to have seen them regularly in a garden centre in Swords. The *Alucita hexadactyla* was quite unusual: its wings were made up of six strands of what appeared to be separate 'plumes'.

'May I get by?' a lady with a shopping trolley said, after she'd already hooshed Horace into the wall beside the ATM as she passed at some awful speed.

The moth must have been disturbed from its nesting place, because it was more unusual still to see them during the day. And yet there it was, resting, near the Westbury Hotel in Dublin city centre, on the bronze hand of a statue of a man with a guitar. Over to the right, flower-sellers filled the gap before the road yawned into Grafton Street, but the moth did not seem interested in their carnations or other blooms. Horace stood, awestruck at the sight of the creature. The colouring of the moth was like an army truck or gun-carriage camouflage net. It sat with its wings open for a moment, staring Horace down. He heard a voice shouting, '*Evening Herald*!' He thought he saw someone he knew standing with a camera taking a picture. The cautious tick of the shutter capturing all it could see was loud in his ears. He knew that his tablets were becoming less and less effective against the tide of his illness.

'It's Phil Lynott, from Thin Lizzy,' a man's voice said, in exasperation.

Horace saw the moth fold its wings, disturbed by the various voices and flashing cameras, and then it prepared to fly away. All around the large statue was a clear space. The Twenty-plume began its take-off and rose away from the cold metal and up into the late afternoon. A crowd of people could have gathered to watch the event, but chose not to.

Horace looked down at the ground, then up into the sky. The moth was only a couple of feet away from his head yet it kept to its flight path. It flew past Horace so closely that he thought he saw its eyes, clear as an epiphany. On the edge of the building opposite, a man leaned out of a balcony opening and shouted up to window-cleaners some floors above in a pulley lift. Horace couldn't hear what was being said. People walked past.

When it began to get cold, Horace realised that the moth was not going to return. He looked around him and saw a Crunchie wrapper swish its way to the wall near his feet. It lay flat on the bricks until the vacuum ended and it slid down to the red-cobble roadway below. Horace noticed a lamplight flickering in the foreground. The bronze man with the bronze guitar had still not begun to play. The evening drew down on Horace, like a whisper, and he felt pain in the backs of his legs. Half-sounds drifted to him: the swirl of a tiny street-cleaning machine driven by a gorgeous black lady with long, dangling, jingling earrings; the scrape of steel as jewellery shops shuttered down for the night.

'Hey, bud, have you got a cigarette?'

Horace heard the words but couldn't see the

speaker. It hurt him to lift his feet and he couldn't find the source of the voice without moving.

'I'm waiting for the moth to come back,' he said.

A man came round into his world from the right. 'She must be some fucking goer if she wants you ready for bed,' the man said. He was the same height as Horace, and had hooded eyes and bushy eyebrows, which had started too early on the left and finished too soon on the right. 'Have you got any money?'

Horace turned to his right and saw that the flower-sellers and their thousands of flowers had all gone. 'I have some savings and a pension. I used to be the assistant manager in the Bank of Leinster branch on—'

Horace felt a crushing pain in his eyes and nose, and blood ran from him into the street. He dreamed of fire, fire running in a line across a field of tarmac to char the wings of moths before they could take off …

A police radio crackled.

'I'm right in front of the Westbury. It's an old guy in pyjamas and slippers. Must have fallen and hit his face. Either that or someone loafed him.'

Later that week, Horace had an appointment at the hospital. They seemed a little concerned about him. As he waited for a number 46A bus, Horace thumbed through a newspaper someone had discarded on the seat of the shelter. It was a regional paper, the *Tipperary Star*, and was full of reports about agricultural shows and bridal-wear fairs. One headline told of the death of a local vet in a single-vehicle collision on a motorway. However, the item that captured Horace's full and undivided attention, arresting his deliberation, was a quarter-page advert announcing the arrival of a circus in Borrisokane the following week for 'One Night Only'. The colour photograph showed two elephants on their hind legs with their trunks hooked together to form an archway. The caption listed some of the attractions, such as clowns and llamas, but most interesting of all was the name of the man in the top hat standing beneath the elephants' trunks: 'Ringmaster Freddie Alexander'. Horace held on to the newspaper for dear life, as though it might disintegrate if he relinquished his grip for even a nanosecond.

CHAPTER EIGHTEEN

Comma Butterfly (*Polygonia c-album*)

Dusky Heath (*Coenonympha dorus*):
underwings distinctive with a single eyespot

Privet Hawk (*Sphinx ligustri*)

Angle Shades Moth (*Phlogophora meticulosa*)

It reminded Horace of a funfair he'd been to once, years ago, with his father. He remembered the *snap* of air-rifles and wondered about the real guns his father, Migsie Spring and everyone else in the infantry had carried. 'Death-sticks', he decided to call them:

tubes of metal, wooden stocks and the power to end life. The noise in the circus was almost unbearable. Children screamed and the smell of candyfloss was everywhere. The large old tent was packed to bursting at its sagging canvas seams. Horace and Amanda sat at the end of a row.

'What's been your favourite act so far, Horace?' she asked.

'I don't really know, but probably the elephants,' he replied, as he munched a bar of Cadbury's Fruit and Nut and hoped the show would end soon so that he could go and speak to the ringmaster. Freddie Alexander hadn't seemed to be much older than himself, although he *was* wearing make-up. He had to be at least twenty years older, although he moved with the apparent ease of a younger man.

Horace was apprehensive about what he might discover about his father from the man in the top hat, who cracked his whip with such panache. Each crack sounded like a pistol shot and Horace wondered whether perhaps it had been that very noise which had enticed the man from his father's regiment into joining the circus after the war had ended. He held the photograph in front of him and looked from it to the ringmaster and back again. There was no doubting that he had the right man. It was a huge step forward in the search for Migsie Spring.

Three tigers emerged from the tunnel cage and trotted cattily out into the ring. Horace closed his eyes as he discovered his fear of tigers.

After the show, Horace and Amanda waited patiently in their seats until the whole tent had emptied. A tall clown agreed to ask the ringmaster whether he would be prepared to meet Horace. He was.

'I'll see you back at the car,' Amanda said understandingly, and she caught the keys as Horace hopped them in his hand.

Moments later, he found himself in a caravan with the ringmaster, who was taking off his make-up in a mirror surrounded by brightly coloured bulbs.

'I think you were in the Second East Yorkshires on D-Day when they landed in France?' Horace began.

'Nope,' the man said, looking at him suspiciously over his own shoulder in the mirror. Horace saw instantly that he had been mistaken. This was an even younger man than himself. 'My father was, though. Did you know him?'

'No,' Horace replied, 'but my dad did.' He

produced the photograph and handed it to the man, who scrutinised it carefully before handing it back.

'Which one's your dad? Is he still alive?' the man asked.

'The one on the left, and I'm afraid not,' Horace said. 'He died a long time ago. And yours? Is he ...?' The man turned back towards the dressing table and wiped some more make-up off with cotton wool. He seemed more comfortable talking to Horace in the mirror. As he continued, he revealed three blotchy moles on the back of his right hand. Horace pegged him as a Comma butterfly. *Mainly haunts the areas around hedges and laneways. Strong jagged outline.* From the photograph, Horace reckoned Fred Alexander Senior had been the very same species.

'My father took his own life almost thirty years ago. He suffered badly from ... you know ... well, depression, I suppose. Nowadays, they prob'ly call it something fancy like post-traumatic stress.'

'Did he work in the circus all of that time, I mean until ...?'

'Until then, yes. I've never known any other life. Family business, you could say.'

'And your mother,' Horace asked, 'is she ...?

'She's in a nursing home in Hastings. She'll be eighty-three this year. What was your dad's name?'

'Robert Winter,' Horace said. 'Corporal Robert Winter.'

The man shook his head. 'Means nothing to me, mate. Dad never ever spoke about the war, not a blinking word. Perhaps that was part of the problem, keeping it all bottled up, like. I'm pretty sure Mum wouldn't know anything about it either. She's not really herself now anyway, if you know what I mean. I'm sorry I can't be of any help to you, whatever it is you're looking for.'

'It's the man in the middle I'm trying to track down,' Horace said. 'Corporal Matthew Spring.' He pointed to Migsie and tapped the old picture. 'My father left a letter for him and I want to see that he gets it. I've been looking for a while now but I can't find any trace of him. I'd hoped you might be able to help me.'

'All I can offer you is a couple of free tickets for our next performance,' the man said, and smiled. He took the passes out of his hat and gave them to Horace. 'Is there any chance you could send me a copy of the photograph?'

'Of course,' Horace said. The man wrote an

address on the back of one of the tickets. 'Thank you for seeing me, Mr Alexander.'

'No problem.'

Horace returned to the car.

'Any luck?' Amanda asked.

Horace shook his head sadly. He started the car and began to drive across the bumpy grass towards the gate out onto the main road. As he indicated to turn left, and waited for a gap in the traffic, there was a tap on the driver's side window. He rolled it down.

It was the ringmaster, this time wearing slacks and a woolly jumper. 'I just remembered something after you left,' he said.

'Yes?' Horace said.

'I don't know how long ago it was, maybe fifteen years or even more, we were appearing in Grantchester, a tiny village just outside Cambridge. I remember it because I had the flu, a real dose. It was so bad I had to stay in bed so I couldn't do the show. Well, anyway, the following morning, the girl in the box office gave me a note someone had left for me. I forget the exact words, but it was something like, "Knew your dad in the army. Top bloke he was." I know it was signed but I can't remember the name. What was the lad in the photo called?'

'Matthew Spring,' Horace said.

'Nope, that doesn't ring a bell. I think it was just one name like a first name but I don't think it was Matthew or Matt.'

'Migsie?' Horace suggested.

The man's face lit up against the supine gloom of the evening sky. 'Yes,' he agreed exultantly. 'Migsie. I'm almost certain that was it.'

During the drive home, Horace checked that the letter was still around his neck in the pouch. It seemed to feel ever so slightly lighter.

Later that week, Horace read in the newspaper that Max had escaped from Frostfield Abbey. The article did not give any details about the method he had used but Horace knew in his heart that his plan had succeeded. He wondered whether the boy had managed to return to his home. On the news that evening, the announcer said that a nationwide search had been launched to locate the boy. A spokesman for the HSE was interviewed by the newsreader.

'Do you think it's appropriate to house an eleven-year-old child in a facility that caters for teenage offenders?'

The man from the Health Service Executive looked distinctly uncomfortable with the question. 'Er, um, the matter is being investigated by the HSE and *all* aspects of the situation are being reviewed. However, it is the policy of the HSE not to comment on individual cases.'

'Will an effort be made to find a suitable foster home for the child if he's found?'

'Again, let me restate that it is the policy of the HSE ...'

There were three M. Springs in the Cambridge area and no definite Matthew among them. The world wide web has narrowed it down that much and now it's up to me, Horace reckoned, as the train from Stansted airport drew into the station of that peerless university town. He recalled his journey by rail months earlier into the wilds of North Yorkshire. It would be easy to think of it as a failure, ending as it had among cribbage players and ale poured from porcelain jugs, but now he knew that it was just another piece of the jigsaw; a puzzle that, when solved, would endow him with a better understanding of his father. Amanda had decided to remain in Dublin and to spend a couple of days pottering around the annual Bloom Festival in the Phoenix Park.

'Don't be too disappointed if you don't find anything, Horace,' she'd counselled, before he left. 'You've done everything you can to try to deliver that letter.'

'Except actually deliver it,' Horace had countered ruefully to himself, in the taxi to the airport.

He was booked in for the night at the Garden House Hotel. It proved to be a large smart modern establishment, right in the heart of Cambridge. He put his suitcase in his hotel room, then set off with his list and the packed lunch he'd brought all the way from Edenvale Road. He was delighted that the flask had not been harmed in the cargo hold on the flight over.

He walked down King's Parade and stopped outside an outfitter's called Ryder & Amies. Lists of the teams selected to represent the university at various sports, including real tennis and boxing, were stuck to the window. As he walked through the town the vast sandstone façades of the various colleges filled Horace with a wistful malaise. If only he had not failed English in the Leaving Cert ...

The village of Girton took quite a while to walk to

and Horace had to stop and rest a number of times on the journey. He was sorry he hadn't taken a cab. He found the address easily enough and rang the doorbell, which was situated in the middle of a now-welded-down knocker shaped like Jacob Marley's face. From within came the sound of a bolt being undone. The door opened. A lady stood in the doorway wearing absolutely nothing, apart from an orange apron. She was about the same age as Horace. He was unsure where to look.

'Yes?' she said insouciantly.

'Erm, I'm looking for Matthew Spring,' Horace stuttered. 'Does he live here?'

'There's no one of that name here,' the lady said, with a thriving smile. 'I'm *Mavis* Spring, *Miss* Mavis Spring, if that's any help to you.'

'No, not really,' Horace stammered. He was glad Amanda was not with him to witness this display of … of … He didn't know of what exactly.

His hostess seemed perfectly at ease and she reached out a hand and took one of his. 'Are you responding to the *personal* advertisement I took out in the *Chameleon Newsletter* last week?'

'Certainly not,' Horace said, affronted, reclaiming his hand.

'Oh, what a pity,' the lady said. 'Never too late for a second bite of the cherry, I always say.' She gave Horace an enthusiastic wink, then closed the door. Jacob Marley stared down and appeared to smile.

Horace left. Definitely a Dusky Heath butterfly, he thought. What else could she be?

The second address was out on Abbey Road on the Newmarket side of town and quite near to a football stadium. It was a tiny semi-detached house, with a pretty garden full of red and orange geraniums. Horace knocked on the door but there was no reply. There was a bell, but it appeared to have become wedged in its setting and now served no useful purpose.

Horace considered trying to find the third and final address on his list, then coming back here in the morning, but opted to stick to his original plan. He sat on a park bench across the road and waited, counting twenty-three Grayline coaches during that time. He had all but decided to return to his hotel when a young man pulled up in a car directly outside the house and unloaded a lawnmower from the boot. He wheeled the machine up the tarmac drive and opened the garage door to put it away.

Horace got up and went across the road. He was

halfway up the drive when the man came out of
the garage. He looked suspiciously at Horace, then
started to advance down the incline towards him. His
expression demanded an explanation.

'I'm looking for the home of Corporal Spring,'
Horace said.

'Yes?' the man answered. 'This is where he lives.
It's Lance Corporal actually.'

'I wonder if I might speak with him,' Horace
asked.

The man's face began to go red. 'You're bloody
well *speaking* with him now,' he said.

'Oh,' said Horace. 'I was expecting someone much
older.'

'Were you indeed? I suppose you're one of those
geezers who goes around taking advantage of the
elderly. What you selling, then? Power-washing
of the fascia and soffit? Equity release? Funeral
insurance? I know your type.' The man advanced to
where his face was almost touching Horace's. He had
a Scottish accent and Horace believed he was now toe
to toe with a Privet Hawk moth.

'No, no, I'm not selling anything. I'm looking
for a man who served with my father in the East
Yorkshires in the Second World War.' Horace was

really and truly frightened now and believed the man was about to assault him.

All at once the man's demeanour completely altered. 'I'm sorry, mate, I shouldn't have flown off the handle at you like that. The truth is I'm absolutely knackered. I'm just off after a week of night duty and my missus is expecting and God knows what else. We just moved here six weeks ago from Edinburgh.'

'You're in the army?' Horace asked hopefully.

'Yes, well, the *Territorial* army. My main job is as a porter in one of the colleges.'

'Oh,' said Horace. 'Then I take it you're not related to a Corporal Matthew Spring, who landed in France on D-Day?'

'I had an uncle who was in the Scots Guards, but he was a Buchan, on my mother's side.'

Horace explained what his search was all about. The man listened intently, then shook his head. 'I can't be of any help to you there, Mr Winter. But I do make a great brew if that's any good to you.'

After a welcome cuppa in the man's kitchen, Horace gratefully accepted a lift from him back to the hotel.

'Best of luck, Horace,' Corporal Michael Spring

of the Territorials shouted out of the car window, as he drove away.

Horace was tired. He went up to his room and ordered some orange juice and toast from room service. Afterwards, he fell asleep with a programme called *Hetty Wainthrop Investigates* on the TV, which he had simply forgotten to turn off.

Number eleven Gough Way was deserted. Two of the windows were cracked and it was the only house in the street not to have a dustbin out for collection. A To Let sign had fallen over in the front garden. Horace had rung the bell but had expected, and received, no response. As a last-ditch effort to cross all of the ts before taking the train back to the airport that afternoon, he decided to knock on the neighbours' door and see if they might know where the occupants of number eleven had moved to.

The door was answered by a young lady who was wearing not only an apron but much more besides. From behind her in the house came the reassuring scent of bread baking.

'I'm terribly sorry to bother you,' Horace began.

'Not at all,' said the woman, 'as long as you're not selling ceramic tiles? We've just had the bathrooms redone.'

She smiled, and Horace was reminded of Rose Burke on Rosslare Strand all those years ago. 'You're funny, Horace,' she'd said. 'A real ticket.' His overriding emotion was regret that he'd disturbed the lady's baking. 'I'm not selling anything. I was looking for the people next door but they seem to have moved away. I just wondered whether they had perhaps given you a forwarding address.' Horace heard the tiredness in his voice.

'Is it the Packhams you're looking for? Or the people before them? What were they called now? Oh, yes, of course, Mr and Mrs Swanborough?'

'No,' said Horace, despairingly, 'neither of them. I was looking for someone else entirely, Migsie Spring. He was a corporal in the—'

'The East Yorkshires?' she offered.

'Why, yes, yes indeed,' Horace said, with surprise.

The lady turned slightly and called over her shoulder down the hallway. 'Grandad, put your teeth in. You've got a visitor.'

Horace stood, glued to the spot, like a gun-turret on an Airfix model of an ancient battleship.

'I suppose you'd better come in, then,' she said. 'I'm Elizabeth Spring,' she introduced herself.

'Horace, Horace Winter.' He stepped into the house.

Migsie Spring sat in a wheelchair in a space between the dining-room table and the door into the kitchen. He was a thin but elegant figure of a man, with wisps of pepper-grey hair combed across his head, like a chat-show host. His face was lined with age but was nonetheless strong and proud, dominated by green eyes that could have belonged to a child. He wore an open-necked red and white striped shirt and a corduroy jacket. Across his lap, a travelling rug was neatly tucked down on either side of him. Horace stood at the other end of the room and could not take his eyes off the old man. There was a long shelf on the right wall containing the collected works of Charles Dickens in brown and gold editions but, apart from that, he took in precious little. When Corporal Matthew Spring spoke for the first time it broke a silence that had lasted almost a full minute.

'Perhaps you'd like to tell me what all of this is about,' he said, in a voice that was neither welcoming nor ungracious. Horace cleared his throat and shuffled a little before composing himself enough to speak.

'I'm Horace, Robert Winter's son,' he announced. He had never uttered those exact words in that particular sequence, and it felt like a declaration to the whole universe, an announcement he had waited his entire life to make.

'I'd never have guessed,' the older man said, with a cold laugh. 'You're the absolute image of him. How *is* old Wintertime these days? Still collecting butterflies?'

This last question was delivered with a garnish of animosity that Horace found alarming. He could feel tension rising in the carpeted leeway between them. 'My father died a long time ago,' he said.

'Then why have you come here to my home? And why now?' Migsie Spring demanded. His voice was quieter than it had been but the tone was more unpleasant.

'He wrote you a letter the day before he died, but never got the chance to post it. I only discovered it after I retired and I've spent a good deal of time trying to track you down to deliver it. I have it here with me, if you'd like to read it.' Horace unbuttoned the top three fasteners on his shirt and took out the plastic pouch.

'You know what, son? You can keep that letter.

I've no interest in reading it. I'll not be told in my own house what I have to do or what I *should* do.'

'I'm not telling you what to do,' Horace spluttered.' I just want to—'

'Just want to what? Come marching into my life and tell me to read your father's bloody letter? Why should I? Why didn't Corporal Winter buy a stamp and stick the blooming thing in a postbox? Why didn't he do that, eh?'

'The letter was written on the day before he died,' Horace said stiffly. 'He never got a chance to post it. I've already told you this.' Horace could feel himself getting cross now. He had come a long way to deliver the letter and now this man in a wheelchair was telling him he didn't even want to read it.

Migsie Spring's granddaughter put her head around the door. 'Now, you two, I've got to get to Sainsbury's or there'll be nothing for you to eat. Today's my shopping day, Mr Winter. I hope you don't mind?'

'Not at all,' Horace said.

'Splendid,' she responded. 'You can take the old grump for a walk around the town while I do the shopping.'

Half an hour later, Horace stood on the pavement outside Sainsbury's in the town centre opposite The

Edinburgh Woollen Mill. Beside him Migsie Spring was sullen and petulant in his wheelchair. Elizabeth Spring addressed the two of them like schoolchildren, even though their combined ages were more than four times her own.

'Grandad, you're going to be nice to Mr Winter and you're going to talk to him, make proper conversation and try not to be such a Victor Meldrew. All right?' She poked her grandfather in the ribs with her handbag.

'Fine,' he answered.

She turned to Horace. 'And you, Mr Winter.'

'Yes?' he answered meekly.

'You're going to push my grandfather on his usual walk, along the Backs, then over the Silver Street Bridge, past the Anchor pub and up to Fitzbillie's tea-shop for a chocolate éclair. Understood?' Horace nodded. She must have read the question posed by the expressions of both men, because she concluded by saying, 'If he doesn't co-operate, don't buy him the éclair.' With this, she handed Horace a ten-pound note. 'He has no money with him so the power is in your hands'. The two men nodded and regarded each other with slightly less suspicion than before. Elizabeth Spring looked at her watch. 'It's almost eleven now, so I'll pick you both up outside Fitzbillie's at one sharp. That'll give you plenty of time, Grandad, to defrost.' She kissed her grandfather's forehead and left the two of them alone.

'Which way?' Horace asked.

'Straight on, then take the second left,' Migsie Spring eventually said. And off they went.

Cambridge was magnificent in the sunlight. The colleges were old and imposing yet also charming and inviting with their turrets and towers, gargoyles and Gothic grandeur. Horace steered according to Migsie's directions and they made their way through narrow, winding streets over cobbles. The motion of pushing someone else reminded him of his mother and her wheelchair trips. She had been a much more vocal passenger.

Horace found himself beginning to talk about himself to the back of Migsie's head, encouraged perhaps by his inability to see the other man's expression. In a way, he felt he was talking *to* himself. He was almost certain that Migsie Spring was a moth.

'I retired last year from the bank. I never worked anywhere else. Strange in a way, because during all the time that I did work there it never entered my head to go and work anywhere else. Anyway, since

I've retired I've been trying to get out a little more often ... you know, see new things.'

The other man was silent as Horace pushed his wheelchair over a small narrow bridge at the back of Trinity Hall, then headed for the main footpath along the Backs.

He pushed Migsie Spring at a pace that was comfortable to him. He thought about his father's letter, still in its pouch around his neck and still unread by the person to whom it was addressed. The River Cam flowed considerately through the old university town and, for some reason, Horace thought about those ancient clocks that were operated by the flow of water. Around them, elms and lindens stretched up into the sky from velvet lawns. Stone bridges invited dreamers to step back through centuries of learning into castles of education protected by moats of tradition. A lone boatman pushed his punting pole into the bed of the river in the shade of Trinity Bridge, balancing on the chipped varnish of the punt-end where thousands had stood before him.

The sun beat down on them as sixty-five pushed ninety-two and the day and the strain began to take their toll on Horace. He felt his arms weakening and a short spell of dizziness came upon him. He put a hand into his jacket pocket for his tablets. Up ahead a vendor's stall sold ice-cream and drinks. As if sensing his companion's distress, the older man looked half around at Horace. 'Are you all right, old boy?'

'I'm — I'm fine,' Horace said. But he wasn't. He stopped pushing the wheelchair and put his hands on his thighs and leaned forward, his breathing accelerated by his distress. Composing himself again, he walked towards the vendor's stall, holding his tablets in one hand in their plastic case. Without needing to be asked, the young man on the stand poured water from a bottle into a plastic cup and proffered it to him. Horace popped the pills into his mouth and gulped the water down after them. He reached into his pocket for some coins to pay but the young man waved away the money in a gesture of humanity and understanding.

Something in the scene must have triggered a memory in Migsie Spring. He spoke as Horace came back to him from the stall. 'Your father had a weak heart, young Winter. I saw him often, as I saw you there, taking tablets. Are you very ill, lad?'

'Not too bad,' Horace replied. 'Just a little turn every now and then.' Something in the air between the men had softened, and as Horace recommenced to push the wheelchair, he felt the physical act had become easier, almost as if Migsie Spring had released the brakes and was now assisting instead of impeding its progress. As if to confirm this impression of the alteration in the atmosphere, Migsie Spring began to talk now. Not much at first, but unprompted, and about the war.

'We landed on the left of the First South Lancs. We had support for the landing from two battleships, HMS *Warspite* and HMS *Ramillies*. If it hadn't been for those two ships our casualties on the beach would have doubled, maybe trebled. Most of us would have been killed. The Germans were dug in on the beaches and had a series of defended strongpoints all the way to Caen. The houses at La Brèche and Lion-sur-Mer had been turned into fortresses so that even when we managed to get up off the beaches there was still enormous resistance.'

Horace listened with the ears of someone who had waited for most of his life to find out about his father. Not second-hand from history books, but from someone who had actually, *been there* with him. He waited when the man stopped, and was almost afraid to say anything in case the gentle sorcery of the moment shattered. And yet, Horace realised that he had to keep the dialogue going, had to fill in the silences, otherwise the conversation might end and he might never find the answers he'd come looking for.

'Where's this tea shop?' Horace asked, as they turned and went along Silver Street back towards the river.

'Sod the bloody tea shop,' Migsie Spring said. 'Into the Anchor with us, lad. I'd murder a pint.'

Inside the pub, the air was cold and the light was scarce. Horace pushed Migsie to one of the low tables and went to get the drinks.

'So, you want to know what it was like? Back there in France on the beaches?' Migsie Spring sipped hungrily at his pint, then turned slightly away from Horace as if he were giving evidence in a court, not speaking directly to anyone in particular but to the world.

'Around us in the water were headless bodies, bits of people, arms, legs. I remember the screams of fellas who never even made it into the water from the landing craft, hit by mortar or machine-gun fire. The water all along the edge of the sand was red, like a jam-jar with children's paintbrushes steeping in it. Later, when we'd cleared the beaches, we were ordered to move towards the River Orne and to get into positions to assist Four Commando in Ouistreham as it moved towards the Orne bridges.'

Horace looked at the man's eyes as he spoke. They were glazed and fixed on the middle distance, as though he could actually see Sword Beach and the 2nd East Yorkshires as they made their way inland in a hail of machine-gun fire from a network of trenches and pill-boxes surrounded by thick barbed wire and minefields.

Migsie continued, 'You know, the beach was the easy part in a funny way. At least there we knew what we were supposed to be doing. It was pretty simple stuff. After that, though, everything was less clear. About a month after we'd landed, we were billeted in tents in an orchard. I remember your father sitting on a box of .303 ammo one morning, making notes about butterflies. "Look at this, lads," he'd said, "It's an Olive Blue," or some such bloody thing.'

Horace knew there was no such species. There was an *Alcon* Blue and indeed an Olive *Skipper*, either of which could conceivably have been in Normandy in July, but certainly no Olive Blue. He decided against enlightening Migsie Spring.

'Everyone had the shits. I remember *that*. Not out of fear or anything, mind, just from eating too many apples.' He chuckled at the memory, and it was clear to Horace that, although there were two of them at the table in the corner of a Cambridge pub, Migsie was really speaking to himself and was probably, palpably, in his own mind, somewhere back in 1944 France. 'We were sent out to clear farmhouses, Fred, Robert and me. The day was a scorcher, a right stone-sizzler. We were in great form, I remember that too. Just outside a tiny village called Mathieu, it were. We'd been to more than a dozen farms before this one, found nothing, really. One of them had a well that had been booby-trapped and the farmer and his wife were lying about twenty yards away, not a mark on them, like they'd just lain down and fallen asleep. It was absolutely frightening, like some giant hand had come down from the sky and pulled the life out of them both. Death was everywhere. You just couldn't escape it.'

Migsie Spring's eyes were now frosted and his face carried an expression of horror. 'Robert went to search the outbuildings, just a bit of a hayshed and a pigsty. Fred and I went into the house. In the kitchen, there was this French bird, gorgeous she were, just sitting at the table looking like Saint bloody Thérèse. Like butter wouldn't have melted. She had a bowl of hot chocolate in front of her, steaming it were. I remember the kitchen, all blue and white, enamel and gleamy. Like there was no war at all and we'd just arrived home. The place was all the same colour as my sweetheart's parents' house in Kettlewell. It was Fred who copped it, though, the second bowl drip-drying one side of the sink. It was still warm. "Eh, Migsie," he said. "Something's not right here." He spoke to the girl in French and asked her whether anyone else was in the place. She shook her head. Fred stayed in the kitchen with the girl while I went to search the upstairs. I opened one of the windows in the front bedroom and beckoned to Robert to come in and join us. The rooms were just as you'd expect from one person living in the house on their own. Nothing obvious was out of place. I searched everywhere, under beds, in wardrobes, you name it, and still found nothing. I was just about to go back down to the kitchen when I noticed a panel of wood on the landing wall. It was a slightly different tint and width than the others. To this day, I'll never know how I copped it. It were a very cleverly constructed door, no handle or nothing, just a slight press with your thumb and it opened enough for me to get my fingers behind. "Come out, you Nazi bastard, or I'll shoot until I run out of ammo," I shouted. The sound of the bolt on the Lee Enfield were enough. Out he came with his hands up. A right pretty-looking German he was too. He couldn't have been more than sixteen or seventeen. A deserter he was, all cosy up and riding that French lassie. Well for him. He was absolutely terrified, I could see that. I marched him downstairs and then we took him and the girl out into the yard. Fred and I searched the place top to bottom for guns while Robert kept an eye on them. We found nothing. I remember it clear as day, as if it were all happening again right now in this very room.'

Horace felt for the first time that the man was actually talking consciously to him, not just to himself. And there, in the afternoon sunlight, which poured across the River Cam and strafed into the Anchor through the round, thick window glass, Migsie Spring recounted the events, which had led Horace's father to the point where he had needed to write the letter his son had come to deliver.

'"What should we do with her?" I asked.

'"Leave her here," Fred said. "Her own people will know how to deal with her. We've more farms to clear and it'll be difficult enough to complete the task with one prisoner."

'The girl went back into the house and we prepared to leave. Fred was tying the bugger's hands behind his back with hay twine. I had my rifle on the prisoner, keeping him covered. My back was to the farmhouse. Suddenly the girl was in the doorway right behind me. The only reason I knew that was because Fred roared at your father, "Shoot her! For Christ's sake, shoot her!"

'Corporal Winter was on the opposite side of the farmyard, not forty feet away. He must have had a clear view of everything as it happened. I turned and saw that she had a stick grenade and was in the act of priming it. On my right, I saw your father with his rifle raised, but he was like a statue. I began to fire as I ran towards her, emptying my rifle into her face and her chest. She fell with the grenade still in her hand and the blast blew her back into the kitchen. I remember thinking, You'll never finish your hot chocolate now, you bloody traitorous bitch. The next thing I remember was waking up about ten days later in a field hospital.'

Horace felt tears run down his face and onto his shirt. He now knew why his father had written the letter. It was as plain as a pikestaff. Faced with the choice of shooting the girl dead or endangering his comrades, his father had hesitated. It could easily have ended his comrade's life. Did that make his father a moth, or simply confirm him as a butterfly? Horace simply did not know.

'For years, Horace, I've hated your father. I blamed him for this.' At these last words, Migsie Spring removed the travelling rug from his lap to reveal two stumps of legs, which ended most of the way between the man's waist and where his knees would once have been.

Horace was shocked by the sight but also galvanised into taking the letter from its pouch around his neck. He held it out, trying to avert his eyes from Migsie Spring's stumps, proffering it. The old soldier put a hand on one wheel and swivelled rudely away from him. Horace contemplated speaking but did not know what to say. Perhaps there was nothing *to* be said. He placed the letter on the table beside Migsie Spring's pint, then stood up. He decided to leave and to make his way back to the station. As he moved towards the door, he turned and said, 'Goodbye.'

He saw that the man's shoulders were now shaking and that he was crying, silently and uncontrollably, while looking out at the river and the assembled punts chained together like convicts.

Horace saw, too, the movement whereby Migsie Spring reached a hand onto the pub table, took possession of the letter and laid it on his travelling rug lap. His granddaughter was coming into the public house as Horace left. She gave him a smile he felt he did not deserve.

He decided that Migsie Spring was an Angle Shade moth. The colouring was slightly lighter than might be expected, but he conformed to the shape in every way: *The wings are crumpled when resting and the torso is out of proportion to the legs, with the result that it looks like an old leaf.*

On the Saturday night following his escape, Max Hackett was found by social workers and a garda. He had been sleeping rough in Shanganagh cemetery beside his mother's grave. For the first two nights of his freedom, he had broken into his old house and slept there.

CHAPTER NINETEEN

Scarce Fritillary (*Euphydryas maturna*)

Scarce Copper (*Heodes virgaureae*)

Horace sat in the back of the car with a series of textbooks spread out around him on the green leather seat. He had taken all of his tablets before they'd left Dublin, so that was one less thing to worry about.

'How are we for time?' he asked.

Amanda leaned across and read the clock on the tower through the window, then checked it against her own watch. Horace no longer wore one: it hurt his arm.

'A quarter to eight, you've plenty of time. Would you like a sandwich?'

Outside, it was just beginning to get ever so slightly hot. The previous week had been rainy but today had been promised fine. A series of June clouds moved over the rugby pitches cautiously but with vigour. The school was deserted, except for those few classes who were sitting state examinations. As the clock above the scene boom-clanged eight, they still had the place to themselves. The traditional buzz of camaraderie and mischief-making, which loitered in the dormitories during the exams, had vanished at the flick of a board of governors' whim to abolish boarding some years earlier.

'What's Newbridge famous for?' Amanda asked, as a duck swooped low and came in to land against the flow of the river.

'Cutlery, I think,' Horace replied, as he memorised a couple of lines of a Seamus Heaney poem about a boy in a boarding school who comes home at mid-term for his young brother's funeral.

'And rugby too, I suppose?' Amanda chuckled, as she looked at Horace in the rear-view mirror.

Horace sensed her reflected gaze and returned it with a wry glance of his own. 'I suppose so. I think they won something absolutely years ago.'

As the witching hour neared, a dribble of students made their way from the cutlery town into the school grounds. The car park began to fill. Horace imagined the scene flipped onto its side and flooded with water; each newly arrived vehicle displacing a car's worth of the river. Eventually there wouldn't be enough water to cover the Morris Minor so that he and Amanda could escape by climbing over the cars and away up to the bell-tower. He imagined, too, clambering in through the doors of the church. But what would he do when he got there? He didn't often think about God. What was there to believe in? Was it all any more than some stories written down and passed through the hands of successive generations as a form of comfort blanket against the inevitable? He had asked himself all the questions when he was younger: why doesn't anyone ever come back to tell us what it's like? If there *is* a God, then why does He let bad things happen to good people? Why did children sometimes die? And if there was more to death than just an end of life, why did people have to go through this life to get to the next? Why couldn't they all be born in the afterlife? He heard the clock strike nine.

'You'd better get ready, Horace.'

For a moment, he didn't know who had spoken, before he realised Amanda was addressing him from the front seat of his own car. English, Paper One, loomed.

Write a composition choosing one of the following as a starting point or topic:
1. Hip-hop is not a valid art form.
2. 'When the doorbell rang, he already knew who it would be ...'
3. Every family has its secrets.
4. The colour blue.
5. Fire, earth, water, God.

The Colour Blue

When I was a child, I had a blue hat. It was made of light cloth material and it came into my possession at an age before I was old enough to be conscious of receiving it. For me, it was a constant; something whose presence I took for granted, in much the same way as we think our parents will always be somewhere in our field of vision because they existed before we could see, before we had, in fact, existed ourselves. People crave consistency. They need to know that, no matter what happens, certain things or places or people or sounds will remain exactly the same. These are the thermometers of life against which we measure our own wellbeing. Perhaps, too, in a way, it is this very same craved-for consistency that holds us back.

One day, I lost the blue hat. I cannot say how it happened but I remember being upset for a very long time and thinking that life would now have to end because the one thing I was always sure of in it had been taken away, or simply misplaced forever through my own fault. I am sure that those were not the words I used to describe the sense of despair to myself as a six- or seven-year-old but I know that I was despairing and my world ended, for a time at least.

In the place where I went to school, our rugby jersey was dark blue. One of the greatest moments in my life for a long time was the honour of having been selected to play for my school in a major rugby match when I was in my early teens. The day of that game is imprinted on my memory as if someone had put one of those pieces of paper with slightly oily ink on it, then worked away on one side with a pencil. One of the kindnesses shown to the players on the school team was being allowed to keep the jersey when the cup run was over. I never wore mine again and, eventually, I cut it into strips and squares. It was used variously as dusters and cleaning cloths in my home.

Blue is also the colour of the logo on the headed paper of the institution where I was employed for all of my working life. It was a good place. It was a place where people came when they needed help and I would like to think that I helped people when they met me there. But the truth of it is that I don't know whether or not I was of any help to anyone except the institution itself. I know that I willingly gave the vast majority of my life to it but, at the end, it did not want me at all. They paid my wages and perhaps that is all that anyone can ever hope for or expect from their employer.

I know that in doing my work, I also missed out on doing other things. In particular, I never really took the time to find out how many other shades of blue there are. One day I made a mistake at work and it set in motion a sequence of events that resulted in the death of a young man by gunfire. My decision was brought about by a lack of judgement on my part and also a discrepancy of timekeeping. In a way, though, his death was entirely my fault, although that man's choices were also a factor, I suppose.

Once, on a cold October day, I bought a ticket for the zoo. It was blue and had the word 'Adult' written on it as well as the price. During my visit, I thought I recognised somebody near the polar bears' enclosure. It was a person from my childhood with whom I had fallen in love. I walked after her and called her name but I was mistaken.

In my head, and also in the organ that pumps blood around my veins, I had an image of that person, which I had carried with me since long-ago summer days. On that distant day, an ice-cream van had caught fire on the promenade at Rosslare and we had watched it burn. At some point, perhaps, I imagined that the ice cream would defeat the flames, but it did not. Ice cream, it seems, is not stronger than fire! Those days amid the dunes were among my happiest. I recall the sound of the sea and the rattle of railway carriages in the distance. I still have that ticket from the zoo.

Horace glanced at the clock over the stage in the Newbridge College Theatre and saw that he had roughly twenty-two and a half minutes left within which to finish his essay. He would not make the same mistake twice.

When photographers take pictures from aeroplanes over the South of France their studies, when developed in colour, show 'blue measles' on the landscape. These are swimming pools. They are scattered throughout the countryside. They may appear to be randomly distributed, but of course they are not. Each pool has been planned, dug, constructed and filled with water. Just as the Zephyr Blue is to be found where the climate is suitable, so too are swimming pools. If something or someone could photograph us all together from above, there would be 'blue measles'. These would be the cold patches, or abandoned hats, or even the shirt that has been torn into strips and squares. But best of all would be the bright patches of bubbling blue light signifying the lives that were touched by love; the empty rooms now full of people who are no longer empty themselves, the lucky few upon whom the Zephyr Blue has alighted gracefully and effortlessly, like a transient angel who whispers a song of blue eternity.

Afterwards, Horace and Amanda picnicked on the grass terrace overlooking the weir.

'I bet it's pretty rough water here in the winter,' Amanda said, as she handed him a cheese and tomato sandwich.

'Winter isn't always the worst,' Horace said, between bites.

'No, I suppose it's not,' Amanda agreed. They looked at each other and smiled.

He knew that his body and his mind were getting

weaker, but he felt that somehow his heart was becoming stronger. He knew, too, that there were some things he must sort out before it was too late. Once he had had too much time. Now he did not have enough.

Horace and Rose Burke had a magical two weeks of summer. And then one day she was gone. Horace waited on the dunes for hours before he went to the caravan park to find her. He wondered if he'd said or done something wrong. Perhaps he should not have told her how he felt.

'Ah, no, they've gone home,' the man who collected the bins at the site had said. 'I think that someone belonging to them died.'

Horace felt that it had been him. 'Do you know where they're from?' he asked the man.

'Someplace in County Galway.'

Horace didn't know exactly where they lived but he thought he'd heard her mention the name of the village Dunmore. What if she had been lying about that or even about everything? He had no way of reaching – physically – across the country, at sixteen. So he wrote dozens of times but received no reply. He had no specific address for her beyond his recollection of the name of her village and the fact that it was in County Galway. It was all to no avail; an endless journey of paper, pen and heartache.

Ahead of him in Dublin lay the prospect of the Leaving Certificate in less than a year's time and the possibility of life beyond it as a doctor or an engineer or a lawyer. 'Something better than we are', his mother called it. All through the winter of 1958, he'd thought about Rose Burke and her red and white polka-dot dress and the way she chewed bubble-gum and how she'd looked across the fire engine at him as the ice-cream van smouldered in the sunlight, and of how they had taken a new and powerful journey together on the train to Wexford. He was miserable and angry all at the same time and did not know what to do about it.

Despite receiving no response to his letters, Horace went back to Rosslare the following summer just to see. Strand View Caravan Park had vanished. It was now a graveyard of concrete being poured, and of hoardings that promised a hotel for the 1960 summer season. By then Horace would have finished school. With the gobbling up of the caravans, Horace Winter's world, too, was devoured and discarded.

He'd sat among the sand dunes that summer and cried for a girl he had lost the previous August and still couldn't find. He knew that whatever was wrong with him, it was more than enough to drive away anyone he loved. And what was the answer to that?

He thought of Rose Burke now as a Scarce Fritillary: *Confined mainly to sunny open lands and difficult to spot outside the main summer months.* He couldn't imagine any worthwhile future without her.

Horace had met other women in his life, but somehow none had been able to hold a candle to Rose. He had been press-ganged into double dates with his cousin Stephen, grim outings with civil-service ladies, who wore layers of make-up and talked only about themselves. Sometimes he had made plans in his head about his future and had drawn them up so that they would include a girl he would meet, fall in love with and marry, but nothing ever came of them. Whenever he got dressed up and ready to go out with Stephen, his mother would look sad. She usually said something on those occasions that made Horace acutely aware of the consequences his actions might have for her.

'For some people home just isn't good enough,' she'd said once, in the late 1960s, as he'd been about to go to the pictures with Stephen and two girls, who worked in Bewley's Oriental Café. He couldn't remember now what the film had been.

Once, when he was still quite junior at the bank, maybe in his second or third year there, he'd encountered a lady at the butterfly display case on one of his visits to the Natural History Museum. She'd lingered a little longer than Horace believed she had originally intended to.

'Hello,' she'd said, as they looked up at each other.

'Oh, hello,' he'd replied.

She'd been wearing a smart pleated two-piece suit in a sort of orange brown. Looking back now, she reminded him of a Scarce Copper – the upper wings in the females were usually that colour. Of course, they were almost never seen in Ireland, but the combination of the extreme heat of the day and her Spanish or Italian accent had reassured Horace in his categorisation. She'd had a lovely face, all kindness and warmth.

'I think I've seen you here before,' she'd said,

smiling. 'Somewhere between the butterflies and the moths.'

Horace didn't know *what* to say in reply, so he'd said nothing. Nothing at all, until eventually the lady left. He had never seen her again.

CHAPTER TWENTY

Grey Dagger (*Acronicta psi*)

Burnished Brass (*Diachrysia chrysitis*)

Horace found the golf club easily enough. The entrance was on a winding road between Maynooth and Dunboyne, but it was well signposted. He looked at the clock in the car and realised he had lost about half an hour as a result of his detour.

As he'd come off the motorway, he'd seen a sign: 'Butterfly Farm'. He had heard that such a place existed but had never been there. He had allowed himself to be distracted from the true purpose of his journey and sought it out. He wondered if they might have an Odd Spot Blue among their collection. It was one of the rarest species of butterfly. A sign on the gate to an old-looking bungalow sandwiched between two fields informed him that the opening of the butterfly farm would be delayed until much later in the summer because of 'planning difficulties'. Only in Ireland, Horace thought.

Back on track, Horace manoeuvred his Morris Minor carefully as he drove around a sharp corner. According to an orange sign, the road was still liable to frost even though it was the middle of July. The gates into the golf and hotel complex were impressive. His car bumped over speed ramps and he began the trek into the heart of the old estate.

Over to his left, he saw a golfing academy and, in the distance beyond it, enormous new lodge-style houses, with electric barriers and expensive vehicles. The car park was quite full but Horace found a place between a large black Jeep and an awkward-looking silver Jaguar. It had taken him quite a while on the telephone to locate the man but, eventually, after he had rung eight other people with the same surname, Horace had got the right number.

'Oh, he's playing golf in Carton House,' the man's wife had said. 'He was due out at eleven so I suppose twelve, one, two, three, four … He might be back around teatime.'

Horace glanced at the Rolex clock in the courtyard as he passed it. It said ten to five. He made his way through the swishing automatic doors and found the lounge without any trouble. A helpful young man behind the bar pointed out the person whom he had come to see. He was engrossed in conversation with three others. Horace bought a cup of tea, sat and waited.

At about seven o'clock the group of men dispersed and the person to whom Horace wanted to speak was left momentarily alone at the table in the corner of the room. Yes, he could see the face now: some features remained as they had been – the closed thin mouth and the right ear a little more prominent than its compatriot on the other side of the thinning hair.

'Mr Dodd?' Horace enquired, as he covered the last few yards between them, crossing the point at which a sumptuous carpet met functional wood flooring. He noted that the man still seemed reasonably fit and well, and had managed to keep most of his shape, despite the interval since Horace had last seen him.

'Yes?' The man looked up from his drink.

Horace sniffed the air and got the faintest hint of ginger. 'Alan Dodd, who went to St Columba's in the 1950s?' he asked.

'Yes, that's right. I was in Columba's. Can I help you? Are you a member here? Do we know each other? Would you like to sit down?'

Horace remained standing. 'My name is Horace Winter.'

The man's face assumed a quizzical expression. 'I'm afraid I don't really—'

'I was on the left wing on the Junior Cup team in 1957.'

A slight pause.

'No, you weren't,' the man said, in a cold snap. 'James Sefton was on the left wing.'

'He was injured in the quarter-final against St Mary's. Remember the tackle he made on their prop? He broke his collarbone,' Horace countered.

'Billy Redshaw!' Mr Dodd, with the thinning thatch, announced. '*He* was the replacement. That's who played on the left wing.'

'You're greatly mistaken, I'm afraid,' Horace

parried. 'Billy's mother died the week before the final and he had to go home to Tipperary. I was on the subs' list at that stage and was called up to replace him.' Horace watched for the slightest of quivers at the edges of the thin mouth that would signal a dawning on the other man of the truth of what he was saying.

Alan Dodd's visage remained impassive and he began to shake his head slowly from side to side, as if trying to remember. 'What did you say your name was again?'

'Horace. Horace Winter. I was in the year behind you in Columba's.'

'Ah,' said the old outside centre. 'That would explain it. You must have been on the team the *following* year. It's such a long time ago now. They all seem to blur into one, don't they?'

'Not for me,' Horace said bitterly. 'I remember it as clearly as if we were back there now, in Donnybrook, on the eighth of February 1957.'

'I remember the final, all right,' the other man said. 'We lost by a point.'

'Two points,' Horace corrected him. 'They kicked a drop-goal and that put them two ahead. Do you remember what happened then?'

'Not really. I think that was very close to the end of the match.'

'We had one final attack,' Horace said. 'Although it was their put-in. Does this ring a bell?'

The man shook his head with an unclenching of his lips, as if desolated by his inability to be of any assistance.

Horace continued. 'We won a heel against the head. Lennon picked the ball from the base of the scrum. You know who I mean?'

The man nodded. 'Yeah, Fincy Lennon. He went on to play for Bective after school.'

'He made a break to the short side and gave this fantastic pop pass for the wing forward ...'

'Trevor Something ...'

'Lawless?'

'Yes, Lawless.'

The man's left hand went out to grip his glass and he raised it to his mouth but didn't seem to drink any of it.

Horace continued. 'The scrum-half got the ball from the ruck when Lawless was tackled and he passed it to the fly-half and then we made an incursion into their twenty-five. The Newbridge backs couldn't get there quickly enough, and the crowd was baying, and eventually the ball came to you. Do you know what I'm talking about now?' Horace was frustrated by the other man's calm.

'Yes. Yes,' the man said. 'You're talking about the Junior Cup final of God knows how long ago and what players were called, and you weren't even *on* the team.'

'I *was* on the team,' Horace insisted. He felt the eyes of all of the other people in the room turn on him. A waiter came from somewhere behind him and stood to the side.

'Is everything all right, sir?' He had addressed the second centre and ignored the winger.

'Yes, Paddy, everything's fine. Would you like a drink?' he asked Horace.

'No, no thank you.' Horace felt hot now and sensed the onset of a headache. He sat down. His right arm felt strange.

'A glass of water, Paddy,' Alan Dodd called, after the departing figure.

The air settled between them and, moments later, Horace felt the alien sensation of fizzy bubbles in his throat as he gulped down some of the sparkling Ballygowan, with its clinking ice-cubes and deformed slice of lemon. He swallowed a clip of ice, then took a deep breath before continuing with his narrative.

'We were inside their twenty-five, with just the full-back to beat. You had the ball and moved towards the left a little. He shadowed you and prepared to tackle. I was just behind you and to *your* left, waiting. All you had to do was draw him in the tackle and pass the ball to me and I'd have gone over in the corner and we'd have won. But you didn't. You just kept going.'

'It's a long, long time ago, Horace. With the best will in the world the memory distorts things. Sure, I can barely remember what I had for breakfast this morning.'

'Thick pulpy central stems, perhaps?' Horace suggested.

'Sorry?'

Horace knew him now, the Frosted Orange moth: *Prefers to frequent open waste ground. Sometimes found in gardens. Occasionally mistaken for a butterfly.*

'You should have passed the ball to me,' Horace said. 'But you didn't, you just kept going. And before you committed yourself to trying to barge through the Newbridge number fifteen, you gave me this look of pure, unadulterated contempt, as though I was the world's greatest failure. Ever since that moment, I've always wanted to know why you refused to pass.'

Horace flopped back in the armchair, exhausted. He searched in his pockets for his tablets and a waiter brought another glass of water.

Alan Dodd watched Horace as he gulped down his medicine.

'Look,' Alan Dodd said, 'this is obviously very important to you. I don't know why, but it seems to be. Am I right?'

'Yes,' Horace replied.

'You're ill, aren't you?' the man said. Horace let the question answer itself as he pocketed his pills. He gazed at the lines on the man's face, and a look passed between them that told him the other man remembered.

'I just want to know why,' Horace said quietly.

Alan Dodd tapped his fingers on the table as if trying to make up his mind about something. 'Do you remember the summer of 1956, Horace?'

'Not really.'

'Well, I do. I injured my left leg in a fall from a bicycle. I'd been racing down a hill in the Phoenix Park, like an eejit, on the grass slope to a bandstand. You probably don't know the place – it's just opposite the entrance to the zoo. Anyway, they weren't sure whether it was a fracture or just a bad sprain. As a precaution, I wound up in a cast and on crutches for a month. One day, towards the end of August, my family went to the seaside at Bray. It was a fucking scorcher, Horace. The kind of weather you wouldn't get in Africa. We drove out and the place was absolutely jammers. My dad drove at a crawl up and down the esplanade trying to find a place to park the car, and, after ages, we managed to find a slot right up on the grass at the Greystones end. You know where the prom ends and there's a path up the hill?'

Horace nodded.

'Well, anyway, everyone went down to the beach, but I was left in the car because of my leg. I had piles of books with me and I was happy enough because I wouldn't have been able to *move* on the beach, not with the crutches and the cast and all. I read a few pages and that was when I saw you.'

'Me?' Horace was surprised.

'Yeah. You were with another boy, about the same age. He had red curly hair and freckles. Do you remember that day, Horace, and what you were doing?'

'No, I don't.'

'Well, I'll remind you. The pair of you had a comic each. The *Beano* was one of them, I remember that much. Both of you were standing at the dead end of the promenade, just where the countryside began. I was only about the length of one of those eight-man rowing boats away from you, in the car looking out, with my leg in a cast up on the back seat. I'll never forget it. You were standing beside the wall at the end of the prom and had obviously discovered a nest of wasps or bees in the wall itself. I could see them, flying in and out. One landed on the front of my father's car where some kid had dripped ice cream – I'm nearly sure they were bees. Anyway, there you were, like two sentries guarding a tomb, and then the pair of you rolled up the comics and started your ritual. It must have lasted, God, I don't know, an hour, two hours?'

'What ritual?' Horace asked.

'Each time a bee emerged from the wall, you killed it, taking turns like men with mallets hammering in the stake on a circus tent. On and on and on and on and on. You never let up, not for an instant, in case one might escape out into the afternoon and survive. The world and his wife were down on the beach, swimming, sunbathing, sleeping. But your face was concentrated with a thirst for death and killing. I sat in the car, unable to do anything to stop you. I could have shouted – I *should* have done something, anything, sounded the horn – but I didn't. The thing that bothered me most about it afterwards was that they decided the following week that my leg wasn't broken at all. The cast came off and I went back training. So I suppose I *could* have stopped you but I just didn't know it at the time.'

It began to come back to Horace now: the slam of reinforced paper on stone, the creatures dropping to the pavement. He and his cousin Stephen behaving like madmen. He had never thought about it before. Horace remembered that teenage version of himself. He'd wanted to lash out at the whole bloody world that day as the heat of the afternoon boiled up all of the feelings inside him. But why? About what? Whatever had possessed him? He felt the stirring of another memory now, another occasion altogether. More bees, different bees.

'And then, when there were hundreds and hundreds of dead bees on the paving stones of the promenade, it began to rain. Completely out of the blue, as though something or someone wanted to save the rest of the swarm. They stopped coming out and I thought, That's it now. The rest of them will be safe. But they weren't, not one of them. You stuffed the comics into the opening of the nest and set them on fire.'

Horace looked at Alan Dodd and wanted him to stop speaking but he went on and on and on and on and on.

'So that's why, six months later, in the Junior Cup final, I didn't pass to you. When the ball came to me and I drew the full-back, I looked out and saw you on the wing and thought, Well, I'm fucked if I'm going to pass to someone like him just so that he can score the winning try. So I didn't. I kept going and went for glory myself. It was a brilliant tackle, I'll give him that, the bollox.'

Suddenly and ineluctably, Horace now realised what he himself was: a Burnished Brass moth: *Found commonly in woodland and marshes and almost anywhere that nettles grow. The defining characteristic is its inability to ever comfortably blend into its environment.* After years of designating others on sight as butterflies or moths, he had ever so conveniently avoided passing judgement on himself. And yet, somewhere in his darkening heart, perhaps he had always known which of the two categories he fitted into.

Horace hunched forward and moved his drink into the middle of the table, squinted a final time at the Frosted Orange through the tall glass, then stood up. Wordlessly, he gathered his coat around him, left some money on the table for the drinks and turned away. He could not feel his right arm at all now.

The arc-lights in the courtyard illuminated the path to the car park, past abandoned golf trolleys and obscenely useless buggies, which crammed against each other in the pools of false light that managed to reach them.

★

In the past week, a new family had moved in next door. After breakfast, Horace went into the front sitting room to see whether any Hornet Clearwing moths had been attracted to the poplar tree the new owners had planted in the front garden of number fifty-nine. Yet another removal truck was parked on the pavement, in front of Horace's own car, and two enormous bronzed men with shaved heads were unloading a piano from it. Horace hoped that he would not be plagued for the rest of his life with sonatas and jazz coming at him through the party wall.

The removal men looked quite formidable. One wore a bright orange football jersey. The other had tattoos on his arms. Horace thought he could make out a cross. Perhaps they're Large Copper butterflies, he mused. They could equally be Lappet moths, although it would be unusual to see them early in the morning. He went upstairs to his bedroom to find his *A Beginner's Guide*.

He watched the men from the window as they continued to unload the van. At one point, a car came up the road but was unable to get past the truck. One of the men signalled for the driver of the car to reverse back the way she had come. The other, without hesitation, climbed into the van and drove it off up the road and right round the block to enable the car to proceed.

'One butterfly and one moth,' Horace said to himself, although he was surprised it had been the man with the tattoos who had done the right thing and moved the lorry.

Horace had just taken off his shoes, and put them on an old newspaper on the table to polish them, when he thought he heard the doorbell ring. He wasn't always sure any more. He walked in his socks along the hall and opened the door. No one was there. He stepped outside onto the short path and went as far as the gate, then looked up and down the street. He could see no one. The removal men and their truck had gone. Horace had wondered whether one of the tanned two might have rung his bell to query his diagnosis of them.

As he turned to go back into his house, a movement on a spike of the railing of Amanda's house across the street caught his attention. Horace opened his own gate and continued into the middle of the road. He approached the opposite pavement and craned his neck as he walked as slowly as he possibly could. In an open-winged repose, on top of the fence rail, a tiny flutter gave away the presence of a species of moth Horace knew all about but had never seen. It was the Grey Dagger. He stood, motionless, and recalled the markings from his memory – he had read the description dozens of times: *This moth has a basic deep grey colouring. This is in sharp contrast to the segment colouring break of a bright red spot contained within a black border. In the female, the hind wings are flecked with brown. The markings on the fore wings look like daggers. This species despises its offspring.*

Horace leaned forward ever so slightly and looked intently at the moth. He glared at the hind wings, daring it not to be the female of the species. But it was. His mind raced with possibilities and likelihoods. What if he left it alone and pretended he'd never seen it? What would happen if he tried to capture it now with his bare hands? If he went back to the house to get his net, would it fly away? The moth made the tiniest flutter of its wings but remained where it was. Horace knew that if he pounced and managed to grab it he would probably destroy one or perhaps both of the wings. He needed to capture it alive. That last thought decided him, so he retraced his steps, walking backwards across the road in his socks, keeping the Grey Dagger in his field of vision all the time. As he retreated into the garden of his own house he lost sight of it for a moment when a passing car cut it off from view. He was worried that the noise or movement of the vehicle would scare it away. But it did not.

The net was in the drawer of the hall sideboard just inside the front door and Horace was able to retrieve it without losing sight of his prey. The thin gauze netting was frayed at the junction of the Y-piece and the frame ends, but otherwise did not appear to be too damaged. He picked up an umbrella from the stand in the hall and forced the point of it into the single end of the Y. It was better than no handle at all, he thought. He began to manoeuvre himself back out into the street in what he hoped was his original line of retreat. He was conscious of trying to maintain a constant presence, without deviation, in the horizon line of the Grey Dagger moth.

As he went through his own gate, and out onto the pavement, he stood on a stone or a piece of glass, piercing his left foot through his sock. He stifled a yell, by biting the back of his left hand. This action hurt him even more than the original injury but at least now his mouth was full and thus unable to release sounds that might frighten away the moth. He crossed the street once more, his socked feet making no noise on the reddish tarmac road surface.

The moth had a wing span of just a few millimetres, yet Horace had managed to see it from across the street before he'd gone to fetch the net. He was amazed that it hadn't flown away. Perhaps it, too, was keeping an eye on him. He wondered about reincarnation. Some people believed in that, didn't they? He worried for a moment that Amanda might come out of her front door and cause the moth to flee, but then he remembered she'd probably gone to work in Herbert Park.

Horace Winter advanced with his net at the

ready. He eyeballed the moth and slowly began to lift the umbrella with both hands while keeping the net out to the side so that the moth wouldn't see it until the last moment. He noticed a flicker of red and grey as he raised the net slightly above shoulder level. In a confluence of instinct and movement, Horace and the moth jumped at the same exact time. Horace pounced with the net as the moth lifted off from her perch. The ancient umbrella handle was lost in the attack but the net lodged on the railing and forced the moth downwards. Horace thought she would simply turn around and fly towards the ground, thus escaping, but she did not. Instead, the Grey Dagger flew up against the netting as if trying to break through. He could hear the moth's wings battering against the gauze.

Back in the garage at number fifty-seven, Horace took down the killing jar from its perch. He did not know whether the cyanide would work quickly, or at all, after so many years. He saw that the cotton wool had deteriorated so that in places the plaster of Paris was exposed. He knew that this could damage the moth. He looked around for some suitable material to cushion the bottom of the jar. In a drawer he found strips of blue cloth and stuffed in three. He turned towards the net as he continued his task and began to speak to the trapped moth.

'Why did you throw out my collection of butterflies and moths, Mother? I know you hid the net too. Do you recognise it now? What's wrong with big families? Why were you always so angry with me?'

Horace looked around the garage for something that might enable him to transfer the Grey Dagger into the killing jar. He needed some conduit, perhaps a cardboard or plastic tube. He thought of rolling up a newspaper. Would that work?

'What was wrong between you and Dad? Why were you always shouting at him? I'm going into the house now for a moment. Don't leave. I'll be back in a minute. I know you don't want me to go, but it's only for a short while, Mother.' In the house, he managed to unclip the vacuum-cleaner pipe, then carried it back to the garage, discarding the metal nozzle in the garden as he walked.

'Just take your time, Mother,' Horace said, as he undid the netting from one of the legs of its frame and closed the fabric around the pipe with his right hand and slid it into the space where the Grey Dagger sat staring (unblinking) at him. The other end of the pipe fitted neatly over the opening of the killing jar. Horace kept his body in the way so his mother couldn't see her destination. Despite this, however, the Grey Dagger moth was reluctant to fly up into the dark tunnel presented to her as a channel of escape. Eventually Horace loosened the remainder of the netting and began to reduce the size of the prison by gathering it. The moth had no option but to enter the pipe and, as soon as she did so, Horace put the palm of his hand over the end she'd flown into, so that the only light she could see came from the jar. He lifted the end of the pipe so that the line was straight. After about two minutes, the Grey Dagger flew out the other end. Horace withdrew the pipe and put the airtight stopper in the mouth of the killing jar. He carried it across the back yard and into the kitchen, where he placed it in the centre of the table.

'Why did you throw out my collection of butterflies and moths, Mother? Why did you make me go to work in the bank?'

The moth flew around inside the jar, then landed on the blue cloth and looked out through the glass at Horace.

'What was wrong with you and Dad? Why were you always shouting at him? I want to know why you were so ... so ...' he searched for the word '... controlling. Yes, that's the word I was looking for. Why, Mother, why?'

The moth flew up to the rubber stopper, then hovered in the middle of the jar at eye-level with Horace. Perhaps she's trying to explain, he thought. Then he was shouting: 'Do you remember that time when we were in the museum, Mother? You got cross with me about not getting the right film for your camera. Do you remember? Was it so important? Why didn't you want me to have a life of my own? What do they all matter now? What does anything matter now, Mother?'

The Grey Dagger alighted on a stiffened tuft of cotton wool and fluttered its dagger-laden wings with less vigour than before. Horace could see she was getting weaker. He wondered whether she could feel any pain as the crystals of cyanide worked their ancient magic and filtered fumes up into the air she breathed. He knocked on the jar with his knuckle, trying to distract his mother's attention for long enough to allow her to answer even one of the questions he had in his mouth and his heart.

The Grey Dagger flapped her wings and tried to rise but could not. Horace's head was filled with a thousand things. *He* was a moth and *she* was a moth and she had hated *him* and he had tried to love *her* and to keep her happy but he had failed. *This species despise their offspring*. And what now? What was the answer to all or any of those things? Was the solution for him to kill her? To capture and interrogate her, then to murder his own mother with cyanide, was that the answer? He didn't really know what he thought or felt any more about her or about anything. He'd loved Rose Burke, too, but she hadn't loved him back. He loved Amanda, but in a different way from how most people loved others. His father was dead; his mother was dead; he was nearly dead himself, if truth be told.

Suddenly Horace remembered the day he and Amanda had found the letter to Migsie Spring and also Horace's Leaving Certificate results. He had to ask her about that. He looked back into the killing jar and saw the shadow of death beginning to invade the interior of the glass. He *had* to ask her about the letter.

'Did you put that letter there so that I'd find it and try to discover more about Dad? Is that why you put it in the bookcase near where you kept the Leaving Cert? You wanted me to find them, didn't you? You know, Mother, I've repeated that exam. I really think

I might pass this time. *And* I delivered the letter to Migsie Spring. I've tried to make things right, Mother. I really have. Why didn't you love me back? Was it because of what happened in the bathroom?'

Horace asked the questions but no answer came. He saw the tiny creature stagger across the cloth strips and remembered the bees on the promenade. Was he a murderer of moths as well? He looked at the Grey Dagger moth and saw her stumble around the ancient killing bottle, looking for a way to avoid death.

With a sudden violent movement, he swept the jar off the table with his right arm and it shattered on contact with the diamond-shaped black and red tiles on the kitchen floor. An explosion of glass sprayed up and out and covered the room with a carpet of splinters and chunks of old plaster of paris. Two of the strips of his rugby jersey ended up stretched across each other. They made the sign of a cross, like the tattoo on the removal man's arm. Horace got down on his hunkers and then his hands and knees, looking for the Grey Dagger moth, but he simply could not find her, no matter how hard and long he looked.

CHAPTER TWENTY-ONE

Bee Moth (*Aphomia sociella*)

That summer in Rosslare had been the happiest of Horace's life.

Rose Burke was as carefree and wild as he was conservative and overwrought. Horace allowed himself to be carried with the current of his feelings, and, with each hour he spent in her company, he felt himself becoming stronger and more confident than he'd felt in his whole life. He wanted to stay with Rose Burke forever and to protect her from anything that might threaten her happiness.

One day, she seemed slightly melancholy and distant as they walked along the railway line. They were keeping an eye open for stones shaped like flatfish.

'Is everything okay, Rose?' he asked, as they held hands and Rose balanced on one of the rails. She thought for a moment, then looked as if she were about to cry.

'My father gets very angry sometimes,' she said. 'That's why my mother never comes on holidays with us now. Sometimes when we're at home, she goes and stays with her sister for a few days.'

'Is he ... Has he ever been angry with you?' Horace asked.

Rose looked away as she answered. 'No,' she said, 'but sometimes I wish he would just die.'

Horace did not know whether either of those things was true or not but he did not wish to press her on the subject. He wanted to say something to her that would take her mind off her sadness. 'My father died because I disappointed him,' he said.

Rose looked at him incredulously. 'That's the maddest thing I've ever heard,' she said. 'That can't be right. How could you disappoint someone to death?'

'I'm afraid it's true,' Horace said. He told her about the last few moments of the rugby game.

She listened intently. After he finished, she took one of his hands in hers. 'How on earth can you blame yourself for your dad's death?' I bet your mother doesn't blame you the way you blame yourself.'

'My mother blames me for more than that,' Horace said. But he didn't tell her that part. He'd never told anyone that part.

Horace was upset. A great deal of darkness surrounded him at night. Not just the darkness of night, but a deeper quotient of some thick absence of light beyond what everyone else had to contend with. At least, that was what it felt like. He could make out names on the rectangular prescription stickers of the pill cylinders on top of the bedside table: dexamethasone, cyclizine, Codipar, OxyContin, diazepam, co-danthramer. These were his daily nourishment now. The existence of this extra layer of blackness frightened him. Horace wanted to discuss something with Amanda, he reckoned it would be easier to talk about it away from his house.

They caught a bus at the Triangle to the city

centre. After they alighted on Leeson Street, they did not speak until they reached St Stephen's Green. Horace led the direction of their walk, with a silent steely resolve. He took a plastic bag out of his pocket.

'What have you got there, Horace?' Amanda asked, as they neared the bridge at the centre of the park.

'Bread, ' he replied, and kept walking. She was barely able to keep up with him. At last, they reached the duck pond and Horace divided the hunks of stale bread into two. Together they began to feed the ducks. They came from all corners of the park to feast on the remains of Brennan's Traditional White Sliced Pan.

'I remember trying to hoosh a bee out of a window upstairs at number fifty-seven Edenvale Road.'

'Did it sting you?' she asked.

'I simply can't remember any more than that,' he said. 'I think I must have been still in primary school.'

'Is that all you can remember, Horace?'

He thought and thought and thought. Then something extra came back to him. Amanda gazed at him expectantly.

'I remember that I was in the bathroom and so was the bee. The sound of it was so loud and I was ...'

'Yes?'

'I was frightened, really, really terrified.'

Amanda took his arm and began to walk with him back towards the bridge. 'Real friends are friends forever,' she said. 'Little things or big things from long ago make no difference to that. Okay?'

'Okay,' said Horace, feeling in his pocket for his bus ticket.

They walked like that, arm in arm, oblivious to the children rollerblading along the paths between the flowerbeds and unaware of, or at least ignoring, the tears streaming down Horace's face as they made their way home.

Back at the house, Amanda put on the kettle. Horace wandered up the stairs and stood on the landing outside the bathroom. He put his ear to the door and, hearing nothing, came back down to the kitchen.

Amanda watched him as he slowly pulled out one of the chairs from the table and carefully sat down. The pot of tea brewed on a coaster in the space between them. For a moment, there was absolute silence in the room. Then Horace looked across at his friend and spoke in a quiet voice, which seemed barely that of an adult. 'I'd forgotten all about her,' he said.

'About who?' Amanda asked. Horace continued speaking as though he'd not heard the question.

'Her name was Helen. I remember when she came home from the hospital with my mother. She was so tiny. She had pink cheeks and her eyes were the same colour as yours. We had a seat for her that was made of wire bent back on itself so that when she moved it bounced her up and down. I used to stand in front of her in her Bongey-Bongey seat, and I'd hold my hands by my sides and just jump on the spot, and she'd laugh and laugh and laugh. She had the most wonderful laugh. She was my baby sister. I'd forgotten all about her, just blocked her out completely.'

Horace swallowed twice in succession and caught his breath. Amanda reached across the table and placed her hand on his.

After a moment or two, Horace continued. 'One day when I was about five or six – she was just over a year old – my mother was giving her a bath upstairs. I don't think I was in the bathroom ... no, I'm nearly sure that I was in my own room. It was hot. I remember that. Probably July or August.'

Amanda poured tea for both of them. Horace became quiet again. 'It's okay, Horace. You can tell me, but you don't have to if you'd rather not.'

Horace looked into the middle distance and travelled back to an afternoon when the sun had shone so vehemently through the window on the return that the carpet on the stairs had been warm to the touch.

'The telephone rang, one, two, three. "Horace, mind your sister while I answer it," Mother said. I went into the bathroom just as she left. Helen was splashing, with an orange duck in one hand, and smashing down with her other. I can see and hear her now, shrieking with absolute delight, you know, screaming out her infant joyfulness, water everywhere. Then I heard the bee. It was up above my head, circling around the lightshade. I *knew* it had come to do her harm. I had to do *something*. I closed down the toilet lid, stood up on it and tried to shoo it out of the bathroom. I was too small to reach the high window. At one point, the bee flew straight at me and I wanted it to sting *me* and then Helen would be safe. "They only have one sting," Dad used to say. It flew round and round the room and down over the bath, making a dummy run, just waiting for the chance. I picked up the facecloth and stood beside the bath trying to fend it off. The first time I swiped at it, I missed, then I sort of clipped it but that just made it more ill-tempered. Eventually, it seemed to be flying after *me*, so I ran out of the bathroom and across the landing into my parents' room. Somehow, I managed to close the door of their room just after it flew in right behind me. The window was so hard to open. The cord was broken. I had to push and pull that old wooden sash and, all the time, the bee was flying at my face, taunting me, scaring me. Finally, I got the window open and as soon as I did, it flew past my face and out. I watched it descend into the garden and land on some flowers. That's the place for you, I remember thinking. When I was going back into the bathroom, Mother was coming up the stairs. "I *told* you to look after your sister," were the last words she said before she started screaming. All the splashing had stopped. There wasn't any splashing left. I just stood there in the doorway watching my mother yelling and shouting at my little sister to wake up, to cry, to "bloody live", but she couldn't.'

Horace's life came headlong down at him along a telegraph line to his heart and he saw everything clearly. He re-experienced the feelings, the disbelief, the completely isolating rules of chaos that ushered in a childhood in which it seemed his mother had never stopped screaming at him, blaming him, because of the way in which he'd failed to look after his sister when she'd told him to. She hadn't wanted to know about the bee. What she'd wanted was her baby back.

He stood up slowly from the table and made his way out into the hall. He climbed the stairs, pulling and dragging the past as though it were a set of irons welded around his ankles. When he reached the return, he put one hand down to feel if the carpet was warm. It was not. Slowly and sadly, Horace Winter ascended the last few steps to the landing. He did not want to go on but he knew that somehow he had to, as if his very life, or what was left of it, depended upon it. He took the key from the ledge on the top of the bathroom doorframe. It was heavier than the keys of Hell. He undid the lock. He opened the door. The decay of abandonment was everywhere, stretching in cobwebs across the years he'd been afraid to open the door. He expected that someone would be waiting for him in the shadows, but nobody was.

Horace stepped into the centre of the room and looked at the empty bath. Silently and deliberately, he closed the door behind him, then sat down on the closed toilet lid and wept.

CHAPTER TWENTY-TWO

Red Admiral (*Vanessa atalanta*):
found almost everywhere

'We've removed as much of the tumour as we can,' the surgeon said.

Horace saw the room in absolute white terms: the blind on the window, blithe in its moment of repose, and the brass antlers on the wall relieved of the pressure of the taut string for now. High in the air, a television screen on a bracket leered out of the wall at him, like a grotesque jack-in-the-box. His arms felt heavy, although they were already under

the covers and supported by the best bed that Plan
C of the voluntary health insurance cover had to
offer. Down at the foot of the bed, the cold grey
curve of the handle on his chart clung to the rail. The
walls of the room were almost entirely bare, except
for a picture of a lady holding a baby. The woman
wore a blue cape with a hood, and the child lay on her
lap with its eyes pleading up. Horace wondered how
old the baby was. The door of the room was open
and he could smell detergent. In the corner, there was
another door, a cupboard, which was also painted
white. It was almost impossible to tell it apart from
the wall, except for a thin strip of the handle, which
peeked out brown where the painter had missed. A
floor-polisher groaned in the distance and the blind
tinkled against the window, like distant jingling bells.

Horace put a hand to his head and felt the wrap
of the bandage, like the Sellotape overlapping around
the loose battery cover of his mother's remote control.

He did not know how long he had been there
before the surgeon had spoken. He remembered
someone asking him to count to fifteen and how he
had tried. 'One, the loose-head prop. Two, the hooker.
Three, the tight head. Four and five, the locks', and
on. Before he'd reached the backs, it had ended in

black and new bliss. He knew that he had dreamed heavily but did not know what of. His torso was tight, constricted by more than just the bedclothes. It lay at a slight angle. Horace had a feeling that parts of his body belonged to someone else, who was in another room, deciding how they should behave. He couldn't move his left arm. He recalled the pitch and toss of the ambulance journey.

Time was truncated now as he tried to lay it out in his head, and postcards of seaside towns book-ended the part he could actually see. There was the golden apple, in the dead centre of the piece, hanging from someone else's Christmas tree. He saw beaches, all of them, sand seamlessly sewn together to where the tides came and went at different times on each. Zero seven hundred hours was the time the invasion was due to begin. Butterflies hovered over the bookcase, then landed, laughed and took off again.

Away from there, he had another life. Out of that room, down however many floors, up the road and across the city, that life was still waiting for him. He knew that. He also knew he'd made a mess of some things but not how to fix them or even whether they could be repaired. He had been able to see the Clarence Hotel, but not from his office, no: it had been from another room full of champagne and shaking hands. The smell of pâté on slightly stale salt biscuits had been too much to take.

Apricot sunsets and old photographs were there, too, somewhere, out in the heave and hustle of that other life. He was proud of his car, with its new tyres. There were places to go and things to listen out for, trains in the distance and apples being toasted by teenagers lost in the marram grass. He had a moment now, in the grip of his thinking, a little bit of there and then that needed mending. Mending and mitching, he thought. He wondered about the man who had stolen the brown leather purse with the spinning-top tag. Days were pop-passed by the wing-forward to the boy, who passed to the boy, who passed to the boy who wouldn't pass. Horace Winter lurked in the top right-hand corner of his own life.

There was a movement in the room and the blind clittered against the wall on one side, then bounced back into place. His throat was dry and he smelled water.

'We've removed as much of the tumour as we can,' the surgeon said, although Horace did not know if this was the first or second time he'd spoken those words. The ticker-tape parade of share prices beneath the silenced newsreader on the television in the corner told him that it was 1 October.

A bandage around his head. He put up his hand to feel for it, but it was not there now. A piece of death had grown bigger and closer inside him but had been beaten back. He wondered if he had really just had the operation or whether that had been ages ago at another time. He didn't feel happy now, though. A portion of contentment had to be out there somewhere, he thought, then spoke aloud: 'Like a bundle of feelings in a term deposit account.'

'Are you all right, Mr Winter?'

A lady's voice from somewhere else in the house carried to him with the sound of a toilet flushing. She entered the sitting room. She wore blue trousers and a white top and he couldn't see her feet and didn't know whether or not she was wearing shoes. She was not Amanda. Horace thought about the bee in the bathroom upstairs and wondered if it was still there. Was his sister still in danger? He would still be able to get up and about, but he would, most of all, try to be better. Pain in his head jolted him for a time.

'Would you like to use the toilet?'

He didn't know this woman.

'Would *you* like to go and disembowel yourself

with whatever you can find in the fridge?' Horace said. He hadn't meant to say that and wasn't even sure that he *had*. He looked into the lady's face and she was smiling.

'Someone brought you flowers,' she said. They were yellow and orange, and when they merged they made the shade and hue of the Coxcomb Prominent. *Ptilodon capucina*.

The zoo was always deserted in October. Horace visited once or twice a year and had found that the late autumn carried with it a distancing between people and animals. Of course, most butterflies had vanished by then, too, except for the Common Blue and the Speckled Wood. The Clouded Yellow (or *Colias croceus*) could be seen sometimes, particularly in coastal areas, right into the first week or two of November, but most species had disappeared by this time of year. He knew that the animals in the zoo weren't seasonal but, nonetheless, he figured that, on some days, no one at all might come to visit them. Horace had always tried to organise his visits for mid-October because it came just before the Hallowe'en rush and the Christmas boom, two of the times, he imagined, when visitors would be in abundance at the Zoological Gardens. He preferred to visit when the animals were more likely to be in need of company. He had also always liked the park near the zoo, where the grass sloped sharply down to an old bandstand.

One day in late October, years earlier, Horace had taken a half-day from the bank. He was supposed to attend a training course at Head Office to be instructed in the provisions of new legislation. Instead, he decided, as he crossed Capel Street Bridge, that he would not bother with the seminar because the weather was so fine and he was feeling a little rebellious.

Looking back, he reckoned it was probably around the same time as the result of the internal enquiry into the bank robbery.

Rather than continuing in the direction of Parliament Street, he suddenly, and without warning, turned right at Sunlight Chambers and walked the half-mile along the south bank of the river to Heuston railway station. It had been well before the Wood Quay controversy and the building of those civic offices, he was sure. (Unlike the rest of the free-thinking world, Horace did not think these buildings to be an eyesore. The Vikings had had their time and place, and enjoyed it, so why not afford the same courtesy to Sam Stephenson, the architect of the new headquarters of the local authority?)

Up along the footpath, against the flow of the Liffey, he strolled and, as he did, he inhaled the coffee-like nose-filling warm pleated *whoomf* of hops that escaped all day long from the panting towers of the Guinness brewery.

Mitching, yes, that was what he was about that day. And what a wonderful day it had been, too. Horace was thirty-one years old and deserved a day off.

In the green funnel of the rice-grass lawn, the bandstand hosted a concert by a jazz quartet. The flyers, handed out by smiling footmen, announced the programme. Horace thought it was the most wonderful sound he had ever heard. The piano player made the whole park sing with combinations of chorded thrill that Horace could never have imagined. His ears were cleansed of the melodies of *The King and I*, played incessantly by his mother on the radiogram. Horace felt truly alive that day. His sensation of guilt about missing the detail of the provisions of boring new legislation, began to ebb away when he moved beneath the thinning but continuing canopy of the music towards the red-brick arch that was the portal to the zoo. As he entered the Zoological Gardens, through the black kissing-gate beside the thatched admissions hut, he'd heard a jazz arrangement of 'Hey Jude' drifting after him from the bandstand.

Horace thought he wouldn't be able to sleep that night, after the trauma of the surgery, but was out like a light as soon as his head hit the pillow.

In the same city, at the edge of one of the largest urban parks in Europe, the polar bears, too, were asleep, and there was still no sign of Rose Burke between their enclosure and that of the sea lions.

'We think the surgery has been a success,' the surgeon had said. 'Only time will tell.'

Horace wasn't sure whether he had been in hospital for days, weeks or months.

It was a perfect morning. Horace sat at the kitchen table and ate a bowl of cornflakes. He was getting weaker but, at the same time, he felt invigorated by the sunshine that trespassed into his house through the back window. Even so early in the day, he could feel the heat on his face as he poured more milk on his cereal. He tried to put the top back on the plastic carton but could not. He had arranged for the newspaper to be delivered to him each day now because he found it tiring to walk down to Ranelagh village and back.

Amanda called to see him and brought him the newspaper. He saw that it was Tuesday. She now had a key to his house because sometimes Horace wasn't well enough to get up and answer the door.

'What would you like to do today, Horace?' Amanda asked, as she came into the sitting room and stood beside the low table, which held a tray with cups and a pot of tea. Horace looked from the tray to the door and saw a stream of blue steam. It led across to the table where his mother had set down cup after cup after cup while she'd waited for his return on the day of the Leaving Cert results. The line of aquamarine stayed in the air.

'I think I'd like to go to the cinema,' he said, as he poured the tea for himself and his guest and snapped a chocolate biscuit in half. His father looked across the room at his son from his position against the road sign in the photograph. The blue and white enamel letters bleached through the bodies of the soldiers so that the word 'Ouistreham' was now as clear as day and it obscured the three men. Things had moved ever so slightly forward now in the bigger picture, too, and Horace felt as if he were finally beginning to understand a little of the vast world around him. Horace treated Amanda to a trip to the Light House Cinema in Smithfield Square.

At one point in the film, there were sheep everywhere. The main character had stumbled into a girls' boarding school in his attempts to evade capture by his pursuers. It was all to do with a message in a toy battleship beneath the funnel, which had led to the death of 'Nanny' early on. Now, Richard Hannay was handcuffed to Miss Fisher in Scotland and it all looked a little hopeless. Horace nodded off but came round again when a man in one of the boxes in the theatre shot and killed 'Mr Memory'. Horace felt relieved to have woken up.

Amanda squeezed one of his hands in hers. 'Are you okay, Horace?'

They left the Light House Cinema and walked through the city. Temple Bar was a maze. Horace wanted the moment not to end. He saw a shop called Books Upstairs and thought about *Macbeth*, the play he'd studied for the exam. Two girls walked near them on Dame Street and he heard one say, 'You see, he was ringing me at the same time as I was ringing him so we cancelled each other out.'

Horace wondered if that wasn't what everyone did to someone else in the end, cancelled them out.

He knew that he was dying. He had known it for a while now but had tried not to think about it. He was alive, here in Suffolk Street, now Nassau Street, round the corner, turning right and striding up the hill towards the Luas stop. The lights of early evening were unnecessarily on in some of the houses they passed on their journey home. Some people were frightened of the dark. The city lay all around Horace and Amanda, reaching out, like handfuls of houses taken from a bag and scattered from the central point of Edenvale Road. Impulses raced along the lines of lives and back across hearts and hands into the middle, then out again once more, pulsing thoughts and hopes against the growing gloom.

On the bedside table, at number fifty seven, a

diminishing troop of tablets held the line between the grainy film footage that was Horace Winter's life, and the approaching end credits.

A card arrived in the post. It was a get-well wish from an old customer of the bank – the lady whose lottery win Horace had dealt with so discreetly: 'If there is anything I can do to help, please let me know by return.'

Horace was overwhelmed that, for the first time in his life, someone else was thinking of him enough to write him a kind card. He recalled the letters he'd written to Rose Burke all that time ago to which he had never received a reply.

Once, on holidays perhaps, or maybe in a dream, he had seen a sky-blue parachute or paraglider above him. The person attached had been screaming with delight and Horace had wanted to jump up and join with them to share in their thrill. It was as if someone on their glide through shared air had tossed down a piece of themselves to him: 'Please get well soon.' He had always liked the taste of strawberries but not that of strawberry jam. Perhaps it was the sugar that repulsed him. And now this card, with its strawberry-shaped design, was trying to reach him from somewhere else. He thought of replying:

Dear Mrs_____
Please send me a lifetime's supply of halogen bulbs. Do not worry about me now because I shall be safe within their glare.
Yours (light-heartedly)
Horace Winter (Asst Mgr, Retd)

Horace had the car fully serviced. Up to then, it had performed adequately, but this adventure would be in a different league. To anyone else, it might have seemed a funny time to start repairing things, but Horace was planning a trip. An important trip. He had to think of others as well as himself. He'd never imagined that a fully equipped garage could exist in a street-end back yard in Ranelagh.

Barry, the mechanic who serviced the car, was enthusiastic about his work. 'She's a cracker, Mr Winter,' he said, as they stood back and admired the newly inflated and uplifted Morris Minor with its brand-new tyres and freshly polished bodywork. Horace had feared that the car would not be up to the task, but he was reassured by the mechanic's response.

'The only thing that's beyond repair is Southampton Football Club, and that's a fact. These cars were built to last.' The oil-stained overalls made the young man look like a moth, but Horace was fairly sure he was a butterfly. Rows of canisters of WD-40, and brake-fluid lined the shelves of the workshop, like so many runners at the starting line of a race. Barry got into the old car and turned the key in the ignition. It started first time, and the contented moan of the engine disturbed a couple of magpies that had been sitting on the garden wall, gawping at the shiny chrome cover of the wing mirrors. Horace wondered whether they'd followed him from the pub in Yorkshire.

The birds lifted off, away from the scene, past flapping clothes drying on the line behind the house next door. Horace thought about the army mechanics who must have had to repair jeeps and trucks under fire in Normandy.

'Have you got insurance?' Barry asked.

'I'm not sure. I'm afraid it's most likely lapsed by now.'

'No probs. I'll stick it on my own and put you

down as a named driver. That'll keep you right until you get round to organising yourself.'

That kindness on the part of the youngster struck Horace as uncharacteristic of moths. Definitely a butterfly, he thought. The bowl of overripe peaches and bananas, which sat on top of the small Coors fridge in the workshop, convinced him that the mechanic was a Red Admiral.

CHAPTER TWENTY-THREE

Clifden Nonpareil (*Catocala fraxini*)

Small Tortoiseshell (*Aglais urticae*)

'Jesus Christ, Horace. Look out!' Amanda shouted.

Horace was surprised to meet a truck head-on when he turned left onto the small roundabout just after driving off the ferry at Cherbourg. The vehicle was laden with chickens. He braked hard and the car stalled. The driver of the lorry shook his fist out of the window as the wheels of the truck mounted the roundabout kerb. The noise of the chickens seemed to hang in the air even after the truck had driven away. Horace sat still for a few moments, then started the engine once more and began to drive on the wrong side of the road, like everybody else.

'Sorry about that,' he said to Amanda. He looked across at his passenger and saw that she was covering her eyes with her hands.

'Why don't you let me drive?'

'Absolutely not,' Horace replied. 'I know this old warrior better than anybody. There's a real trick to keeping her steady.'

'Well, the sooner you learn that trick, the better,' Amanda said, in a sort of cross voice.

He had never been to France before. What he noticed most in those first kilometres was the huge number of dilapidated buildings and the army of signs he could not understand. An elderly man stood outside one little bar, which he passed about ten minutes after the incident on the roundabout. Horace only saw him because he moved. Otherwise, he would have blended seamlessly into the colour of the paintwork. A Clifden Nonpareil, he thought, *commonly found in northern and central Europe. Difficult to see in daylight when at rest on tree trunks.* Sometimes moths were everywhere.

On the ferry, he had tried his best to sleep but had woken several times during the night in his tiny cabin. The creak and groan of the great ship had been a comfort to him in a way because he'd not interacted with anyone, apart from Amanda, during the voyage. Before they'd retired for the night, they had eaten in the linen-tablecloth restaurant. There was little chance of being left alone in the Emerald Cafeteria, he imagined. The chaos of ketchup and children filled him with dread and horror. It would be like trying to find a spot on the beach at the height of a sunny summer.

He decided to go down the corridor to Amanda's cabin to see if she, too, was unable to sleep. She didn't respond to his knock – which was probably just as well. Not the done thing, he thought, before returning to his berth and trying once more to find sleep.

He followed the signs and drove into the square in the centre of the town. All around it, tourists loitered in the cold of the autumn sun. Horace watched a bus pull up in front of the church. Elderly people disembarked with helpers, and began to shuffle across to a large tent, erected to one side of the square, like an extension to the small hotel. Horace parked the car and watched the old people disappear one by one into the tent. He spotted a large vehicle with a German registration plate and wondered if they would try to follow him and Amanda. The dead paratrooper on the church steeple moved slightly in the breeze.

Later, after they'd left Sainte-Mère Église, Horace slowed as the road curled down towards the sea and the bend of it drew him closer to his father's memory. A meadow of withered yellow flowers greeted them around the next corner. It lay like a silk handkerchief on a putting green, almost perfectly square.

'Oh, what a magnificent view, Horace. Can we stop for a minute?'

He brought the Morris Minor to a standstill. A small and noisy moped driven by a teenage boy passed, travelling in the opposite direction. The rider wore an orange T-shirt. The noise of the engine dimmed in the distance, and then the moment, the flowers and the sound of the English Channel belonged solely to Horace and Amanda.

They got out and walked across the road to the field of flowers. Using an old stone stile for support, Horace stood as tall as he could and gazed across the countryside at the horizon. Amanda stood beside him. Somewhere in the middle of their view, a sailboat skated from left to right. In his head, Horace heard the noise of flapping wings, as though he'd suddenly acquired an inner ear so sensitive that it could discriminate between the waves splashing and a bird or a butterfly in flight. He shaded his eyes with one hand and tried to scan the flowers for movement. He saw, or thought he saw, a figure dressed in army fatigues struggling up the incline away from the water at the other end of the field.

'Look, Amanda.' He pointed at the figure. 'Whatever do you think he's doing?'

'Who?'

'See? There he is, at the bottom of the field. He's wearing army fatigues.'

Amanda, too, used her hand to shade her eyes and looked intently in the direction he'd indicated. 'I can't see anyone,' she said. 'Perhaps it's a trick of the light.'

To Horace's right, the hand-smoothed surface of the stone fixed to the top of the stile gleamed like diamond dust. He closed his eyes and listened to the murmur of the swaying flowers and the hum of the sea. When he finally opened them, he saw that a butterfly with deep blue and narrow black-edged wings had settled on the shiny stone and seemed to be looking directly at him. The insect lifted its wings to reveal pale brownish-grey undersides with rows of orange spots near the outer limits and black spots near the centre. A Reverdin's Blue, he thought. There could be no doubt about it. He looked for Amanda and saw that she'd walked down through the field towards the sea for a better look.

'Why don't you let me drive for a while?' she said, when she returned. 'I think you're getting tired.'

They were booked into a guesthouse in Lion-sur-Mer. Horace had a printout of a map of the village, which showed the exact location of the house. He imagined his father and the East Yorkshires with maps in their pockets and fear in their hearts, readying themselves for the trip across the Channel. They would not have known whether all or any of them might return when the war was over. What did you think of first when it might be the last thing you'd ever think?

The lady who ran the guesthouse was smaller and older than Horace, and this made him smile. Their lodgings were on the main street.

'Your room is at the top of the stairs,' their host said, in very clear English.

'We need two rooms,' Horace said, becoming a little embarrassed. He saw Amanda smiling as he spoke. The landlady, too, smiled and indicated that Horace was to follow her upstairs to his room. On the wall of the small hall hung a barometer and an ancient rifle, its smooth walnutty stock like a cricket bat. Horace had never played cricket.

That afternoon, they took a brief trip to Ouistreham. There were very few people around, as if the whole town were wary of some impending catastrophe. Horace wished he could speak French. He imagined a language card, like a bankcard, which you could have for travel abroad. When inserted into a local ATM, the card would enable its owner to use the language of the country in which he found himself. He thought about the radiotherapy and the surgery and wondered whether it would have helped his brain to understand the language of de Gaulle and Bardot if he'd had the treatment in France. He also knew that he probably should not be driving. He walked down a street and glanced at the sign that declared its name: 'Rue du 11 Novembre'. Horace understood the name immediately. (Maybe the ATM machines *did* have magical powers here.) On the stroke of four, by the huge bells of the church nearby, Horace found himself in the Rue Jean Mermoz. There he found the type of shop he'd been looking for.

Later that evening, upon their return to Lion-sur-Mer, Horace had a snooze in his room at the guesthouse. He woke to a soft knock on his door.

'Fancy a ramble before dinner?' Amanda asked.

It was getting quite dark outside as they strolled around the seaside village. Large, tired-looking buildings sheltered the main street from the sea. Horace saw an old lady stacking jars of mustard in a small shop whose sign said '*Fermé*'. The streets were deserted and only a marmalade cat crossed their path as he wandered languidly.

'It's lovely here,' Amanda said, as they turned to face the sea.

'Yes,' Horace agreed, 'it certainly is.'

The promenade was chilly, with the inhospitable lights of the streetlamps casting a pale, thin glow on the concrete wall that bordered the sandy beach. About halfway along, there was a strange edifice, a lookout tower of sorts that one mounted via a set of precast stairs. It was like the cockpit of an airship, standing proudly at the edge of the town and looking impassively out to sea. Amanda went first and then Horace began to climb the steps but felt the beginnings of numbness in his right arm and leg.

'I don't think I can do this,' he said. Amanda came back down the steps and took his arm. A large sheet of paper, newspaper perhaps, tumbled angrily towards them along the promenade. Horace sidestepped the danger. He had been unable to climb the steps but was unsure as to why. The little town of Lion-sur-Mer seemed asleep. To himself, Horace hummed the tune he'd heard when he was a boy in Otterton: 'A Wicky Wick Wack Wack Woo.'

'Let's get back to the guesthouse', said Amanda.'

The following morning, his alarm clock went off at five. Horace had actually woken up marginally before that. He shut off the noise before it had a chance to give its third beep. He turned on the light on the bedside table, rubbed his eyes and got out of bed. The numbness in his limbs had vanished and he felt quite refreshed. Despite his tiredness earlier, he had carefully laid out all of his purchases before he'd gone to bed and now began to dress methodically as the lights of a passing car raced up the wall and door of his bedroom.

There was no real uniformity to his uniform. The tunic was British all right, with loose threads hanging out where the rank stripes had been ripped from the sleeves. The shirt he wore beneath it was dark blue and had belonged once to a French fire fighter. The combat trousers were baggy and light, almost certainly American from an era after the Second World War. The boots were the best fitting element of the outfit. They were comfortable and seemed exactly the right size. Horace fastened a belt around his waist and filled the water canister, before clipping it to the belt. He pinned a gas mask to his chest. The final piece of the jigsaw was the helmet. That was definitely British and even had a couple of dents where it had either been dropped or shot at. It was a little too big for his head and slipped down over his eyes until Horace took a pillowcase and stuffed it under the canvas webbing inside it. He picked up his car keys from the dressing table, with its tarnished mirror, and began his quiet trek downstairs. As he was about to leave the house, he had the wonderful idea of 'borrowing' the rifle from its hitches on the wall in the entrance hall. He closed the front door and quietly marched towards his car. It was certainly quite chilly out.

The location Horace had chosen for his visit lay just east of Colleville Plage. It was a wide stretch of sandy beach that had been protected by four German bunkers. It was not near to a village or museum, and it was certainly not one of the main 'landing' tourist attractions. For these reasons alone, it was perfect for Horace's purpose. However, even more importantly, it had been key to the success of the day in question, and it had been along this particular stretch of beach that the East Yorkshires had disembarked. Among them had been Corporal Robert Winter, Fred Alexander and Migsie Spring.

Horace locked his car but put the keys under the left front tyre. He looked at his non-waterproof watch. It was ten minutes to six. He made his way over the low wall to the beach. He felt himself sink in the sand as his army boots made contact. Up the coast were Juno, Gold, Utah and Omaha. Horace stood on the section of Sword known as Oboe. He witnessed faint light arriving as dawn approached. He began to walk down the beach towards the emerging day. The tide was coming in and he walked against the flow and out into the sea. The first thing he felt was the heaviness of his legs and feet as his clothes became soaked and began to inhale salt into the soul of their fabric. The water was bitterly cold. Horace held the rifle above his head so that it would not get wet. Some of the photographs he'd seen showed soldiers with rifles wrapped in canvas bags treated with wax to keep the water out. When the water reached the level of his chest, Horace Winter turned to face France and prepared to play his part in history.

On the shore, he saw smoke vomiting from craters where shells fell, creating mayhem. Overhead, the constant drone of bombers and fighters gave the impression that an enormous cloud of swarming bees was shadowing them. All around him and his comrades, the sky was lit up by the race of tracer fire and by rockets soaring into the wall of aircraft. Horace put one hand to his mouth and pulled out a piece of seaweed that had become lodged there. The mouths of the other floating transports yawned down into the sea and their men moved forward, too.

There was a loud yell to his right, and he saw that a shell had exploded in the centre of the next landing craft. The water was full of men now, all walking forward, like giant insects stuck in soup. He saw a young private with no arms talking to himself as water bubbled around him. He was pulled under and did not reappear.

Horace pedalled with his feet for a bit and the men behind him ushered him forward. He was unable to run, but even walking seemed pretty fast as they moved in their thousands into the shallow water and began to pick up their feet and splash to the edge of the beach. All around him, men yelled obscenities and screamed as bullets approached, carrying death.

There were obstacles like giant iron crosses ranged across parts of the beach. Farther up, a line of barbed wire lurked. In front of him, Horace saw a man's face in profile. It was Fred Alexander. A man to Horace's left caught a shell full in the chest, which turned him into a mince of flesh and tunic. A piece of one of his hands lodged in Horace's uniform below the left breast pocket. The force of the explosion laid him on his back at the edge of the water, among the froth and blood.

He turned in the middle of the mayhem and horror. His father was helping a wounded soldier load his rifle so that he would have some protection when the main force moved ahead, leaving him on the sand.

'Dad? Dad!' Horace called.

His father looked up from his task. 'What is it, Horace? What's wrong?'

'Remember that time you came to see me play in the cup Final?'

'In Donnybrook?'

'Yes. Do you remember that as soon as we'd lost, immediately after the final whistle, you started to leave before we'd even come off the pitch?'

'What about that, Horace?' His father fired a shot with his revolver over Horace's shoulder. Someone screamed in German.

'I could have scored the winning try. But the other boy wouldn't pass.'

'It doesn't matter, Horace. None of that matters now.'

'I'm sorry, Dad. I really am. I should have made you proud that day, but I didn't. I found out why he wouldn't pass. Years later he told me.' As Horace spoke, he began to cry slowly as if he were just learning how. 'And by the time I reached the stand someone had put their coat under your head and an ambulance was on its way. I know it was disappointing for you, the fact that I didn't win the match for us. I didn't know what to say when I got up into the stand and saw you lying there. It was all my fault.' Horace continued crying and his father reached across to him and wiped away the tears with the back of his hand.

'None of it was your fault, Horace. I had a weak heart, anyone will tell you that. I could have dropped dead at any time. In a way, I lasted longer than I ever expected to. I was *always* proud of you, Horace. It was only a bloody rugby match. Now I don't want you to start worrying again about the bees and your mum and all that.'

'I'm sorry about Helen, Dad,' Horace said. 'I was only trying to save her from the bee and then it flew out so I followed it, and when I came back she, she …' Through his tears Horace remembered the sight of his tiny sister's lifeless body lying in the water in the bath. 'I was just trying to help,' he said.

'I know you were, son,' his father said. 'You did everything you could. None of it was your fault, Horace. For God's sake, you were only six years old yourself. I know you loved Helen. So did I, we all did. And we all miss her so much.'

'What should I do now, Dad?' Horace asked, as the Germans began to intensify their defence of the beach. All around Robert and Horace Winter, bullets whinnied, kicking up spits of sand as they missed their targets.

'Just keep going, Horace. That's all anybody can do. Here you are, still battling. Keep going for as long as you can. Life is a funny kind of race, Horace. Whoever finishes last is the winner.'

Horace remembered Migsie Spring now. He remembered the letter his father still had to write, and the farmhouse, and the girl with the stick grenade, and everything else. This was his opportunity to warn his dad in advance, to tell him what was going to happen in a month's time. Horace now possessed the power, the knowledge, to change everything. All he had to do was to talk to his commanding officer, Corporal Robert Winter, tell him what to expect and how to make it happen differently. All he needed to do was warn him and everything would be all right. Migsie Spring would keep his legs and Horace's father would never have to apologise. He began to formulate the warning in his mouth but something both great and awful stopped him: it was the explosive realisation in his own heart that everything happens for a reason and that mere mortals should never interfere in what was always meant to be.

'Goodbye, Dad,' he shouted above the gunfire. 'I'll see you when you get home.'

Horace turned away as he spoke those words and set his face against the enemy. The real enemy was time. Somehow he'd always suspected it. He began to pound his way up the sandy slope and into the future.

As he ran, he had an extraordinary experience whereby he was able to see everything in vivid colour. The pathway to safety across the sand became a clear and sparkling yellow corridor of translucent beach in the midst of carnage and terror, as if someone were shining a torch to assist him in his journey. And in that moment, Horace realised that his father was a butterfly, a Small Tortoiseshell to be precise. Of course he was a butterfly! How could it ever have been otherwise?

Flies unhindered across the countryside and occasionally even across the sea. A solitary species, uncomfortable in colonies. The adult male is smaller than many other rivals who feed on Buddleia (commonly known as the butterfly bush), but it lacks nothing in bravery.

CHAPTER TWENTY-FOUR

'It is not always easy to tell the difference between a butterfly and a moth!'

Butterflies and Moths: A Beginner's Guide

In a small village in County Galway, a man came into a kitchen to put on the kettle.

'How's it going, John?' his mother asked, as she walked through the back door to the scullery and deposited a Spar bag of groceries on the worktop.

'Not too bad. Just a couple more questions to set for the Christmas exam, then I'm done. Ali's just taken the little lady upstairs for a feed. She's going to have another go at getting her to sleep in the cot.'

They stood back to back, she unpacking the milk and marmalade and Clonakilty black pudding while he stirred sugar into instant coffee.

'That reminds me, Ma, do you remember telling me once about an ice-cream van going on fire?'

'Yes. That was a long, long time ago. It was down in Rosslare. Whatever made you think of it now?'

'Yeah, yeah, that's right, Rosslare. I meant to say it to you ages ago but I suppose we haven't really had much time to think since the little lady arrived.'

'What is it, John?'

'I was correcting scripts for the Leaving Cert during the summer and I came across an essay that had a line in it about an ice-cream van going up in smoke in Rosslare. I know I shouldn't have, but I photocopied it. I meant to send it to you but I forgot all about it. I think I still have it in a box in the boot of the car. Hang on a minute till I go and get it.' John left the room and returned a few moments later with a copy of an exam he'd corrected. 'Listen to this. "I had an image of that person which I had carried with me since those long-ago summer days. On that distant day, an ice-cream van had gone on fire on the promenade at Rosslare and we had watched it burn."'

'Can I have a read of it myself, John?'

'Sure, Ma. Do you think it's the same incident?'

'I don't know, love. But I'd like to look at it anyway.'

Rose Burke knew in her heart that it must be Horace who had written the essay. She took off her coat and sat down at the kitchen table.

★

On the motorway, Horace saw a Morris Minor, like a tortoise among hares, going the other way.

'Don't worry, Horace,' Amanda said, as she smiled at him and held his hand. 'Everything's going to be fine.'

'There's the sign. Nearly there, bud,' the driver said in the mirror.

Horace recalled a visit from Emma Kelly just after he'd come back from his trip to Normandy. Had the solicitor been with him and Amanda in France? He knew that she'd visited him at home one evening. Dr Caulfield, his GP, had been there too. The solicitor had drawn up a will for him.

It began to rain heavily and the windscreen wipers fought valiantly. Down the road, they turned left at a sign for Straffan. It was a pretty village with stone walls and neatly bordered flowerbeds. Horace saw that the rain had eased.

On Edenvale Road, the rain began to rise up from where it had fallen on the pavements and the roadway. It cast a vapour into the sky, completing the cycle. The cold winter sun was working double time.

*

Miles away, on the other side of the country, Rose Burke was reading Horace's essay. Suddenly she was a young girl again, toasting apples on an open fire and feeling the rasp of coastal grass against her legs as she ran.

*

The taxi slowed and turned right into a field. The makeshift car park had an assortment of occupants, including a red van bearing the name 'DL Woodwork'. Horace saw the folded wheelchair lurch as the car came to a stop. He listened for the sound of the rain but did not hear it.

'Welcome to Straffan Butterfly Farm', a sign on a stick greeted them.

'The driver will help you out, Horace,' Amanda said. The man slid open the great door and began to unload Horace's mother's wheelchair from its lodgings in the back seat. The wheelchair made a crushing sound as Horace was pushed along the gravel path to the museum.

Inside, near the postcard display, a couple was trying to attract their child's attention away from where he was engrossed in one of the display cases. In turns, they tapped him gently on the shoulder but to no avail. The child stood with his back to the rest of the room, scribbling furiously in a notebook that lay open on the glass top of the display unit. Horace watched as the couple looked at each other; Mother pointing to her watch with a smile and Dad grinning while shrugging his shoulders and raising his hands, palms upwards, in front of him in a gesture of happy helplessness. When the boy had finished writing, he closed the notebook carefully and turned.

It was Max Hackett. Horace could hardly believe it. He was much taller now and seemed content and confident. The couple looked at Max with affection. Horace wondered whether the boy would recognise him, but he did not. In fact, Max walked right past Horace, laughing with his new family. Horace was delighted that the boy no longer needed his help. He was overjoyed, too, to see Max's interest in butterflies. It vindicated Horace's decision to send him the latest *Butterflies and Moths: A Beginner's Guide* in the escape package.

Amanda wheeled Horace between the displays. He saw an iguana standing on a branch in a hot glass box, its shoulders hunched like a front-row forward. Donnybrook. James Sefton had been injured in the quarter-final. The whole field was marked out in a grid of whitewash squares. Old soldiers bent over, pushing boxes of whitewash up and across to mark out the playing pitch. Some of the people on the field would disappear through the trapdoors. He felt Amanda's hand on his shoulder.

'Would you like to go into the Tropical Room, Horace? There are live butterflies there.'

Horace nodded, then leaned his head to the right to make contact with her soft skin. She stroked his cheek with her palm, then began to wheel him out through the double doors towards the Tropical Room. A man and a lady, holding hands, were coming out as they went in. They stood back, unclipped the other door and held them open for Horace and Amanda. Horace looked down at his hands and saw that they had withered almost beyond use. He had thought he would be afraid, but he did not feel fear now.

As they were about to leave the Exhibition Room and Shop, Horace noticed a man to one side, arranging the contents of a display case. The glass lid was open and resting against the wall.

'I want to look at that,' Horace said, inclining his head in the direction of the activity. The wheelchair was swivelled to the left. The couple let go of the doors.

The man looked up from his work, as Horace approached. 'You're welcome to have a gander,' he said. 'It's a brand new collection, given to us by Hugh and Mary Bevan.'

He stood to one side so that Horace had a clear line of sight. The display was beautiful: a mix of butterflies and moths that represented the sum of the donors' life work and interest. He looked at the exhibits in turn, trying to identify each one from memory before allowing himself to read the labels held in place by white-topped sewing pins: Scotch Argus; Comma; Duke of Burgundy Fritillary; Glanville; Swallow-tail moth; Scarce Merveille du Jour; Dusky Heath; False Ringlet; Chalk Hill Blue; Geranium Argus; Brimstone; Green Hairstreak. What a marvellous collection. And then he saw it. It was just below the top right-hand corner of the layout. The only element of the collection that was as yet unlabelled. It was like looking into a miniature mirror. Horace pointed with one of his withered hands.

'Ah, yes,' said the man, and grinned. 'That old rascal. Not everybody knows what it is by sight. Any ideas?'

'Burnished Brass moth,' Horace slurred through his teeth.

'I'm afraid not,' the man said. 'A good guess, though. A totally understandable mistake. In fact, it's not a moth at all.' He opened his right hand and revealed a label: 'Lulworth Skipper butterfly'.

'They're very alike, but if you look closely enough, their markings are different. In the Burnished Brass, they take on the appearance of scales. But the key difference between them is that, while alive, the moth has a voracious appetite and rarely settles. The Lulworth, meanwhile, forms settled colonies ...' Horace was delighted that he'd been mistaken.

In the Tropical Room, heavy ferns and palm trees dripped with humidity because of the heaters. On leaves and branches, and in the air, the symphony of colour was fantastic. Horace saw a Violet Fritillary and a Southern White Admiral and a Bath White and a Large Grizzled Skipper, all within two feet of each other. He moved among them and noticed a Camberwell Beauty and a Queen of Spain flying side by side in the air level with his eyeline. The silver patches under the wings of the Queen easily distinguished it from all other fritillaries. He thought he heard a noise, turned his head and saw the red and green stripe of the Six-spot Burnet moth. An Emperor moth whispered to him to look behind the people who were squeezing by.

As the departing visitors went past, a space opened in the mist and the unmistakable colour and form of the Large Copper, or *Lycaene dispar*, fluttered into view and landed on the edge of a variegated fern. This is impossible, thought Horace. He had only read about this species and seen drawings or paintings of it because it had become extinct in Britain in 1864. 'I must be mistaken,' he said to himself. Perhaps it is actually a *batavus*, the similar Dutch subspecies introduced into Wood Walton Fen in Cambridgeshire in the late 1920s.

In Dunmore, it was almost teatime. In her hands, Rose Burke held the essay about the colour blue. Her son and daughter-in-law had gone for a walk. She'd read and re-read the piece all afternoon, wondering if she could be mistaken about the identity of the author, but in her heart she'd known, from the moment John had mentioned the ice-cream van burning on the promenade, that no one but Horace Winter could have written it. She closed the photocopied answer-book for the last time and saw the grade in the box on the front below the added marks. Through the baby monitor on the work surface she heard her granddaughter crying. She hurried upstairs.

'A B2? That's pretty good, isn't it?' she said to her son, after he and his wife had returned from their walk.

'They deserve it, whoever it is,' he said. 'They really went for broke with the essay.'

Rose Burke took off her glasses and wondered about what might have been. In that tiny scullery, her whole lifetime ran away to Rosslare, to a time when ice-cream vans caught fire and almost anything was possible. She thought once again about that summer, half a century away, when she'd finally given up learning music at the Angelus upright piano in their front room and had decided to live. It made her sad.

'They're called Protestants, Rose, because they're *protesting*. Against *us*. They hate us.' Her father had repeated this all the way across the country as he'd driven them home from a holiday by the sea, cut short. The caravan park was being sold and she would never see it again.

She had been in love with Horace. She knew that. Even after she'd had to deal with the realisation that he didn't love her. What other explanation was there for his failure to write? She had waited and waited, never knowing of her father's instruction to the postman: bigotry sealed with a pound note.

Years later, she'd gone on a shopping trip to Dublin with two of her closest friends, girls she'd known since primary school.

'Let's go to the zoo,' Rita had suggested. And so they had gone, the three of them, Rose, Rita and Cathleen, after choosing material for the bridesmaids' dresses in Clery's department store in O'Connell Street. Rose had already decided to wear her own mother's wedding dress when she was married that coming December.

They'd had lunch in a tiny cafe in the Phoenix Park, overlooking a grassy dip with a bandstand. As they strolled past the penguins, she saw him. A good bit older, of course, as she was herself, but it was definitely him. Her heart began to race uncontrollably and she wanted to march right up to him and grab him by the lapels of his long coat and ask, 'Why?' But what would have been the point in doing that? She was weeks away from marrying a good, steady, local, boring schoolteacher at home in Dunmore. And so she said nothing, nothing at all. Instead, she had walked right past him, certain he wouldn't remember her. But he had. And even when he'd run after her and tapped her on the shoulder and used her name, she'd simply shaken her head and pretended he was mistaken. She had made her choice and would be happy with it.

And *was* she? Her husband had drunk himself into an early grave, but she had a son she loved and now a grandchild she adored. She also possessed a lifetime's worth of memories from an amazing summer when she had encountered a boy who had captured her heart. It was evident now that he had never let go of it.

They'd kissed among the sand dunes to the sound of curlews and the hum of the sun. She wondered where he was now, right at this moment. Maybe they could finally meet again and be reunited. Perhaps it *wasn't* too late.

Amanda stood in front of him. A tiny Map butterfly landed on her shoulder and Horace stared intently at its wings, where the reddish-brown undersides, with their white bands and yellowish edges, looked like the plan of a large city. He thought about a Tarzan film and a boy whose foot had been crushed. He thought, too, about honeybees and telephones and second centres who wouldn't pass the ball, and boys and old men clambering up the sand to save the world from jackbooted ruination.

He saw Morris dancers with bell pads on their shins and handkerchiefs in their hands, skipping down the main street of an English village while onlookers drank real ale and listened on their transistors for the latest on the cricket from Lord's.

He saw in his mind's eye the orange and yellow striped dustjacket of *A Beginner's Guide*. He heard the sound of an ambulance and a train in the distance, both ultimately racing towards the same destination.

In the stifling heat of the Tropical Room of the butterfly farm in Straffan, County Kildare, it seemed then as if all of the butterflies had stopped flying or moving for one long humid and intimate moment. The wings of the Map butterfly assumed the pattern and design of the map of Dublin City on the wall of his office at the Bank of Leinster on Ormond Quay. The corridor, within which he'd lived a narrow, lonely life for many years, stood out on the wings and then began slowly to dissolve into the wonderful and happy colours of a life finally realised.

Horace found that he could barely use his voice but he did not need to. He looked at Amanda and knew that the moment had finally arrived for him to say goodbye to her. Just as he had come into the life of Max Hackett when the boy needed help, Amanda had come into Horace's when *he* was most in need. If, indeed, angels *did* exist, she was certainly one of them. She was part nurse, part memory, mixed with the imagining into adulthood of a little sister who had lost her life in six inches of bathwater. Some of her was certainly drawn from Horace's own fear of facing retirement and illness alone. Above all, she was an emotional hologram of Rose Burke, the only woman he'd ever loved. And so, just as the boy no longer required Horace's presence, there was nothing more that Amanda could do for Horace. Of course, she was entirely real to him, but nobody else could see or hear her. It was time to let her go, to allow her to return to the imagination from which she'd arrived. The Map butterfly rose from her shoulder and flew away. Amanda reached out a hand to touch Horace's face, but before contact could be made she, too, had disappeared. It was as if a picture slide had been removed from a projector and all that remained was empty light.

As the heat of the Tropical Room bore down upon him, Horace sensed the spirit of Corporal Robert

Winter, late of the Yorkshires, late of fifty-seven Edenvale Road, Ranelagh. The presence was nearby and was more than just a feeling. Horace heard the sound of the sea and was not afraid of the campaign that lay ahead of him. He embraced the past, *his* past, every last bit of it, and felt it settle around his shoulders like a scarf. Within this embrace lay an understanding of things, of unspoken phrases that did not now need to be uttered, and a common cord binding father and son forever, regardless of what else existed or did not. It was a silver thread of gossamer, like the trail of a rare butterfly that may or may not have been observed, identified, noted, crossed off or queried. The heat began to subside and the reduction in temperature stemmed from a realisation by a former assistant bank manager that he was in the presence of, and yet also at the epicentre of, a simple and wonderful phenomenon: mortality smiling in the shade of a life well lived.

And now, once more, there was movement in the room. A Zephyr Blue floated above the wooden bridge in the centre of the scene and was joined at last by a Lulworth Skipper.

Horace felt himself being inhaled out of this world without fuss.

AUTHOR'S NOTE

Butterflies and Moths Motif

Many years ago at a funeral, in the month of February, I saw a butterfly in the church and wondered perhaps if those we lose ever come back as butterflies to tell the people who mourn them that they're fine. That's where the idea for Horace's habit of evaluating people as butterflies and moths came from. I am indebted to Messrs Frohawk and Bunn-Richards for their wonderful book, *Butterflies and Moths of the British Isles* (published by Ward, Lock & Co. Limited in 1959), which I used as the primary source of my research for Horace's comparisons.

It has resulted in my own viewing people in this way sometimes. Since I began writing about Horace Winter, I have noticed more real butterflies and moths than I ever did before. I suppose we'd all like to think we are butterflies, but it's also hard to admit some of us might be moths. Maybe we've all got a bit of both in us!

Leinster Schools Junior Cup Final 1957

In the 'real' Junior Cup final in 1957, Blackrock College defeated Terenure after a replay.

ACKNOWLEDGEMENTS

A great many people have been involved in one way or another in getting Horace Winter into your hands, so that you can say hello to him before he says goodbye to all of us. I wish to acknowledge their help.

Mary Honan has known Horace since he was just an idea and has always been there to support and encourage both him and me. Thank you so much for your part in his upbringing.

Rita Considine, Cathleen Noctor, John McMenamin and Mark Sanfey all read early drafts and made encouraging noises.

Kate Lyall Grant provided editorial help and other crucial advice when I was close to the edge of giving up. Billy Ryan helped me find Kate.

Helen O'Mara and Hugh O'Keefe allowed Horace to live in their house.

Thanks to sculptor Rowan Gillespie for your advice and your name. Stephen McCullough also kindly allowed me to use his name. Alan Dodd let me use his name and was happy to be moved from full-back to second centre.

Karen Stephenson: you are the inspiration for the character of Amanda.

I am indebted to Deirdre Caulfield, Juliet Bressan and Brendan Gormley for medical and pharmacological advice about Horace's illness.

My warmest thanks to John Minihan for taking my photo for the cover. You are a man who has seen ten lifetimes' worth of things.

The Tyrone Guthrie Centre in Annaghmakerrig provided space and time and food and welcome and inspiration. (Thank you, Lavina McAdoo, for the best jelly in the world; you're the reason I go back!)

My agent, Claire Anderson-Wheeler of Regal Hoffmann & Associates, said 'yes' after one hundred and forty three other people had said 'no'. You believed in Horace and me when we doubted ourselves. You're an angel!

Vanessa Fox O'Loughlin worked with Claire to find a home for Horace. Thank you so much for your energy.

Thanks to John Murphy for your friendship and unfailing positivity. If the glass was three-quarters empty, you'd see it as a quarter full.

To Sylvia and the weasels for putting up with me. Keep an eye out for the Morning Elf!

Finally, I would like to thank Breda Purdue, Ciara Doorley, Hazel Orme, Siobhan, Ruth, Joanna and everyone else at Hachette Ireland for falling in love with Horace Winter and minding him.

You are all butterflies.

Lots of love,

Conor xx